Praise for
Kiss of the Rose

"Kate Pearce gives historical romance some serious fangs with *Kiss of the Rose*. Better plan on losing some sleep, because this is a guaranteed all-nighter!"
—Jessica Andersen, author of
the Nightkeeper novels

"A marvelous blend of historical and paranormal makes this story a must read."
—*New York Times* bestselling author
Hannah Howell

"A book you can really sink your teeth into! It has everything: adventure, romance, history, and Druids and Vampires too!"
—Brandy Purdy, author of *The Boleyn Wife*

"Wonderfully dark and intriguing . . . a fascinating, sensual world filled with adventure!"
—Colleen Gleason, author of the
Gardella Vampire Chronicles

continued...

Kiss of the Rose

THE TUDOR VAMPIRE CHRONICLES

KATE PEARCE

A SIGNET ECLIPSE BOOK

SIGNET ECLIPSE
Published by New American Library, a division of
Penguin Group (USA) Inc., 375 Hudson Street,
New York, New York 10014, USA
Penguin Group (Canada), 90 Eglinton Avenue East, Suite 700, Toronto,
Ontario M4P 2Y3, Canada (a division of Pearson Penguin Canada Inc.)
Penguin Books Ltd., 80 Strand, London WC2R 0RL, England
Penguin Ireland, 25 St. Stephen's Green, Dublin 2,
Ireland (a division of Penguin Books Ltd.)
Penguin Group (Australia), 250 Camberwell Road, Camberwell, Victoria 3124,
Australia (a division of Pearson Australia Group Pty. Ltd.)
Penguin Books India Pvt. Ltd., 11 Community Centre, Panchsheel Park,
New Delhi - 110 017, India
Penguin Group (NZ), 67 Apollo Drive, Rosedale, North Shore 0632,
New Zealand (a division of Pearson New Zealand Ltd.)
Penguin Books (South Africa) (Pty.) Ltd., 24 Sturdee Avenue,
Rosebank, Johannesburg 2196, South Africa

Penguin Books Ltd., Registered Offices:
80 Strand, London WC2R 0RL, England

First published by Signet Eclipse, an imprint of New American Library,
a division of Penguin Group (USA) Inc.

First Printing, August 2010
10 9 8 7 6 5 4 3 2 1

This book is dedicated to my family:
Dermot, Alex, Kit, Gregory and Sophia Rose.
Thank you.

ACKNOWLEDGMENTS

First, thanks to Deidre Knight and Tracy Bernstein, for providing me with this opportunity to write about some of my favorite things—love, Tudor history, and Vampires. Also thanks to the Hot Writer Babes—Amy, Susan and Dana—who read the original proposal and were kind enough to tell me it was good to go. I also received great help from Crystal Jordan and Dayna Hart, who not only read the finished manuscript, but had to keep reassuring me that I wasn't delusional and that NAL was not going to ask for their money back.

On the research front, I received great help from Kathryn Downs, who saved me hours of plowing through information on Tudor clothing and compiled a handy-dandy shortlist when Herbert Norris's *Tudor Costume and Fashion* defeated me. Also, to my mother and sister, Ceri, for additional Tudor information direct from the UK. I found Alison Weir's *The Six Wives of Henry VIII* very helpful. For the Druids, I mainly used Peter Berresford Ellis's book (what a coincidence on the name) *The Druids*.

I'd also like to acknowledge the help of a real Tudor poet George Turberville, whose song I "borrowed" for Christopher Ellis to sing to Rosalind. I've tried as much as possible to use real places in the book, and to be as historically accurate as a work of paranormal fiction can be. All historical errors are my own, and I apologize for them in advance.

Prologue

He needed a miracle.

Here he was, on the brink of a battle for the crown of England, and it was increasingly obvious that God wasn't listening to his desperate prayers. Henry Tudor rose from his knees, made the sign of the cross, and backed away from the altar. A single tallow candle illuminated a handful of dilapidated pews and a ragged altar cloth, tattered and chewed by vermin.

There was only one thing left to do, and it would be the biggest gamble of his life. He'd left the Earl of Oxford in charge of his pitifully few troops, and brought his Welsh companion, Sir John Llewellyn, as his guide. They were the only two men who knew he had left his sleeping army and gone out into the countryside, ostensibly to pray at the church, but in reality to do so much more.

"Are you ready, my lord?"

Henry relaxed as John's familiar dark-featured face emerged from the gloom. John's knowledge of the Welsh countryside had proved invaluable. He'd found

Henry the perfect place for his needs, a place where the old religion of the Druids lodged uneasily alongside the new.

"Is it true there was a battle fought here, John?" Henry asked as his friend led him away from the church and down into the all-encompassing darkness beyond.

"Aye, my lord. *Parc-y-Meirw* means Field of the Dead. A fitting omen for your upcoming victory over King Richard."

"Indeed." *Or a reminder of just how quickly an over-ambitious man could fail . . .*

John stepped aside to reveal a low huddle of stones. "This is the Holy Well I spoke of. It is said the spring leads directly to the old gods, who will listen favorably to the prayers of anyone who offers them a tribute."

Henry strained his eyes to make out the dimensions of the less than impressive stone arch that covered the entrance to the spring. The sound of water trickled and echoed deep in the ground below his feet. He crouched down and shuddered when his fingertips slicked over decaying plants and dipped into ice-cold water.

"I shall make an offering, then." He found a coin and threw it into the small gaping mouth of the well. Was he throwing away his immortal soul as well? Richard Plantagenet was a formidable opponent on and off the battlefield.

"Are you all right, sir?"

"Go back to the church and wait for me there. I will do what I must do alone."

"Nay, sir. I promised Lord de Vere I wouldn't let you out of my sight."

"Even if what you see will imperil your soul, your chance of paradise, and the glorious resurrection?"

To Henry's surprise, John smiled. "Sir, I am prepared to walk through hell itself to protect you."

Henry let out his breath. "All right, then, best get on with it. Do you have the vessel?"

"Aye, sir."

"Fill it with water and give it to me."

Henry withdrew his dagger. Strange that both the old and the new religions demanded blood. He slashed the blade across the fleshy pad of his thumb and allowed his blood to drip into the narrow opening of the pot. He was unsure exactly how much was needed. Tales of the Druids draining their sacrificial victims dry were commonplace. Even the Christian God had allowed his precious son to be crucified, bloodied nails hammered through his wrists, a sword thrust in his side . . .

Henry took a deep, steadying breath and sucked his thumb into his mouth, waited until the sickly coppery flow slowed and stopped. "Show me where the stones are."

He could see better now, and did not hesitate as he followed John toward the ominous row of shadows bordering the field. He reached the first stone, which was about one and a half times his height, and put his hand on it. The stone quivered and warmed to his touch as if he had somehow awakened it.

He snatched back his hand and examined the smooth surface of the bluish gray rock. "How many stones are there?"

"Eight, sir."

"The color reminds me of the great stone circle I once saw down in the West Country of England," Henry whispered. "A circle built by giants, as legend would have it."

"These stones came from the same quarry, and there were no giants involved. Just mortal men."

"You seem to know a lot about it, John." Henry knew he was procrastinating, but his first touch of the stones had proved almost too much for him, had made him doubt his purpose once again.

"Like you, I was born here, sir. I learned all the ancient tales before I could speak."

"Then tell me. What must I do to call the Druids?"

A moment of silence met his challenge and he tore his gaze from the stones back to John.

"Near the bottom of the third stone is a small crevice. Kneel and pour your blood offering into the hollow."

"And then?"

"We wait."

Henry found his way to the third stone and knelt in front of it, used his fingertips to discover the crevice and the worn hollow at its bottom. He closed his eyes and poured the contents of the pot into it, was surprised when none of the liquid seeped out or ran down the surface of the rock. He wanted to pray, but hesitated to offend the old gods he was trying to reach.

Suddenly the wind began swirling and squalling around the stones. A humming sound in his head grew louder and louder until he staggered to his feet and broke off contact with the rock.

Something coalesced out of the wind in front of him. Henry couldn't move as the thing took shape and became a bearded man dressed in flowing white robes, a long staff covered in ivy in one hand. His form was as indistinct as a flickering candle flame, but his voice was commanding.

"Greetings, Henry Tudor, Duke of Richmond."

Henry bowed his head and tried to answer through the stark terror that closed his throat and threatened his ability to breathe. He clenched his fingers around the rosary beads concealed in his palm. How strong was the Christian God against the ancients? If he prayed now, who would win? He was no longer sure.

"I need your help."

Inwardly, he winced at his own abrupt words. But there was no time for subtlety or false praise. Already faint streaks of light were visible in the night sky. He had no illusions as to the precarious nature of his cause. He needed to get back to his army before they deserted him.

"What do you want, Henry Tudor?"

Henry forced himself to meet the specter's glowing eyes. "I want the crown of England and Wales."

"And what are you prepared to offer the Druids in return for our help?"

"What do you want?"

"Your solemn vow that you will aid us in our fight to wipe out the Vampire race."

Henry frowned. "I do not understand." He'd anticipated being asked for many things—money, power, even his soul—but not this. "What is a *Vampire*?"

"A fair question, mortal." The Druid inclined his head. "They are an abomination, a race of parasites that prey upon humanity. Many centuries ago, some of our Druid brethren forsook the traditional blood sacrifice of humans when they discovered that *drinking* the blood of living humans gave them a different form of religious ecstasy. They gained new powers and became immortal."

As he tried to imagine such monsters, Henry struggled to breathe. "I still don't understand. . . ."

"These 'Vampires' have grown in numbers and live among humans everywhere. Our seers have knowledge that they will attempt to overthrow the monarchy, set up one of their own as king, and enslave the human population."

"You wish me to stop them?"

"We wish to join with you to defeat the Vampire

threat. Our numbers have dwindled, and we are no longer strong enough to fight them here in the mortal world."

"If they threaten my realm, I'll deal with them myself."

The Druid's eyes glowed red. "You will fail. They will either kill you or steal your immortal soul and make you rule for them. However, if you accept our bargain, we will send to your court a family of Vampire slayers to protect you."

Henry stared at the apparition, his mouth dry, his heart racing. "This seems a small thing for such a huge boon."

"It is not small, Henry Tudor. According to our prophets, having the king's ear may save our race from extinction. In return for protection against the Vampires, you and your heirs must shield this family, keep their secrets—and heed them always when they warn you of danger."

Henry shook his head to clear it. Could he really accept that such creatures existed?

"They exist, mortal. Do you accept the bargain?"

Henry flinched. Had the Druid read his very thoughts? He tried to weigh the options even though he knew what his answer would be. If he was fortunate, the Druids might never need his assistance against those monsters. But news of his invasion had surely reached the ears of King Richard by now. Without the support of the Druids, his small army faced certain defeat, and he would die a traitor's death. "I agree."

"Then kneel beside your servant, Sir John Llewellyn, and accept your fate."

Henry knelt shoulder to shoulder with John and closed his eyes as the Druid began to glow and shimmer. Suddenly a jolt shot through him and he gasped as he witnessed his victory, saw King Richard abandoned, his broken, bloody corpse dragged through the streets and vilified. Then a blast of heat seared his left wrist and he cried out.

When he opened his eyes, the shimmering form had disappeared. Cursing, he slapped at the sleeve of his smoldering leather coat and stared at the three parallel lines now etched in his skin.

Slowly, John rolled back his sleeve and displayed the same sign to his astonished lord. "It's called the symbol of Awen. It represents the rays of the sun and the balance between male and female. It marks those of us bound to destroy the Vampires."

Henry got to his feet and pushed down his sleeve. His hands were still shaking, but John seemed unperturbed by what they had seen, and Henry had always trusted his Welsh servant. It was lighter now, and he could clearly see the row of eight stones, feel the subtle pulse of their energy around him. If he believed he had just bargained with an ancient Druid, surely he should believe in the Vampire threat too?

He glanced at John as they walked back up the slight incline to where their tethered horses awaited them by the church. "It is you who will stay with me, then, and fight these 'Vampires'?"

"Aye, sir."

Henry watched John's face as he tightened his horse's girth and untangled his reins. "You truly believe they exist?"

"I know they exist."

"You've seen them?"

"Seen them and killed them, sir."

John's matter-of–fact tone made Henry blink. "Since you have served me?"

"Of course, sir. The Vampires have their prophets too.

They are well aware of your existence, and your place in history. So far I've managed to stop them. When you are king, I expect my job will be a lot harder."

"When I am king . . ." Henry mounted his horse and kicked the beast into a canter. He couldn't quite believe what he'd done, but he would do his best to honor both his true religion and his promise to the ancients. A surge of hope shuddered through him.

He would be *king*.

Chapter 1

"Lady Rosalind? I'll take you to the queen."

Rosalind Llewellyn stood up, shook out her skirts, and followed Sir Richard out of the oppressively crowded anteroom into the wide hallway beyond. She hoped she didn't look as nervous as she felt. At court, presenting the right appearance was essential, and with the kind of enemies she had, any sign of nerves could prove disastrous.

Despite Rosalind's familiarity with the palace, it seemed at least a mile before they reached the queen's apartments. Strains of a lute and the hum of conversation died as she entered the largest of the rooms. Queen Katherine sat by the window surrounded by her ladies. Her embroidery lay on her lap as she compared shades of blue silk thread held up to the light by one of her waiting women.

"Your Majesty."

The queen smiled. "Lady Rosalind. It is a pleasure to see you again."

Rosalind sank into a deep curtsy. "You remember me, Your Majesty?"

"How could I forget? You had the most charming singing voice I have ever heard and the sweetness of disposition to go with it."

"Sweet as a country bumpkin or a freshly picked turnip."

The queen looked up sharply at the whispered interjection, and Rosalind felt herself blushing. One of the dark-haired Spanish women clustered around the queen barely bothered to conceal her laughter behind her fingers.

"Hardly a country bumpkin, Lady Celia. Rosalind was born at court and lived here for the first fourteen years of her life. She only returned home to nurse her mother through her final illness." The queen smiled gently. "Isn't that so, my dear?"

"Yes, Your Majesty. I—"

Rosalind stiffened and slowly inhaled. She could sense the presence of the undead in the room, the scent of stolen blood, the peculiar dry aroma left by an animated corpse. She studied Queen Katherine closely to make sure that the scent of Vampire was not coming from her. It never hurt to be cautious, and she hadn't been close to the queen for several years.

She forced her attention back to the queen and smiled. "In truth I could probably find my way around these halls blindfolded."

"That skill might be useful if the king decides to hold one of his wild masques." The queen nodded at Sir Richard. "Please ask the king if he can see Lady Rosalind today and give his formal approval of her appointment to my household. I don't think he'll object," she said to Rosalind. "Your family has always served us well. Lady Clarence will find you a bed for tonight, but until then, reintroduce yourself to my ladies and take your ease."

"Thank you, Your Majesty." Rosalind had always loved Queen Katherine and had no intention of deserting her now, even if—especially if—the rumors were true and she had lost favor with the king because she had failed to produce a male child. She'd always been a most gracious and kind friend to Rosalind.

"Oh my goodness, Rosalind, it is so good to see you again!"

Rosalind turned and found herself in a warm embrace. She enthusiastically reciprocated. "Margaret, how are you?"

"I am well." Margaret Sinclair tilted her head to one side and studied Rosalind critically. "You have grown into a beauty."

"Hardly." Rosalind shrugged. "I've just grown."

She'd known Margaret since they were five years old, when her friend had been made a ward of the king's court to protect her considerable inheritance. They had been inseparable until Rosalind's abrupt departure five years previously.

"And how is married life?" Rosalind asked. Margaret was glowing, her blond hair concealed beneath a French hood while her ample bosom was displayed above her silver and blue bodice.

Margaret's smile widened. "I am very happy. Robert is an excellent husband." She blushed. "We are expecting a child in the summer."

Rosalind took Margaret's hands and squeezed them hard. "That is wonderful news. I am truly happy for you."

Margaret led her away from the queen and toward the quietest corner of the room. "You aren't married yet, then? Is that why your grandfather sent you back to court, to find a husband?"

"Perhaps. But you know how difficult I am to please."

Rosalind tried to keep smiling. At almost twenty, she was already considered far too old to be unwed. It didn't bother her; she had important secrets to conceal, a monarchy to protect, and many dangers to face. Somehow she suspected a conventional husband would not approve of any of that.

Margaret gave her an encouraging pat. "I'm sure you'll find someone. Several of the gentlemen present looked very pleased to see you when you arrived."

"Only because I am an untried delicacy."

"You are so distrustful, Rosalind. Show a man a pleasant face and a willing disposition and you will find your love match in no time."

"But I am not willing," Rosalind grumbled, and Margaret laughed. It occurred to Rosalind that if she wanted to conceal the real reason for her attendance at court, she would at least have to entertain the idea of encouraging a few suitors.

There was a disturbance around the queen and Margaret looked up. "I have to go and attend Her Majesty. She will no doubt be taking a stroll in the gardens. Would you like to come or will you rest from your journey?"

"If the queen permits, I think I'll remain here and accustom myself to her apartments again."

"That is an excellent idea. I'll ask the queen."

A few moments later, the queen's court streamed out into the pale sunlight chattering and laughing, leaving Rosalind alone in the pleasant receiving room. She picked up the altar cloth the queen had been embroidering, folded it carefully, and set it back on the stool along with the tangle of silks.

To her relief, the faint scent of Vampire had disappeared with the exodus of the queen's court. She had no idea yet whether the threat came from a male or a female. To her delicate and well-trained nose, there was a slight difference in the odor. Females smelled more like plants, the males like animals. Unfortunately, experienced Vampires could conceal their scent among the overperfumed and underwashed bodies of the court. It would take her some time to sift through the courtiers and discover exactly who was threatening the king and queen. She could only hope she found the culprit before any damage was done.

With a sigh, Rosalind wandered through the large suite of rooms, but there was no further evidence of Vampire occupation. She paused in the queen's bedchamber and closed her eyes. How close had this Vampire gotten to the queen? If she was a trusted member of the household, she might have been the last thing the queen saw at night before she slept. The last thing the queen ever saw . . .

"What are you doing in here?"

Rosalind blinked and swung around to see a tall young man dressed entirely in black leaning against the door. His crow black hair matched his tightly trimmed beard and he had the brightest blue eyes she had ever seen.

"You startled me, sir." Rosalind advanced toward him, but he didn't move away from the door.

"You shouldn't be in here."

She raised her eyebrows at him. "And you should?"

He blinked as if taken aback by her boldness and his amiable expression disappeared. She guessed he was too used to dealing with the simpering maidens of the court to tolerate a direct challenge from a woman.

"In fact, yes. I'm a member of the queen's household and I'm sworn to protect her." He studied her from the tip of her French hood down to her feet. "You, however, are a stranger."

"To you, perhaps, but not to the court or the queen." She marched right up to him. "Excuse me, sir."

His hand shot out and he gently grasped her elbow.

"Not before I know your name and your reason for being here."

Rosalind gave an exaggerated sigh. "Now you are being ridiculous. If you let go of me, perhaps I won't embarrass you in front of the queen by insisting on an apology."

Up close, she saw his skin was olive and that within his fine eyes lurked an intriguing strength of purpose that matched her own. He smelled of exotic spices and leather, not Vampire, for which she was profoundly grateful. Tangling with a Vampire without her weapons— and in the queen's bedchamber in broad daylight—was hardly the way to begin her mission.

"Sir, the queen is in the gardens. If you insist on being difficult, why don't we go and find her? Then you can make your apology and be done with it."

"That's an excellent idea."

Rosalind met his gaze, her own unflinching. "Then let go of me."

"Not until you tell me your name." He inhaled slowly and his blue eyes narrowed as he scrutinized her face. As if he couldn't help himself, he trailed his fingers along the line of her jaw, paused to feather his thumb over her lower lip.

"It must be Helen, because your beauty is unsurpassed." He leaned in closer until his lips almost brushed hers.

She resisted the urge to nip his thumb, instinct telling her that inviting him into her mouth wouldn't be wise. Was he trying to intimidate her, or was he as intrigued by her as she was by him? She managed an unsteady breath. For some reason, his mere presence made it difficult for her to remember her own name, let alone why she was annoyed with him.

"Do you normally kiss any woman you find unprotected?"

His smile was an invitation to sin. "Only the pretty ones. Now tell me your name."

"Why is it so important for you to know who I am?"

"So that I can couch my apology to you in an appropriately abject manner?"

She couldn't help herself. Her mouth quirked up at the corners. "I am Lady Rosalind Llewellyn."

He dropped her arm abruptly. *"Llewellyn?"*

"Indeed."

He started to laugh, his teeth white and even against his tanned skin. "I don't believe it."

"What on earth does that mean?"

He bowed low and stepped away from the door. "Just that I was expecting someone far more . . . exciting."

Rosalind glared at his handsome laughing face. "I do not excite you? In truth, I am relieved to hear that, as I find you rude, ignorant, and totally beneath my interest."

His expression sobered. "Oh, you'll find me of interest, my lady. I'm Sir Christopher Ellis. I'm sure your grandfather has spoken of my family."

"I have no idea what you are talking about." Oh, but she did, and the thought was utterly terrifying. She fisted her hands within the folds of her gown.

"You are lying, Lady Rosalind. Your kind has lived in fear of mine for generations."

"My *kind*?"

"You know what I mean, my lady." He bowed again. "But I'm not going to discuss it here."

Her cheeks heated at the implication that she was naive enough to speak openly about her family's secrets in the queen's bedchamber. *"You* accosted *me*, sir. I was merely reacquainting myself with the queen's domain, with her permission, of course."

"Of course." He stepped back and she forced herself to step past him calmly, without betraying her unease. "How old *are* you?"

She should have kept walking, but found herself looking back over her shoulder to get one last glimpse of his long, elegant frame lounging in the doorway. "That's none of your business."

"True, but I was anticipating a challenge, a worthy competitor, and instead I get . . . a child."

"Do you often kiss children?"

"I didn't kiss you." He slowly straightened. "Though you could sorely use it. And I think I might enjoy kissing you—if you weren't a cursed Llewellyn."

This time, Rosalind kept moving. When the occasion arose, she would enjoy shoving his mocking words down his throat. How dared he suggest she needed kissing? And how dared he underestimate her fighting skills? But that was the way of all men. As the first Druid female born with the mark of Awen, she had worked twice as hard to earn the respect of her teachers and her grandfather.

She reached the palace gardens and drew in great big gulps of fresh air. He might think himself superior to her and he might be the most handsome man she had ever seen, but it made no difference. If it came down to a fight between her and Sir Christopher Ellis, she would win.

"The king will see you now."

Rosalind entered the small private chamber, sank into a low, graceful curtsy, and held it, her gaze fixed on the dusty floorboards. "Your Majesty."

"Lady Rosalind."

King Henry took her hand and brought her upright. He towered over her, his chest twice the width of hers, his thighs in their tight brown hose as thick as her waist. She blinked at his doublet, which was embroidered with golden thread and costly embedded jewels, and slowly raised her eyes to his face. Four years had changed him, had deepened the suspicion in his hooded eyes, pursed his small, petulant mouth, and added flesh to his once pure profile.

"According to my chief gentleman of the bedchamber, if the need arises, members of your family are always to be given immediate access to my presence. Why is that? I wonder."

Henry led her across to the fireplace and then took possession of the only chair. Rosalind clasped her hands together and faced him.

"I believe it is because of the relationship between my grandfather, Lord John Llewellyn, and your father, the late king."

"So I've been told." The king's keen gaze traveled over her, and she forced herself to look steadily back at him. "Lord John served my father faithfully and received many honors for his loyalty."

"That is true, sire, and we are very grateful for your royal patronage."

"I assume your grandfather wishes you to resume your duties at court and perhaps catch a husband this time, eh?"

Rosalind bit her lip. "He does, sire, but there is another reason."

The king's expression darkened and inwardly Rosalind winced. It was well known that King Henry considered himself intellectually superior to most men. The idea that a mere woman knew something he didn't wouldn't sit well.

"By your leave, Your Majesty." She held out the sealed parchment her grandfather had given her. The king took it and turned it over.

"This is my father's royal seal."

"Yes, sire. King Henry wrote the letter and gave it to my grandfather for safekeeping."

"But it is addressed to me."

"Yes, sire."

The king looked up. "Do you know what the letter says?"

"Some of it, sire, but not the exact words. As you can see, the seal is intact."

The king slid the blade of his dagger under the seal, unfolded the parchment, and began to read. Rosalind tried to relax and watched as a bee banged endlessly against one of the tightly closed leaded windows. She itched to set it free, but she couldn't move until the king finished reading the letter.

After a long while, the king lifted his head. "This is madness."

"I know it seems a little unusual, sire, but—"

"*Unusual?* This letter suggests that my father acquired his throne using sorcery." His hand clenched around the parchment, crumpling it within his massive palm. "Is this an attempt to blackmail me?"

Rosalind swallowed hard. "No, sire. It is the truth written in your father's own hand."

"The hand of a lunatic, rather. God knows my father was many things, but he was as sane as you or I." The king rose to his feet and started pacing the opulent room. "It must be a forgery."

Rosalind gathered her courage. "Sire, it is the truth. I swear on the Bible."

King Henry swung around to confront her and she forced herself not to cringe. "These creatures your family is supposed to protect me from, these *Vampires*. How is it that I've never seen one?"

"Because my grandfather protected your family so well."

"A convenient answer, my lady, but hardly a convincing one." The king started to pace again. "Is that why you have returned, then? To save me from these monsters?"

"Yes, sire."

His laughter was meant to hurt and to humiliate. "*You*? How old are you, sixteen?"

Rosalind raised her chin. "I'm almost twenty, sire, and I've trained my entire life to protect you from the Vampire threat."

The king glared at her. "This is ridiculous, a fairy tale, an abomination perpetuated in my father's holy memory."

"It is the truth," Rosalind repeated. "My own father died in this service." She couldn't fail her family now, couldn't return to Wales and admit she'd been unable to convince the king to let her guard him. It had been difficult enough to persuade her father to train her as a Vampire slayer, being as she was a girl, and not the eldest son he had hoped and prayed for.

"If you don't want to believe me, sire, will you at least let me stay at court?"

"To protect me?"

"If the need arises, yes."

His biting sarcasm made her want to lower her eyes and concede defeat, but her cause was too important. The king had no idea the havoc a nest of Vampires could create or how vulnerable he truly was. It was her job to ensure that he never did.

He held her gaze, his golden eyes so cold she suppressed a shiver. "And if I should suspect this is just an attempt to gain my trust and then assassinate me? It would be a simple enough matter to have your whole family executed."

Rosalind tried to swallow. "That is true, sire. But your father swore an oath to protect my family, as we protect yours." In desperation she glanced down at her left hand and pushed up her sleeve. "Do you remember your father having a mark like this on his wrist?"

The king leaned closer to look. "Yes, I believe he did," he said grudgingly. "It says in the letter that the Druids marked him with the sign of Awen when he accepted their bargain."

"That is correct, sire. My family has the same mark, although some of us are born with it."

"This is madness. My father is dead. I am king now."

"Of course, Your Majesty. But ... are you prepared to risk his heavenly displeasure and the wrath of the Druids if you break his sacred vow?"

The king glared down at her for a long endless moment. "You are a brave little thing, aren't you?"

Rosalind lowered her eyes respectfully. "My grandfather describes me as headstrong and willful."

"And he is right." The king sighed. "I will read the letter again, and see if I can make any more sense of it."

Rosalind took a step toward him. "If it pleases you, sire, the contents are for your eyes alone. No one else should know about this."

" 'If it pleases me ...' You are an impertinent chit, aren't you?"

"I am only trying to protect you, sire." Despite the fact that her knees were shaking, Rosalind risked a hopeful smile. "And may I have your permission to stay at court?"

Henry nodded as he folded the letter and tucked it into a leather pouch hung around his waist. "You may attend the queen. I cannot have you following me around like a lost dog."

She had no intention of doing otherwise. By all reports, the latest Vampire threat came from within the aging queen's court. "I understand, sire, but if you ever have need of me, please do not hesitate to let me know."

The king laughed, his good humor apparently restored. "In case one of those creatures you supposedly hunt jumps out at me?"

Rosalind's tentative smile died. "If one of the Vam-

KISS OF THE ROSE   21

pires gets that close, it would probably be too late to save you, sire."

Henry raised an eyebrow. "That dangerous, aye?"

"Indeed, sire." She knew he was humoring her, but there was nothing she could do about it. She could only hope that when the time came, she would be able to protect him.

"Thank you, Your Majesty." She curtsied low and backed out of the room, leaving him staring after her. She stumbled into the anteroom and let out her breath. A hundred pairs of eyes studied her, assessed the success of her meeting with the king, and gauged his mood from hers.

With a gracious smile, she nodded at Sir Richard and walked out into the palace gardens. Her knees suddenly gave way and she sank onto the nearest bench with an audible thump. The king was even more formidable than she remembered, his power palpable and his threat to destroy her all too real.

She shivered at the thought of her grandfather and younger siblings rotting in jail or, even worse, facing execution. Would the king become more amenable when he read the letter again, or would he rescind his permission for her to reside at court?

Rosalind's heart fluttered against the stiff brocade of her bodice and she concentrated on slowing her breath. She had to find Rhys, tell him what had happened with the king, and, even more important, reveal the unexpected presence of one of her family's most deadly enemies.

Chapter 2

Rosalind managed to avoid the queen's party by taking a shortcut through the kitchen gardens to the stables situated behind the oldest wing of the palace. She paused behind a low brick wall covered in ivy and whistled. The lyrical song of a blackbird floated back to her, and she followed the sound to the farthest stall in the stables.

"Rhys?"

"In here, my lady." Her redheaded groomsman pushed his way past the horse he was brushing and emerged at the door of the stall. "What's wrong?"

Rosalind paused to take a deep steadying breath, one hand braced on the door. "Why do you assume something is wrong?"

He studied her, his head cocked to one side. "Because your face is all red and you are panting."

"I might've been running for pleasure."

His grin was taunting. "The only time I've ever seen you run was from six—"

Rosalind brought her finger to her lips. "You don't know who might be listening."

Rhys chuckled. "Indeed, who knows what this horse might tell the other horses tonight?"

"I'm serious. We're not at home now and we have to be careful."

"Are you being careful with your reputation as well? Chasing me down in the stables might raise a few eyebrows."

Rosalind sighed. "You're right. I should have been more circumspect, but I was so worried. . . ."

Rhys took her hand and opened the door of an empty stall. "We can talk in here. The horses will warn us if anyone approaches."

Rosalind was grateful for his calm strength. He was five years older than she was, but they had become close in the years she'd lived at home to nurse her mother. When he heard she was to return to court, he'd offered his services as her groomsman and servant. He came from another old Druid family and was well versed in the art of destroying Vampires. Rosalind had once wondered if he resented her because she bore the mark of Awen, but he'd never shown any sign of it. With his fighting skills and her ability to scent Vampire activity—not to mention her special access to the king—they were a formidable team.

"How did it go with the king?"

Rosalind grimaced. "He didn't execute me on the spot, but he certainly didn't believe a word I said."

"Why would he?" Rhys upturned the water bucket and invited Rosalind to sit on it. He perched opposite her on a bale of straw, hands resting on his widespread knees. "Would you believe such a fantastical tale?"

"Then why am I here if no one will listen to me?"

"You're here so that when something does happen— and according to the prophecies, it will happen very soon—the king has someone to protect him whether he believes in you or not."

"I suppose that's true." Rosalind smoothed her gown over her legs. She shivered. "I thought he was going to kill me."

"But he didn't and you are still alive, so what else is troubling you?"

Rosalind sniffed. "Sometimes you are horribly practical, Rhys. Had you not a care for my safety at all?"

"You know I care."

She looked hurriedly away from him, aware of the sudden intensity in his voice, and the warm look in his eyes. He was a quiet, patient man and the change in his feelings had happened so gradually that she had been slow to realize he no longer saw her as a fellow fighter, but as a woman. Anxious to avoid the complications of his concern, she quickly changed the subject.

"I am to serve the queen."

"So I heard."

"It gives me the perfect opportunity to seek out the Vampire traitors and dispose of them."

"I believe that was the general idea."

"When I was first introduced to the queen, I sensed a Vampire presence."

Rhys sat forward. "Male or female?"

"I couldn't tell. It was just a trace, a remnant rather than the real thing." She frowned. "Mayhap it is one of the older ones who can conceal their scent. I hope not."

"The Vampire Council would send their best against the king."

"That is true." She sighed. "And I haven't told you the worst of it yet."

"What could be worse?"

"I met a man who is a member of the Ellis family."

Rhys paled, his freckles standing out plainly in his appalled face. "A damned Druid hunter? What in God's name is he doing here?"

"I don't know. It was hardly a topic for discussion in the queen's bedchamber."

Rhys scowled. "He's probably a member of that accursed Mithras Cult the Romans set on us as well. I hate them almost as much as I hate the Vampires."

"As if the Vampires need any help against us these days." Rosalind sighed. "Why on earth does the Ellis family still support them?"

Rhys frowned down at her. "Originally, I suppose, their hatred of all things Druid led them to ally themselves with our greatest enemy. And, as time passed, and the races dwindled, both sides have needed their human allies to do their work for them." He shrugged. "We aid the Druid priests, and they aid the Vampire Council. What's the name of this particular devil's spawn?"

"Sir Christopher Ellis, or so he said."

Rhys nodded. "I haven't heard much about him. I'll find out what I can for you. I don't suppose he told you why he was here, did he? The Ellises only usually turn up when there is a problem the Vampire Council can't solve alone."

"No, he just insinuated that he'd been looking forward to a good fight with a Llewellyn and that I was a big disappointment."

Rhys laughed. "Then he doesn't understand you at all, does he, my lady? And that gives you a distinct advantage. If only we knew why he was here . . ."

Rosalind wrapped her arms around her legs and rested her chin on her knees. "It can't be a coincidence that Vampires return to court and so do their accursed protectors." She shivered. "I've never understood why any human would choose to defend the undead, have you?"

"The Ellises are said to be direct descendants of Julius Caesar, who hated the Druids with a passion, and set the cult of Mithras after us for all eternity."

"But we are so few. . . ."

"And they do not care."

Rosalind met his gaze. "I'm sure you're right, but it is a distraction I don't need. How can I concentrate on killing Vampires when I have to worry about being killed myself?"

Rhys grinned. "You are more than capable of handling a hundred Christopher Ellises *and* the Vampires he's vowed to protect. You are one of the best Vampire slayers I've ever trained." He held out his hand to pull her to her feet.

"Thank you."

He smiled down at her and started picking bits of hay out of her hair. "If you don't wish everyone to assume we had an assignation, perhaps you should tidy yourself up."

"I will." She looked up at him and then regretted doing so as he kissed her nose. She stepped out of his reach and pretended to fuss with her skirts. When Christopher Ellis had tried to kiss her, she hadn't stepped back, she'd just stood there like a fool and breathed him in. "I need to get back. I will try to see you tomorrow."

Rhys nodded. "Dawn is probably the best time. I'll be up grooming Geithin for your morning ride and I can accompany you out."

"Do you think I should write to Grandfather and tell him about Christopher Ellis?"

Rhys opened the door, peered out, and gave her the signal to move past him into the deserted passageway. "As soon as I've secured a safe way to pass on your messages to him."

She shivered as they came out into the sunlight. "How am I going to be able to train amongst all these people?"

Rhys patted her shoulder. "We'll find somewhere. There are many secret places in an old palace like this and I have plenty of ideas."

Rosalind shaded her eyes and looked back toward the palace. Had anyone seen her enter the stables? Was she already being watched by the Vampires and the Ellis family? A stable boy came around the corner carrying a bucket of water. Rhys cleared his throat and spoke loudly, his usually refined Welsh accent suddenly almost unintelligible. "Aye, my lady. Your horse will be ready at dawn."

Rosalind smiled at him. "Thank you, Williams."

Rhys bowed. "You're welcome, my lady."

Rosalind strolled back across the park to where the queen's court was gathered to enjoy the spring sunshine. Rhys made an excellent servant, but in truth, he was her social equal and a potential husband, a fact her grandfather had pointed out to her on several occasions recently. She'd never considered Rhys in that light and found his sudden interest in her unsettling.

Could she learn to see him like that? Rosalind paused to glance back at the stables. During the years of her training, the thought of marriage and all it entailed had never appealed to her, but Rhys was a good man and he understood her well. . . .

When she rejoined the queen's court, there was no sign of Sir Christopher Ellis, but Rosalind spotted Margaret and waved. When Rosalind reached her, Margaret slipped her arm through Rosalind's and walked her toward the shade of an old oak tree.

"I spoke to Lady Clarence and offered to share my bed with you tonight."

"Won't Robert object?"

Margaret poked her in the ribs. "Robert is away at our house in the countryside, setting things to right for our return in the summer."

"When will he be back?"

"In about two weeks, I believe. Until then, I'm lodged with the queen's household."

"Thank goodness. I'd hate to share a bed with a stranger." Rosalind squeezed Margaret's arm. "At least I'm used to your snoring."

"And I'm used to your sleepwalking."

Rosalind concealed a smile. Her sleepwalking had proved a very convenient excuse to get her out at night whenever necessary. She might need to use the ruse again. She stiffened as she recognized a tall, dark figure walking away from the palace and toward the queen.

"Do you know that man, Margaret?"

"Which one?"

"Sir Christopher Ellis, the one dressed in black."

Margaret gave her a speculative glance. "Would you like me to introduce you to him?"

"Not really. Even from a distance he looks rather arrogant and completely disagreeable."

"It's not like you to take an instant dislike to someone you've never met."

"Oh, we met earlier in the queen's bedchamber," Rosalind said airily. "He assumed I was up to no good."

Margaret gave a trill of laughter. "He is quite arrogant. His father was English and his mother Spanish, which is why he has found such favor with Queen Katherine. He speaks her language impeccably as well as several others. She believes he will have a great future as a diplomat."

"Indeed," Rosalind muttered. He had reached the queen now, and was speaking to her. Rosalind blanched when he gestured in her direction.

"Hurry, Margaret."

"What?"

Rosalind picked up her skirts and headed straight for the queen, smiling as she dropped into a low curtsy. The queen beckoned her to her feet.

"Sir Christopher was just asking about you, Lady Rosalind."

"I'm sure you were able to reassure him that I was not a thief intent on stealing your jewels, Your Majesty." She raised her chin and looked straight into Christopher Ellis's cornflower blue eyes. "Don't you have something to say to me?"

Sir Christopher shrugged. "As I was explaining to Her Grace, my primary concern is always her most sacred welfare."

"And yet I'd still appreciate an apology."

The queen laughed. "Perhaps you should oblige the lady, Sir Christopher. Rosalind could never be a threat to me. I love her like a daughter."

"Thank you, Your Majesty." Rosalind bent to kiss the queen's hand. Sir Christopher bowed and turned slightly away from the queen. Rosalind followed him, placed her hand on his arm, and steered him to a quieter spot. Despite his slender appearance, muscles flexed and coiled beneath the fine black velvet of his sleeve.

"Well, are you ready to apologize?"

He grimaced. "The queen has no idea what you are, does she?"

"Neither do you."

He stepped closer until they were toe-to-toe. "Unfortunately, I've seen what your kind does to those you seek to destroy."

"And your family's legendary atrocities against my people are any better?"

"You've remembered who we are now?" He shrugged. "No matter. We all do what we must."

She stared up at him. "Your arrogance is truly astonishing, sir. Do you ever stop to think that what you are doing is wrong?"

He went still, his gaze fixed on hers. "Do you?"

"Of course not."

He brought her hand to his lips and kissed it, grazing his teeth lightly over her knuckles. "Which is why our families will continue to fight and you will continue to lose. We have protected the Vampires for centuries; you can hardly expect us to give up now just because you don't like it."

She tried to pull away, but his fingers tightened on her wrist. He turned her hand over, and this time the hot tip of his tongue circled the center of her palm.

"We shall see about that," Rosalind managed to gasp.

His eyebrows rose. "Is that a challenge?"

She wrenched her hand free and curtsied. "Oh no, sir, it is a promise. I will never cede this court to you and the monsters you protect."

He stared at her for a long moment and then walked away, leaving her breathless and so angry she wanted to run after him and slap his face. She had done nothing to him, yet he thought he had the right to destroy her simply because she came from Druid stock. But she had right on her side. Protecting the king and queen from the Vampires was a just cause.

"Are you all right, Rosalind?" Margaret asked. "You look a little fierce."

Rosalind forced a smile and turned back to Margaret. "I'm fine. Sir Christopher obviously isn't the sort of man who finds apologizing easy."

"What man does?"

Rosalind laughed. "How true."

As the sun disappeared behind the clouds, the queen, surrounded by her ladies, headed back to the palace. Margaret and Rosalind followed more slowly and just avoided the first drops of rain as they came into the hall.

Margaret didn't pursue the queen into her suite, but hesitated by the stairs. "Do you wish to go and see if your belongings have arrived in our room?"

"Yes, please." Rosalind accompanied Margaret along

a series of winding and ever-narrowing passageways and up two more flights of stairs until they were under the eaves of the great house.

"Here we are." Margaret pushed open the door to reveal a bed that took up most of the small space. Two chests and several pegs hammered into the thick beams of the lime-washed walls would hold their clothing. Rosalind's belongings sat on the patchwork counterpane, the contents spilling out onto the floor. Margaret looked around. "Did someone start to unpack for you? I wonder where they went."

Rosalind stared at her bag and noted the broken lock that Margaret had overlooked. "It doesn't matter. I prefer to do it myself anyway." She smiled at Margaret. "There is scarcely room for both of us in here. Why don't you go down and attend the queen and I'll finish this?"

Margaret cast a doubtful look at the bag. "Are you sure, Rosalind? I confess I am a little fatigued. Sitting quietly with the queen sounds like an excellent idea."

"Then go ahead." Rosalind maneuvered Margaret out into the corridor, kissed her cheek, and watched her walk down the hallway. Her bright smile faded as she shut the door and leaned up against it.

Someone had been through her bag. Not that they would find anything of interest. Rhys had carried everything that needed to be concealed in his saddlebags, and would hold her weapons for her until she found somewhere safe to keep them. With a sigh, she started to unpack, anticipating an unpleasant surprise with every garment she unfolded, but she found nothing.

She laid her petticoats, stomachers, bodices, and false sleeves in the chest and hung two of her gowns on the vacant pegs on the wall. She checked her jewelry case and was relieved to find it was still locked. She hadn't brought many jewels with her, but the box proved useful for carrying pins, cosmetics, and all the items necessary for a young lady appearing at court—plus the smallest of her daggers.

She pulled back the feather quilts and went to tuck her prayer book under the pillow. A single red rose placed on a large white kerchief lay on the crisp linen. Had Margaret left it there to welcome her? Somehow Rosalind doubted it.

She leaned over the rose, her nostrils wrinkling as she caught the distinct scent of tainted Vampire blood, and saw the red stain spreading on the linen. Avoiding the thorns, she carefully picked up the flower by the stem and dropped it to the floor. The rapidly decaying rose split open to reveal white inner petals, less contaminated by the blood, which began to disintegrate.

"By all the saints, who would do that?" Rosalind whispered. But if Christopher Ellis knew she was here, surely the Vampires did as well, and this was their idea of a greeting.

Rosalind wiped her fingers furiously back and forth on her skirts and then washed her hands in water from the jug in the corner. She picked up the handkerchief between finger and thumb and studied the initials embroidered in black silk on the corner: C.E.E. While she was with the king, had Christopher Ellis searched her personal belongings and left a poisoned rose on her pillow, or had he stood by and watched as one of his Vampire allies invaded her privacy?

She touched the corner of her mouth. He'd almost kissed her. . . . With a shudder she sat down on the bed. He'd already tried to scare her off by being overfamiliar; had he hoped she would run away because of a bloodstained rose? She smiled slowly. She'd seen far worse than a drop of Vampire blood, and she'd been kissed *far* more competently. Rhys was right. Christopher Ellis didn't really know her at all.

ChapteR 3

"I disagree, Roper. Rosalind Llewellyn couldn't have killed this one." Christopher Ellis stared down at the bloated corpse wedged under one of the ornamental bridges in the king's gardens. It was still early in the morning and the gray sky was heavy with the promise of rain. Apart from him and his servant, the grounds of the palace were deserted. They had stolen out early to view the body before the man who'd discovered it officially delivered his report to the king's guard.

"Why not? She's here, isn't she?"

Christopher gave his servant an impatient glance. "She's only been here a day. He hardly looks or smells like fresh kill, does he?"

Roper's face took on its usual stubborn lines. "Something killed it."

"I can see that." Christopher turned away and sucked in a deep breath of clean air through his mouth. "The question is, what?"

"Druids, sir, isn't it always?"

"Not always." Christopher sighed. Sometimes Roper's fanatical hatred of the Druids annoyed even him.

But in some ways the body did look like a Druid sacrifice; despite its bloated appearance, the skin was milky white as if there was no longer any blood left in it. This wasn't the first body that had turned up in this condition, and Christopher feared it wouldn't be the last. It was the reason he had been ordered back to court with such haste.

"Well, I reckon it's her," Roper insisted.

"This man is built like a bull and Mistress Llewellyn barely comes up to my shoulder. How on earth do you think she killed him? Did she drop out of a tree onto his head, or lurk in the bushes and chop him off at the knees with an ax?"

"Now you are being stupid, sir. He still has his legs." Roper, apparently unperturbed by the stench, poked the flabby dead flesh. "And those Druids have powers, sir. You know that. They can perform unnatural acts."

Christopher tried to imagine the petite and beautiful Rosalind Llewellyn killing a man and found it impossible. Yesterday, he'd tried to shock her, but in truth had ended up shocking himself by how quickly she'd aroused him. She was spirited and quick-witted enough to confound even the cleverest of men, but she didn't look like a killer. She looked as if she needed to be bedded thoroughly and often.

"Don't underestimate her, sir. Those accursed Druid families are devilishly cunning."

"I know that." Irritated by the truth of Roper's words, Christopher turned away from the corpse, which was half submerged in the water and too badly decayed for him to determine anything much, and scrambled back up the path. As he walked, tendrils of wet mist attached themselves to his skin like icy fingers that made him shiver.

Was Roper right? What did Rosalind Llewellyn really conceal behind those fine brown eyes? He had to assume she knew her grisly trade, but how well? Perhaps she was a decoy and there was another Llewellyn, preferably a man, waiting in the wings for him to battle. His spirits rose at the thought.

"You just don't want to fight a woman, do you, sir?"

Christopher stopped walking and stared down at the bald head of his servant. "That is complete nonsense. I will fight anyone if it leads to the destruction of the Druid race."

"If you say so, sir, but she's a fetching little thing. I can understand if you've gone all soft on her."

"I haven't gone soft." In truth, certain parts of him had gotten quite hard when he'd sparred with her, but Roper didn't need to know that. "I'll kill her if I have to."

Roper chuckled. "If she doesn't kill you first."

"As you said, she's a fetching little thing, but I doubt she can do much more than scream and run away."

"There you go again, sir, underestimating her. Now, you just be careful."

Christopher's temper crackled to life. "By God's teeth, Roper, stop treating me like I'm five years old!"

Roper's disgruntled expression didn't change as he stared up at his master. "I've known you since you were five years old, lad, and that gives me the right to tell you what I think."

"So you always say, but I'm quite capable of making my own decisions. I'm five and twenty, and my uncle has trained me well."

"Indeed he has, sir." Roper started to walk again and Christopher followed. The sun was rising in the east, adding a silvery outline to the banks of rolling clouds. Christopher drew his cloak tighter around his body as Roper continued to mutter. "Shame it had to be a woman they put up against you, though, sir. Hard to prove yourself against the weaker sex."

Christopher set his teeth and refrained from replying. Roper had a way of expressing his opinions without concern for his master's pride or dignity.

"Do the Vampires know she's here, sir?"

"I should imagine so. Why do you think my uncle sent for me? But I'm confident that together we will be able to vanquish Rosalind Llewellyn and send her home defeated, or in a casket."

"Or maybe they'll make her one of them, sir."

Christopher shuddered at the thought. "Somehow I doubt it. Mixing Druid and Vampire blood is considered dangerous."

"I hadn't thought of that." Roper nodded as he opened the side door into the men's quarters of the palace. "Better to kill her, then."

Christopher pictured Rosalind Llewellyn's expressive face and imagined it laid waste by death. Surely killing her wouldn't be necessary? He'd much rather send her running home and take on a real Llewellyn adversary in her stead. His sympathy toward her waned. Perhaps that was the plan after all. The Druids weren't convinced he was a real threat and had sent a weak female to test him out.

His fingers tightened on the door handle. Was he always going to be suspect? His foreign blood considered tainted? His worth as a Druid slayer doubted by his own people, *his own family*? Christopher's faint smile died. By God, he would show them he was more than capable. He would wreak such havoc in the Druid world that his name would live on for centuries.

Unconsciously, he pressed his hand over his heart where the mark of Mithras branded his skin. He'd vowed, as had his Roman forebears, to defend the Vampires against the Druids. It was true that the Druid threat was much reduced, but he was still bound by his oath. He'd fought hard to be accepted into the cult of Mithras, and he was determined to do its work, whatever his personal qualms about killing a woman.

Christopher slammed the door shut and stomped up the stairs, leaving Roper trailing in his wake. Doubt stirred anew in his mind and he immediately banished it. He could not afford to show any weakness. If he had his way, the Llewellyn wench would wish she had never been born.

Rosalind frowned at the king. "I'm not sure what you want me to say, sire."

King Henry sat down and indicated that she should sit as well. He'd summoned her to his suite just as dawn was breaking, and she'd had no time to do more than throw a cloak over her riding dress and follow the guards through a series of secret passages into the king's presence.

"You heard me perfectly well. I want to know if you believe the Vampires are murdering my servants."

"As I said, it is possible, sire, but . . ."

He sat forward, his massive hand clenched on the arm of his chair. "Five palace servants have turned up dead in the past five weeks, and last night I found a corpse in my bedchamber!"

"Here, sire?" Rosalind looked cautiously around, but could see no evidence of another body, living or otherwise.

"Yes, *here*." The king shuddered and drew his long fur robe closer around his shoulders. He gave a careless flick of his bejeweled fingers. "I arranged for the body to be left in the queen's pleasure gardens. I cannot have my subjects know someone successfully penetrated my private chambers."

"Absolutely not, sire." Even as she admired the king's callous decision to separate himself from the consequences of an unwanted corpse, Rosalind wondered how the queen and her ladies would feel if they unexpectedly came upon a blood-drained body on their way to Mass that morning.

"Did you say there have already been five deaths, sire?"

"Two men and three women." The king lowered his voice. "These Vampires of yours. How exactly do they kill their prey?"

"They have fangs, sire, which they use to puncture the skin and suck blood out of their victims."

The king shuddered. "The body had such marks on its throat. Do Vampires drain their victims dry?"

"Not usually, sire, because—"

"Do they steal their souls?"

Rosalind strove for patience. "Sire, they usually just drink from their victims and leave them alive. It is very unusual for a Vampire to take all the blood from a human unless they plan to . . ."

"Plan to what?"

"If a Vampire wishes to turn a human into a Vampire, he needs to bleed his victim dry and then feed him Vampire blood to revive him and complete the change."

"So it is possible that whoever did this was trying to make more Vampires?"

"It is possible, sire, or the Vampire might simply have gone mad and just wants to kill."

The king sat back, his face pale, his eyes narrowed. "And what do you intend to do about this?"

"Execute the culprits, sire."

"You make it sound so simple."

Rosalind considered the king. How much did he need to know in order to allow her the freedom to operate without obstructions? "Well, it isn't quite that easy, sire. There are hundreds of people attending your court.

Finding even one rogue Vampire amongst them could take some time."

"You have my permission to take whatever steps necessary to keep those monsters away from me. I will also inform my guards and my personal servants that you are to have access to me at all times."

"Thank you, sire. That will certainly help." Rosalind hesitated. "Do I also have your permission to kill the Vampire?"

"Of course."

"Whoever it is?"

The king's brows drew together. "Are you suggesting it could be someone I know intimately?"

"It could be anyone, Your Majesty. Vampires are immortal and make their plans accordingly. Waiting a human lifetime for one moment of revenge or the chance to enslave a king would mean nothing to them."

"Then you have my permission to kill anyone you want." The king met her gaze and the ruthlessness in his expression shocked her. Here was a man who would sacrifice anyone to save himself: a true monarch, a true survivor.

"How do you kill these things if they are already dead and supposedly immortal?"

"You have to decapitate them with a silver-coated blade and stake them through the heart."

"Ah, of course." The king studied her intently. "And you are capable of doing that?"

"Yes, sire. I might appear small and weak, but I have been trained since birth to defeat the Vampires."

"Have you killed any?"

"Yes."

The king's gaze moved restlessly over her. "If these creatures are already dead, what has happened to their souls?"

"Some say that when they relinquish their humanity and become Vampire, their souls are trapped in purgatory for eternity."

"Aye, I can understand that." The king shivered. "Like the soul of an unbaptized child: living, yet not consecrated to the Lord. If the Vampire is killed, do you believe he is reunited with his soul?"

"I don't know, sire." The king's interest in the theological matters of the Church was well known, so Rosalind was hardly surprised by his questions about the Vampire's soul. "Others maintain that a Vampire has no soul because it disappears the moment they become immortal."

"And what do you believe? When you kill one, what do you think happens?"

Rosalind met his gaze. "I believe in hope and the mercy of God. I like to think that the human soul is finally restored to God and can be free of the Vampire taint."

She suspected her family wouldn't agree with her. They believed a Vampire had no soul and deserved the nothingness of death with no promise of resurrection. Perhaps she only wished to justify killing Vampires, but she had to live with her nightmares.

The king stood up and Rosalind followed suit.

"You will keep me informed of your progress, Lady Rosalind."

Rosalind curtsied low. "Of course, sire, and thank you for your trust in me."

The king smiled. "It appears I have no choice but to trust you, my lady. Don't disappoint me."

Rosalind chose to ignore the implied threat in his words and offered him a smile of her own instead. "Thank you, Your Majesty."

She escaped into the anteroom and was escorted by a single guard back down the same secret passageway, which emerged by the kitchens of the queen's main apartments. She had time to wonder just how many women the guard had escorted to and from the king's bedchamber without the queen's knowledge. Rather than venturing back upstairs to awaken Margaret, Rosalind chose to keep going to the stables where Rhys would be waiting for her. The sun was already rising above the roofline of the palace and he would be worried if she didn't appear.

She found him in the stable yard riding his black horse slowly around the yard and leading her mount, Geithin. His auburn hair gleamed like polished copper in the morning sun and his mouth was set in a harsh line. Without speaking, he waited while she put on her gloves and then assisted her into the saddle. He remounted his horse, clicked his teeth, and headed off toward the forest.

Even though she knew he was wise not to question her in the vicinity of the palace, Rosalind would have appreciated a smile or a greeting. She sighed. She was being contrary now and that wasn't fair. She couldn't ignore every sign of interest Rhys made and then be offended when he failed to offer one.

She tightened her grip on the reins, settled deeper into the saddle, and took off after Rhys. She felt her unbound hair spill free of the cloak and swirl around her shoulders. It would take forever to untangle when she got back, but for once she didn't care. This might be her last chance to enjoy herself for quite a while and she intended to make the most of it.

Christopher watched Rosalind Llewellyn canter after her groom, enjoying the glorious sight of her long brown hair streaming out behind her like a war pennant in the breeze. He wondered how it would feel to plunge his hands into her hair, to coil it around his wrist as he trapped her beneath him and spent himself between her thighs. She looked magnificent on horseback, rode with an ease he recognized in himself, as if she were part of the horse.

He'd heard Rosalind's groom had been asking questions about him, and had decided to take a detour to the stables to see if he recognized the man who called himself Rhys Williams. In truth, Williams looked vaguely familiar, but that wasn't a surprise. There were very few remaining human families involved in the struggle between Vampires and Druids. Sometimes, Christopher wished there was none left at all.

There had been no conversation between Rosalind and her groom, which seemed odd. Surely she should have at least apologized for being late? The man had been ready to leave quite a while ago. She hadn't struck him as the kind of woman who would abuse her servants by keeping them waiting.

Christopher stared after her until she disappeared into the gloom of the forest and then turned to go. A hand on his shoulder and the prick of a dagger at his throat made him freeze.

"Sir Christopher."

"Master Warner."

Christopher let out his breath as the dagger was removed from his neck and he was able to turn around. Elias Warner looked as young as ever, his handsome face, blond hair, and merry smile at odds with the flat coldness of his pale hazel eyes. Because he was immortal, his appearance never changed. He served the Vampire Council and had acted as a liaison between them and the Ellis family for centuries.

"Let's go in here." Warner led the way into a recently vacated stall where the warm, fresh smell of horse dung still perfumed the air. "She's a beautiful wench, isn't she, the Vampire slayer? When I searched her belongings, I left her a present."

Christopher frowned. "What kind of a present? Nothing too dangerous, I hope."

"Of course not." Elias smiled. "All women love flowers."

"I suppose they do." Christopher studied the Vampire carefully, but knew he was unlikely to get the full truth of the matter however hard he tried. Like most Vampires, Elias liked to play games a little too much for Christopher's comfort. And, as it appeared that all was well with Lady Rosalind, he decided to ignore the deliberate attempt to distract him.

"What do your masters say about her arrival?"

Warner shrugged. "We wish her dead like all the Llewellyns before her."

"I assumed that. But why is she here? Is there some specific Druid plot afoot I should know about?"

For the first time since Christopher had known him, Warner hesitated. "There is . . . concern."

"Is it the dead bodies that appear to have been drained of blood?"

"Yes."

"And the Vampire Council believes the Druids are responsible? I assume that is why I was contacted."

"That might be true, Sir Christopher, but the Council is also concerned that one of its own might have gone mad."

Christopher struggled to breathe. For Warner to even admit such a thing meant the Council was very worried indeed. Usually if such a situation arose, the Council took care of it and simply executed the rogue Vampire. In Vampire terms, calling in the Ellis family was an act of desperation.

"Is this Vampire so powerful that the Council cannot detect it or control it?"

Master Warner's gaze slid away from his, but not before Christopher recognized the fear laced through it.

"The Council isn't sure what is going on. It might simply be a new Druid plot to draw unwanted attention to the Vampires at court and cause a panic. As a mortal, you are able to gauge the mood of the king and the court far more accurately than the Council, and you can determine if the Druids are at fault."

Christopher didn't believe that for a second. He stared at the other man as thoughts cascaded through his head: a potentially rogue Vampire at the king's court, a member of the Llewellyn family more than willing to slaughter it, and him, stuck in the middle.

"It is a long while since the Vampire Council has requested help from my family here in England," Christopher said carefully.

"That is because that pox-ridden John Llewellyn has guarded the Tudors so well."

"So, what has changed?"

Elias smiled. "Rosalind Llewellyn has arrived in her grandfather's stead."

"And you believe she will be more amenable to helping me investigate these deaths than her grandfather would?"

"She will certainly be more amenable to you."

Christopher frowned. "What do you mean by that?"

Elias opened his hands wide. "Nothing at all."

"I have taken an oath to defeat the Druid race. I take that vow very seriously," Christopher said, his gaze fixed on Elias. "I can promise you, I will do my duty whether the problem has been caused by the Druids or by one of your own."

"I'm sure you will." With a nod, Elias turned away and walked back toward the palace.

Despite his brave words to Elias Warner, the conviction that something was not right lodged firmly in Christopher's mind. During his years of service to his uncle and the Vampires, he'd learned to his bitter cost that nothing was ever as simple as it seemed.

Should he try to solve the problem himself, or would he have to ask for help? He didn't know all the Vampires who inhabited the court, but he'd just made the acquaintance of someone who would be able to sniff them out. He looked out of the small stable window toward the forest and sighed. He hoped to God Rosalind Llewellyn wasn't as stubborn as she looked.

Chapter 4

"Rhys, whatever is the matter?" Rosalind shouted. Rhys finally reined in his horse, cantered back toward her, and drew to a plunging stop that made his mount rear up on its hind legs.

"Nothing at all, my lady."

She sighed. "Oh, please, don't play the servant. What have I done now?"

"You were supposed to meet me at dawn. I was worried."

She pushed her hair out of her face. "I was summoned by the king. A body was discovered in his bedchamber, of all places. The king was perturbed enough to want to question me more closely about the Vampires." She frowned at Rhys. "Did you think I'd gone Vampire hunting by myself? I'm not quite that dim-witted."

Rhys grimaced. "I know that, but I still worry." He looked down at his reins and gathered them more closely in his gloved hand. "I'm being foolish. I missed you. We've spent almost every day together for the last two years."

With a start, Rosalind realized he was right. He'd become such a fixture in her life that she'd begun to take his quiet competence and strength for granted. She'd been so busy dealing with Sir Christopher Ellis and the king and queen that she'd given Rhys little thought.

She shifted in the saddle and pretended to readjust her skirts. "You shouldn't worry about me so much, Rhys. After all, you taught me everything I know."

"And you think that makes me feel better?" His smile was reluctant. "I, of all men, know what a bloodthirsty wench you are."

"Not bloodthirsty enough to go out and search for a murderous Vampire by myself." She reached across and patted his knee. "I'd much prefer you to be by my side."

He covered her hand with his own and then brought it to his lips. "I'll always be by your side."

She carefully eased her hand out of his grasp. "Then please, stop worrying about me."

"Are you afraid of me now?" he asked.

"What do you mean?"

"Because I finally told you that I care for you, and would marry you tomorrow if you wished it?" He sighed. "It's all right. I have no intention of dragging you back home and forcing you to settle down. I know you're too valuable to our race for that."

She met his gaze and tried to be honest. "I do feel a little strange with you. It's as if the person I knew, the warrior and friend I trained with, has disappeared, and in his place is . . . a man."

His smile this time was warm. "Aye, I am that, but I always have been. And I've always wanted you. Mayhap the change is on your side, and now you're ready to *see* me as a man."

She swallowed hard. "I'm not sure about that."

He winked at her. "It's all right, Rosalind. I'm not trying to trick you; I understand the mission must come first. I'll wait." He glanced up at the sky where the sun had finally made an appearance. "We should get back. You'll be late for Mass."

Rosalind headed toward the palace, her attention focused on braiding her wind-tangled hair rather than where she was going. She gasped as she bumped into something solid and was grasped firmly around the elbows and set back on her feet.

"I apologize, sir," she said. "I was not aware . . ." She stopped speaking and went still. The man in front of her had the face of an angel, but the feral scent of a wolf. Rosalind knew her unwise preoccupation with her appearance might just have cost her life. She glanced back at the stables, where Rhys was still dealing with their tired horses. It was too far to run. Would the Vampire be stupid enough to attack her in public?

She met his gaze, glad that she was unaffected by the compulsion in his pale golden eyes to force her to stare at him forever, to willingly offer him the blood he needed to survive. Her hand moved toward the leather pouch hanging from her jeweled girdle.

"There is no need to arm yourself. I have no intention of hurting you."

He held up his hands to show he had no weapon. His voice was warm and compelling, his expression friendly.

"I doubt you would risk such a thing in broad daylight, sir."

He bowed and gestured at the path back to the palace. "May I walk with you?"

"Do I have a choice?"

He smiled at her. "There are always choices, Lady Rosalind. Some of them less bloody than others." He fell into step beside her. "My name is Elias Warner. I represent the Vampire Council at the king's court."

Rosalind glanced at him as the path narrowed and

he paused to allow her to precede him. "I believe my grandfather may have mentioned you."

"I knew him well. We often crossed swords both physically and mentally. He was a fine opponent."

"I don't remember you being here when I was a child."

His smile was wry. "That's because even humans would notice if I stayed this age forever. I reside at court for about ten years and then leave again. I reappear a generation later, as my own son, when those who might remember me have died or left the court."

Rosalind focused on the path ahead of her. "And why did you approach me, Master Warner? It seems unlike one of your kind."

Elias Warner stopped walking and faced her, all signs of humor removed from his expression. "I am the ambassador, if you will, of the Vampire Council. I'm sure your grandfather told you that. In extraordinary circumstances I am ordered to share information with your family. Over the centuries, the Llewellyns have learned to ignore me at their peril."

"And what does the Vampire Council want with me? To stop my investigation of the recent murders?"

He shrugged, the gesture as elegant as a cat's. "Five deaths in just over a month isn't unusual."

"What is unusual is that corpses are turning up right under the king's nose. He is most displeased."

"I should imagine he is."

Rosalind frowned. "You still haven't told me what you want."

"I wanted nothing but the pleasure of introducing myself to you." He raised his eyebrows. "What more could any man desire?"

Rosalind sought for patience. Her grandfather had warned her that talking to members of the Vampire Council required extreme caution and a devious mind.

They had perfected the courtly ability to smile and promise you everything while simultaneously selling you and your secrets to your worst enemy. Which, in this case, meant the Ellis family.

"Have you introduced yourself to Sir Christopher as well?"

"Sir Christopher? I have made his acquaintance." He smiled. "I even suggested he speak to you, but he seemed reluctant."

"That's probably because he doesn't wish to talk about exactly who is killing these people." Rosalind held Elias's gaze. "He refuses to believe it is a Vampire."

"And you are quite certain that it is?"

"Why else would you have summoned the Ellis family? You tend to use them for tasks that might draw unnecessary attention to your race, or are seen as beneath the Vampire Council's dignity."

Elias chuckled. "It appears that you are as quickwitted as you are beautiful, Lady Rosalind. I suspect Sir Christopher will underestimate you at his peril."

Rosalind set her jaw. "Of course he will. I'm a woman."

Elias doffed his hat and bowed low. "A very beautiful woman, indeed." He straightened up and caught her gaze. "Did you like your gift?"

Rosalind fought a shiver of revulsion. "The bloody rose you left on my pillow?"

He opened his eyes wide. "You did not care for it? I thought it a particularly fitting tribute both to your name and your calling."

"And you probably hoped it would send me running home to Pembrokeshire."

His smile this time was slow and full of speculation. "I'm glad you didn't run. I'll enjoy watching you and Sir Christopher match wits."

Rosalind curtsied. "Thank you for escorting me

back to the palace, Master Warner. I'm sure we'll meet again."

He laughed and held the door open for her. "I'm sure we will. Good morning."

She let out her breath. Elias Warner must be a very old Vampire to be so unafraid of the daylight. He reminded her of a predator. All that genial amiability concealed a ruthless streak that found it amusing to leave a blood-drenched rose in her bed. She debated returning to the stables to seek out Rhys, but she'd managed to part with him amicably and had no wish to incur his displeasure by admitting she'd bumped into another of her enemies without a dagger in her hand.

At least Rhys had found them somewhere to train, and had agreed to meet with her later that night to sort through their collection of weapons. That made her feel far more secure.

"Good morning, Lady Rosalind. How was your ride?"

Rosalind raised her eyes heavenward and wondered whether she was destined to meet all her foes in one morning.

"Sir Christopher."

He smiled at her and her suspicion was immediately aroused. Under his black velvet gown, he wore a dark blue silk jerkin embroidered with silver that complemented his eyes far too well. "Would you care to join me in the great hall for something to break your fast?"

"Unfortunately, I'm late for Mass. The queen is expecting me." She curtsied and started walking toward the distant chapel where a few late stragglers slipped through the still open doors.

"I'll accompany you, then."

Rosalind gave him an irritated glance as he increased his pace and came up alongside her. "Are you sure you won't be struck down if you try to enter a church?"

"I was about to ask you the same question." His quick grin almost made her smile back. "It is Vampires who avoid sanctified spaces, not Druid hunters, though I understand that even some Vampires can tolerate them for a short while."

"As long as they don't try to partake of the Blessed Sacrament or cross themselves with Holy Water."

He looked down at her, his blue eyes serious. "I've seen Vampires do those things as well. Some of them still believe in God."

She bit back her reply as they reached the queen's chapel, and Sir Christopher held the door open for her. The Mass had already started and the familiar smells of incense and melting candle wax surrounded them. Rosalind saw the queen and a group of her older ladies-in-waiting at the front of the church. Considering how large the court was, she was surprised at the poor showing. Did the younger members of the court stay away or worship elsewhere? It was yet another sign of the queen's waning influence.

Sir Christopher took her elbow and maneuvered her into a pew near the back, then slid in beside her. He knelt down, clasped his hands together, and bent his dark head, the very picture of pious reverence. Rosalind sighed and tried to attend to her prayers, which was difficult when her mind refused to stop thinking about her meeting with Elias Warner and the intentions of the Vampire Council.

When they sat down on the hard pew to listen to the priest, Sir Christopher turned his head so that his lips brushed her hair. "I saw you talking to Elias Warner."

"Is that why you sought me out? To discover what he said to me?"

"I can guess what he said. Surely the question is, what are we going to do about it?"

"*We?*"

"Yes."

"Don't be ridiculous. I'm not going to cooperate with the likes of you. I'm here to kill a Vampire, and you're here to stop me."

The priest raised his hands and the congregation stood to receive the final blessing. Rosalind barely managed to make the sign of the cross before Sir Christopher grabbed her hand and towed her out of the church. He kept walking until they rounded the chapel and were bathed in the shadows of the small graveyard. He let go of her hand and swung around to face her.

"What if I said you were wrong?"

Rosalind stared up at him. "Why would I believe that? I don't trust you, you don't like me, and most important, I am perfectly capable of catching any rogue Vampire by myself."

Sir Christopher's expression darkened. "What exactly did Elias tell you?"

"He simply introduced himself and told me that he represented the Vampire Council at court. When I questioned him about the corpses, he was remarkably evasive. But that was to be expected." Rosalind watched Sir Christopher carefully. "I should imagine he is extremely old and experienced, and if he has served the Council for this long, he must have exceptional skills."

"I'd agree with that."

"I wish I knew," Rosalind said slowly, "what he's really after. Whatever he says, there must be something more to it than that, because why else would my family and yours be sent back to court? Both of us arriving within days of each other is no mere coincidence."

"I'd also agree with that." Sir Christopher sighed. "What I can tell you is that the Vampire Council *is* concerned about the corpses. They asked me to investigate and determine whether this is Druid's work or Vampire."

Rosalind snorted. "Definitely Vampire."

"Are you sure? Isn't it the Druids who drain their sacrifices dry for their pagan rites? Vampires take only the blood they need to survive."

Rosalind glared at him. "I haven't seen one of these corpses, but the king believes the victim found in his bedchamber had been bitten by something. And let me reassure you that human sacrifice is no longer a part of the Druid religion."

He took off his hat and shoved a hand through his hair. "We still might be dealing with a rogue Druid who prefers the old ways."

"Or more likely, a Vampire who simply likes to kill his victims."

His intense blue gaze met and locked with hers. "Which is why I suggest we work together. The court is large; we will be more efficient if we divide the work and share information."

"And I repeat, I don't want to work with you."

"Why not?" He studied her for a long moment. "I can protect you from harm."

Rosalind took a step toward him. "I do not need protecting." He had the audacity to grin and she fought off a desire to slap his face. "And I do not need your help."

He reached for her hand and his strong warm fingers closed over hers, making her skin tingle. "At least think about it, will you? Even though I detest your faith, I'd hate to see a pretty young woman like you overestimate her abilities and end up dead."

Rosalind pulled out of his grasp and curtsied. "Thank you for your confidence in me. I'll let you know when I've killed your Vampire and you can report back to your masters at the Council."

His expression hardened. "They are not my 'masters.' We simply share a common enemy—you."

"An enemy you have almost completely destroyed."

He didn't have anything to say to that, and Rosalind's anger grew. "We are few in number, and wish only to practice our faith in our own way. Why do you still hunt us?"

He shrugged. "We are all bound by the vows we take, Lady Rosalind."

"Even if those vows are outdated and cruel?"

A muscle flicked in his cheek. "Even then. Please think about what I have said."

Rosalind stalked away, aware that her hair was coming loose again and that she needed to go back to her bedchamber and get properly dressed for the day with the queen. She also wanted to ponder Sir Christopher's extraordinary offer. Did he really think she'd sob gratefully at his feet while he saved her from the evil Vampires?

She ground her teeth so hard it hurt. She was tired of being underestimated and was ready to show her mettle. Tonight, she would get a chance to spar with Rhys and ready herself for the battle with her foe. For now, she had to dress in one of her prettiest gowns and accompany the queen to a musical concert. Her life might be full of contrasts, but she could never forget her true mission. With or without Christopher's help, she would track down the rogue Vampire and kill it.

Chapter 5

"Try it again."

Rosalind gripped the handle of her sword until her fingers hurt and stepped forward, the tip of the blade extended to kiss Rhys's. She focused on mirroring his delicate forays and avoiding his more obvious invitations to lunge for his heart and forget everything she had learned.

Her arm ached from holding up the heavy sword and she was perspiring, but she was not prepared to give up. Sir Christopher's patronizing blue gaze filled her mind and she concentrated even harder, saw the slight hesitation in Rhys's guard and went for the kill. The tip of her blade sliced through the linen of Rhys's shirt right over his heart.

He put up his sword and grinned at her. "That was much better. Now let's change weapons and concentrate on dagger play."

Rosalind paused to sheathe her sword and wipe the sweat from her brow. The abandoned stone cellar Rhys had discovered was the deepest cellar of the old palace. To reach it, they had to descend two flights of narrow stairs concealed within the queen's chapel. It was certainly secure, but it was also stuffy and damp.

Rosalind was used to hunting Vampires, and being underground didn't bother her much. But the thickness of the walls and the silence were oppressive. She was just glad Rhys had provided plenty of light. He didn't know how afraid she was of the darkness, ever since she'd fallen into an open grave and almost drowned when the Vampire had risen from the depths of the mud-filled hole and pinned her beneath him. She still had nightmares of being smothered.

Rhys tossed her a dagger and she tried not to groan. She would receive no quarter if she complained or begged for a respite.

Rhys waited until she stepped fully into the light of the circle of candles and bowed. His auburn hair gleamed, his smile taunted her. "Ready?"

Rosalind gathered what remained of her strength and took up her fighting stance. She watched with a practiced eye as he began to circle her. She might not know what to think of Rhys as a potential husband, but in this arena, he was certainly her master.

When Rhys finally sent her on her way, she was so weary she barely managed to fit her feet onto the curved stone steps that went up toward the chapel. Narrow cracks of light from above showed through the well-fitting flagstone that concealed the second set of stairs she ascended. They followed the same spiral pattern as the exposed staircase to the crypt, but came out under the flagstones rather than in the wall. She raised her arms above her head and heaved up the stone, her well-used muscles trembling with the effort to shift it. When she'd scrambled to her feet and replaced the stone, she paused at the exit to the stairwell.

She heard nothing except a barn owl in the distance and the shrill call of a peacock closer by. Rhys would conceal their hiding space and gather the weapons so that no one would ever guess their purpose in the cellar. Rosalind patted the pocket of her jerkin and withdrew her favorite dagger. At least she was armed now, although concealing such a weapon during the day while wearing her cumbersome skirts always proved difficult. She much preferred the freedom of the men's hose, boots, and shirt she wore for her nighttime exploits.

As there was no sound of Rhys emerging from below, Rosalind decided not to wait for him and to make her way back to the palace alone. Her eyes were now accustomed to the dark, and there was just enough moonlight to see the well-trodden path between the chapel and the queen's chambers.

Rosalind set off, her dagger in her hand, her gaze focused on her goal. After only a few steps, she became aware of a disturbance in the air, the sense of a threat, and the vivid stench of fresh blood. She slipped behind the nearest tree and stayed still, tried to breathe through her nose and seek the Vampire's scent, but there was nothing. . . .

She debated moving onward. Perhaps an animal had recently killed rather than a Vampire. She took another long, slow breath and summoned her ability to pick up the resonance of a Vampire kill and the scent of death.

No, not an animal. She might not smell anything specific, but something was wrong. Something lay dying, bleeding, and screaming, if only in the echoes of her mind. Was it possible that Sir Christopher was right, and it wasn't a Vampire, but a Druid killing humans? She angled her head until she could just see the moonlit path. A blur of movement up ahead made her heart beat faster.

There was something or somebody there. Were they waiting for her, or had she inadvertently stumbled upon the very Vampire she sought? She glanced down at the cut her practice had bestowed on her wrist, and blotted it against her shirt. She had no desire to offer her own blood as a Vampire lure. Using the oak trees lining the path as cover, she slowly made her way toward the shimmering black form that edged closer to the queen's chambers with every heartbeat.

The smell of blood grew stronger, so strong that Rosalind felt as if she were drowning in it. A jagged red line of spilled blood leaked from the Vampire's prize and marred the perfection of the flagstones. A vivid reminder that whatever was up ahead had killed once, and would have no qualms about killing again.

A slight movement to her left had Rosalind bringing her dagger up and spinning to face the new threat. Even though she had her blade at his throat, Sir Christopher didn't flinch as he brought his finger to his lips and shook his head. He wore dull black hose, a leather jerkin, and a cloak devoid of decoration. She glared at him for a moment and then returned her attention to the creature by the palace walls. She had to get closer, and that meant crossing the path and finding shelter in the bushes nearest the wall.

She took off at a run, her tired limbs full of energy again, her hunting instincts on fire. The bushes were dense and woody and smelled strongly of rosemary, which helped drown out the scent of blood, but hindered Rosalind as she frantically tried to sniff out the Vampire's identity.

Sir Christopher arrived in the bushes behind her, but she didn't spare him a glance. At least he was quiet. The hooded figure seemed to be doing something to one of the windows, perhaps trying to open it to get in. Rosalind squinted at the indistinct form. Why was it so hard to see exactly what she was facing? It was almost as if the Vampire had the power to distort her reality. With a quick prayer to all her gods, Rosalind gathered herself to run again.

She'd barely managed three strides when a wave of darkness slammed into her like a closing door and knocked her off her feet. Above her, a black vortex swirled and screamed, sucking the air into its depths and momentarily depriving her of her senses. She wanted to clap her hands over her ears to shut out the appalling noise, but it seemed to be inside her head. She felt rather than saw Sir Christopher grab her around the waist and bring her completely to the ground. Her cheek hit the stone paving as she was flattened under the weight of his far heavier body.

Her dagger was still in her hand and she struggled to move her arm, to bring it up and stick the blade into his flesh. At that moment she didn't care where. He placed his hand over her wrist and with an expert twist, held her fingers immobile until she dropped her weapon. Above the scent of rosemary and Vampire, she smelled his breath, the freshness of the apple he'd recently eaten, and a hint of spiced cologne. She focused on breathing him in, and not on the dark, disorientating magic around her that continued to confuse her senses.

The chaotic roaring noise inside her head abated, and she was able to hear again. Both the black fog and the Vampire had gone.

Christopher grabbed her by the shoulder and rolled her onto her back, his lower body still straddling hers, his hands planted on either side of her head.

"What in God's teeth were you doing?"

"Trying to kill a Vampire. What were you doing?" She shoved at his chest, but he didn't let her up. "I knew you were lying about wanting this monster dead."

"I wasn't lying."

"Then why did you stop me?"

He glared down at her. "Because . . ."

"Because?"

"*Because* that was an extremely old Vampire. Didn't you feel it? I didn't want you to get hurt."

Rosalind studied his enraged expression. Was it likely that he had tried to protect her, or was he merely trying to conceal the truth?

"I'm glad you finally admit it's a Vampire we're after. And I'll assume you're right about its age. I can't judge that very accurately except through scent. The older the Vampire, the better they are at concealing themselves." She realized she was babbling.

Although she'd often fought with Rhys and been put on her back, the pressure of Christopher's muscular body over hers made her feel quite strange. Her heart was beating too hard and her breathing was ragged. She shifted restlessly, her hips arching upward. "Now will you please get off me?"

Christopher lowered his gaze to her body, her unbuttoned jerkin, the dark linen of her shirt, and the black hose and supple leather boots. She made a comely boy. Her legs were just as long as he had imagined them. She wiggled again, and his body reacted far too favorably.

"But I like you on your back," he said. "Aren't you going to thank me for saving your life?"

"You wretched dog . . ." she spluttered.

He raised his eyebrows. "I beg your pardon?"

"You didn't save me. You obstructed me, because you can't bear to watch even one of those monsters die."

His smile faded. "I've seen them die. We Ellises have been called on before to dispose of rogue Vampires."

She gazed up at him, her brown eyes full of fire. "All I know of your family is that you murder mine."

He held her gaze. "Nonetheless, we still must work together."

"If this is your idea of working together, we're never

going to catch anything except a cold from rolling around in the morning dew."

"I wouldn't object to rolling around with you at all." He rocked his hips against hers, wondered if she was aware of the thick length of his cock pressing against the soft wool of her hose.

"Oh, for goodness' sake."

He admired her spirit even as he deplored it. Couldn't she see that they needed each other? He took a deep breath and tried to be reasonable. "Pray reconsider your decision. This Vampire is so powerful that not even Elias Warner knows who it is or how to stop it. We cannot afford to argue. We must prevent it from killing the innocent."

She stared up at him, her teeth worrying her lush lower lip. He wanted to replace her teeth with his own, to devour her mouth, and show her just how much she needed him . . . in *so* many ways.

"Rosalind . . ."

He lowered his head and she brought her elbow up and almost broke his nose. As he recoiled, she rolled out from under him, dagger at the ready, and swiped at his chest. Christopher managed to find his feet a second before she did, and blocked the blow.

She stepped out of reach, her expression furious, and he couldn't help laughing. He held out his hands. "My lady, there is no need to—"

He didn't get a chance to finish his sentence before she launched herself at him, feet aimed at his torso, and kicked his dagger out of his hand. Her forward motion brought her down on his chest and they fell back on the ground entangled together in a heap. As Christopher fought to get on top of her and regain his superior position, he heard someone clearing his throat. Christopher looked up and groaned. Rosalind's groom stood there, a sword pointed at Christopher's heart, his stance all business.

"May I suggest you get off my lady, sir?"

Christopher climbed off Rosalind and snatched up the dagger she'd knocked from his hand. Ignoring Rhys, he repeated, "Please think on what I've said."

She rose to her feet, patted at her clothing, and ignored him in return. "Rhys, we need to see what happened to the Vampire's prey."

Christopher frowned. "It's all right. I can do that."

"We don't need your help, Sir Christopher."

"I'm not leaving you two to investigate on your own. Perhaps, if it won't upset your delicate sensibilities, Lady Rosalind, we should all go?"

"I've seen dead bodies before," she snapped. She glanced at Rhys. "The Vampire was over by the palace wall."

He nodded, his gaze flicking between Christopher and his mistress. "I know. I felt something very powerful."

They all walked toward the wall where the Vampire had last been seen. Bloodstains marred the creamy stone, but there was no sign of a corpse. Rhys frowned.

"Are you certain there was a body?"

"Absolutely." Christopher nodded. "When the Vampire used his magic to hold back Lady Rosalind, he must have managed to escape with his prize." He murmured a quick prayer for the poor dead soul. "I wonder where the body will turn up this time."

Rosalind shivered and glanced up at him. "I hope it isn't in my bed. Margaret would never recover from waking up with a corpse."

Christopher took off his cloak and dropped it over her shoulders. To his surprise, she didn't bother to protest his kindness. He took a moment to trade glances with Rhys and discovered that his considerate behavior was not appreciated. "Shall we escort Lady Rosalind back to her chamber?"

Rhys bowed. "It's all right, sir. I'll see to my lady."

After all the excitement, Christopher wasn't willing to get into a brawl with the man now. "Then I will bid you both good night." He nodded at Rosalind. "Think about what I said."

She nodded, her gaze serious and her face smudged with dirt. For some ridiculous reason, he yearned to touch her grazed cheek, to apologize for having thrown her to the ground so roughly. Instead he bowed and turned back toward his quarters. When he'd seen the dark Vampire magic surround her, he'd acted on instinct to protect her. But Rosalind Llewellyn had Rhys Williams to aid her, and scarcely needed his help. And why would he want to help her anyway? She was the enemy.

He shivered as the wind picked up, and rued his gallantry and the loss of his fur-lined cloak. It was supposed to be spring, but the April breezes felt as bitterly cold as those of winter. For once, the entrance to the men's quarters was dark and deserted and he was able to reach his small room without attracting any attention. Despite his concern for Rosalind, he couldn't help remembering how quickly she'd had a dagger at his throat. It appeared the lady had sharp claws after all.

He paused before he opened the door, glad that he slept alone. He had no wish to speak to anyone. He realized that he was far too agitated to go in and take his rest, so with a sigh, he went back down the stairs and stared out at the night sky. He estimated there were still several hours until dawn. Shaking off his apprehension, he headed back to the queen's chapel where he'd first spotted Rosalind earlier that night. Mayhap he'd use his time to see if he could ascertain exactly what she'd been doing there with her servant in the middle of the night.

Not that he believed Rhys Williams was anybody's

servant. The man was far too confrontational to appear as anything less than what he was—a Vampire hunter in his physical prime. A man who also had a rather proprietary air when it came to Rosalind Llewellyn. Christopher studied the arch-shaped door of the chapel. It was highly likely that the two were lovers as well as fellow Vampire hunters.

He grimaced as he recalled the recent subtle pressure on him to wed a distant cousin of his uncle's wife. Marrying your own kind was encouraged. He supposed it was the same for the Druids.

The main door wasn't locked, and Christopher made his way into the vestibule, caught the acrid smell of snuffed-out candles and nothing more sinister. There were two additional doors in the small space, one that led into the main church. He cautiously opened that door and peered down the brightly painted nave, past the massed ranks of candles and the gold rood screen. He could see nothing out of the ordinary.

He focused his attention on the other door. He suspected it went down to the cellars and crypts below the church. Of course, when he tried the latch it refused to open. He contemplated the thickness of the wood and knew he stood no chance of breaking through it unless he used an ax. Desecrating church property was hardly going to win him any friends in the church or at court. Whatever Rosalind and her surly groomsman were up to, they had it well concealed. He would have to catch them entering the door to have any chance of success.

With a frustrated sigh, he turned to go, annoyed with himself for even imagining that the Druids would make it easy for him. In the flickering candlelight he suddenly noticed a small carving in the stone lintel above the main door. He reached up his hand and traced the Druid symbol of Awen, three dots and three lines coming down from them like rays of light. The carving was old, the lines smooth to the touch, so it hadn't been put there by Rhys or Lady Rosalind.

Christopher frowned. It seemed that his current foes weren't the first to take advantage of the trusting nature of the Christian Church. And that was the real problem, wasn't it? The roots of Druidism were enmeshed so tightly with Christianity that it wasn't surprising the two often coexisted rather than clashed. The unlikely battle lines of his particular struggle had been drawn centuries ago, the Christian church and the Druids on one side, and the Roman cult of Mithras and the Vampires on the other.

He'd joined the Cult of Mithras with great anticipation, only to find that the sect had moved far beyond its original purpose of destroying the Druid race. Its main focus these days seemed to be following the Vampire Council's orders rather than making decisions for itself. He had grown to hate it, hated his younger self for being so impressionable and eager to enlist in such a violent struggle.

With a final glance over his shoulder, Christopher retreated to his quarters. Even vows made in haste were for life, and he was well and truly caught. Rosalind Llewellyn's declaration that the Druids no longer made human sacrifices added to his own suspicions, and made it even harder to justify his hate. He scowled into the darkness, which had lifted just enough to illuminate the dainty touch of frost on the grass and spiderwebs. He needed his wits around him, and speculating about the Druids was not helpful. The Vampires needed his protection. That fact was an absolute truth and it had to sustain him.

He opened the door to his room, and went still as he registered a shadowy figure sitting in the single chair. He drew his dagger and inhaled slowly, catching the unmistakable coppery tang of blood.

"Roper, is that you?" he murmured.

There was no answer, and Christopher fumbled with a flint to strike a spark to light the candle beside his bed. He wasn't too surprised to see a corpse with deep puncture wounds in his throat staring sightlessly back at him. He held the candle high and walked around the body. Unlike the other corpse, this man looked like a gentleman, his flabby belly and soft skin more fitted to an indolent existence than a peasant's harsh life in the fields.

Was someone missing this man? Did he have a wife and family somewhere in the countryside anxiously awaiting his return from court, or was he a gentleman of the king's chamber? Christopher leaned in to study the man's fat fingers, and noticed a signet ring on his right hand. Perhaps the crest could be used to identify the Vampire's victim.

He took a few steps backward and considered the message the body in his room was meant to convey. A warning of some kind? But whether it was to dissuade him from hunting the rogue Vampire, or from getting too close to Rosalind Llewellyn, he couldn't tell.

It didn't matter. He wasn't going to stop now. His mission was far too important.

"Sir, is that you?"

Christopher turned to find Roper at his elbow, and for once, was more than glad to see him. He raised the candle so that Roper could see the ghastly figure in the chair. "We need to get rid of that."

Roper didn't even blink. "Aye, sir, we do. I'll call Murray and Douglas."

"The man is wearing a signet ring. Perhaps you might make some discreet inquiries as to his identity to aid the authorities." Christopher shut the door behind them as they left the room. "I think I'll go and sleep in the great hall or the stables."

Roper nudged him and winked. "I'm sure you can do

better than that, sir. A nice armful of warm wanton like that Betsy who changes the bed linen. I'm sure she'd welcome you."

"I don't think so, Roper. I've had enough excitement for one night." The only bed he was interested in crawling into was Rosalind's and he hardly imagined he'd be welcome there. She'd most likely slit his throat. "Good night and thank you."

Roper's face resumed its normally lugubrious expression and he padded down the stairs, Christopher behind him. Christopher paused in the doorway. He couldn't go to the stables—that was where Rhys Williams lodged, if he wasn't already bedded down with Rosalind. Christopher cursed softly and turned toward the great banqueting hall, where the lesser folk slept with the fleas and the dogs in the rushes. He'd sleep there. At least it was safer than being with Rosalind.

Chapter 6

Before she entered the great hall, Rosalind paused at the doorway to survey the crowded scene. Light from a thousand candles bathed the merrymakers, caught on jeweled collars and caps, glanced off head-dresses and throats encircled with precious gems. Rosalind touched her modest ruby and pearl necklace and looked down at the matching gilt pomander that hung from her long girdle almost to the floor.

She'd never been that interested in adorning herself; a sharp dagger had always seemed a far more important possession than a bejeweled trinket. Despite the magnificence of her favorite red gown, she did feel underdressed. And—if she was honest with herself—a little lonely.

As a servant, Rhys wasn't allowed to attend court functions with her. Tonight he wasn't even here, having set off to London to deliver her letter to the first in a chain of secure couriers who would take it to her grandfather in Wales. For the first time in her life, she felt distinctly vulnerable. She took a deep breath and fought her way through the milling crowds toward the table where the queen's ladies sat together.

She saw Margaret dressed in pale blue, diamonds at her throat and in her French headdress. Margaret patted the seat beside her and Rosalind stepped over the bench to squeeze into the narrow space. Margaret studied her, her cheeks flushed, a goblet of ale in her hand.

"Where have you been?"

"I had to write a letter to my grandfather and then go and find my servant to arrange for it to be sent to him."

"I suppose you had to do your duty." Margaret smiled. "That's another reason why you should marry, Rosalind. Husbands are far easier to please than parents."

"I'm not sure about that."

"Trust me, they are. There are many ways of making them forget their anger." Margaret nudged her. "Most of them in bed, of course, but I'm not supposed to tell you about that."

"I know what happens in a marriage bed. I'm not that naive. All that huffing and panting and groaning. It doesn't sound much different from the horses mating in the fields or the ducks in the pond."

Margaret sighed wistfully. "Oh, you're wrong. With the right man it can be . . . beautiful."

Rosalind made a face, glanced down at the trencher in front of Margaret, and stabbed at a piece of capon. Her stomach growled as she swallowed and she took another piece. When she finished chewing, she looked up to find Margaret staring at her.

"What's wrong now?"

"You eat far too enthusiastically."

Rosalind opened her eyes wide. "But I'm hungry." She scooped up some fish and managed to maneuver it into her mouth on the tip of her knife. "If I don't eat, I'll waste away."

"And that would indeed be a tragedy," Margaret murmured. "You have a figure most women would envy."

Rosalind looked down critically at her breasts, which

threatened to overflow her embroidered bodice. "I wish I was flat-chested."

Margaret pressed her hand to her heart. "No, don't even think that. Men adore a comely display of bosom."

"I know." They might be perfect for a maiden at court, but for a Vampire hunter they certainly impeded her speed and had to be bound to prevent them from jiggling. She sighed deeply and tried to pull up her bodice. A wolfish scent drifted past her nostrils and she looked up, knowing who she would see.

"Good evening, Lady Rosalind. You look very fetching in that gown."

Elias Warner smiled at her from across the table, his gaze firmly fixed on her chest. He wore a pale silver doublet and matching hose and his surcoat was dull gold. He seemed to shimmer in the candlelight like well-polished metal. "Good evening, Master Warner. Are you enjoying the banquet?"

"Indeed, Lady Rosalind. If the king is joyful, we are all content, yes?" Elias nodded in the general direction of the king, who sat at the high table at the end of the hall. A giant stuffed peacock complete with feathers sat on the table in front of him, obscuring most of his face. Occasionally the boom of his laughter drowned out the tentative sounds of the musicians in the minstrel's gallery behind him.

Queen Katherine had chosen not to attend but had sent all but one of her ladies to take their meal in the great hall. Rosalind had offered to stay behind too, but her request had been denied. She'd only left after verifying that the lady chosen to stay with the queen was free of any Vampire taint.

She sighed as she studied the beautiful, unlined face of Elias Warner. She'd been here for almost a week and was no closer to finding the Vampire who hunted the king and queen. It was humiliating. Her grandfather would be disappointed; her family would believe she wasn't up to the task. . . .

"Of course we are, sir," Margaret said loudly, and elbowed Rosalind in the ribs. Rosalind realized that Elias Warner had been speaking and that she had no idea what he'd said. "If the weather remains fine, we will both be there."

Elias Warner bowed. "I will look forward to it, then. Your servant, Lady Rosalind, Lady Margaret." With a last appreciative look at Rosalind's breasts, he sauntered away and was soon engulfed in the crowd of servants who were rushing to clear the center of the hall for the dancing.

"Rosalind!" Margaret sighed. "Elias Warner is one of the richest and most eligible men at court this year, and yet you barely bothered to speak to him. How on earth do you intend to marry if you can't even feign interest?"

"I told you, I don't want to get married."

"But you must!" Margaret grabbed her hand, her expression serious. "You cannot want to remain a maiden, an object of ridicule at court, no home but that which your family provides for you, and subject to the petty tyrannies of your brothers' wives?"

"I hadn't thought of it like that."

"Then mayhap you should. It is not a fate I would wish upon my worst enemy, let alone my best friend."

Rosalind turned to wash her hands in the bowl a servant held out to her. She'd never thought about anything except hunting Vampires, but what would happen when she was old or too injured to fight anymore? What would become of her then? There was Rhys, of course. She knew that he would take care of her, but sometimes that seemed remarkably unexciting.

She climbed off the bench and had bent to straighten her skirts when she found her gaze caught on a pair of long muscular legs in shapely black hose. Of course he was wearing black. Did he ever wear anything else?

"Sir Christopher." Even she had to admit that this particular costume was a very splendid black. The intricately patterned lace and embroidery that completely covered the fabric of his doublet and his black ruff were both costly and unique.

"Good evening, my lady." He inclined his head, his smile warm, his blue gaze at least fixed on hers rather than roving over her bosom. "You look ravishing."

Margaret poked her in the ribs and Rosalind managed a simper. "Why, thank you, kind sir."

He held out his hand. "Would you honor me with a dance?"

Rosalind hesitated, only to flinch and leap forward straight into Sir Christopher's arms as Margaret pinched the soft skin below her wrist. "I would be delighted, sir." As Sir Christopher led her away, she turned to glare at Margaret, who smiled unrepentantly back at her.

The musicians struck a loud chord and began one of the slower dances, a pavane. Rosalind placed her hand in Sir Christopher's and they joined the line of dancers advancing and retreating toward the high dais, their hands linked, their steps in graceful unison.

"Your gown is most becoming."

"Thank you. You look very fine as well."

"Although you always look splendid, whatever you wear." He glanced down at her. "I particularly like you in boy's clothes."

She felt herself blush as she remembered the press of his body over hers and tried not to look at him. He was her enemy. She should not even be dancing with him, let alone finding him so fascinating. But, as she'd just written to her grandfather, she'd reluctantly concluded that Sir Christopher was right and they might need to work together to kill the Vampire.

They reached the head of the line, bowed to the king, and separated only to rejoin hands a moment later at the bottom of the set. The steps changed, bringing them toward each other and then away. His fingers tightened over hers as if he feared she might flee.

"Do you find this as difficult as I do?" he asked.

"Find what?"

"The unfortunate attraction between us."

"I am not attracted to you."

"Aye, you are."

"Whatever makes you think that?"

"You're dancing with me, aren't you?"

"Only because my friend Margaret would be suspicious if I didn't. She's determined I should catch a husband."

"You could have said no." He sighed. "And I have behaved just as stupidly by asking you." He gave her a sidelong glance. "I think I'm still shaken from finding that corpse we were looking for in my chamber."

"In your bedchamber?" Rosalind paused to turn a full circle and for Christopher to reclaim her hand. "Why on earth would the killer put the corpse there?"

"I'm not sure, unless it was a warning."

"Does that mean you're going home?"

He grinned, the expression making him far too attractive. "You'd like that, wouldn't you? Unfortunately, I'm not going anywhere."

"I didn't think you would."

"Because I am so brave?"

"No, because you are as stubborn as most men of my acquaintance."

He squeezed her hand as the dance ended and she sank into a deep curtsy. She noticed his gaze was fixed on her bodice.

"You must have to bind them," he said.

She stood up and he kept hold of her hand. "I beg your pardon?"

He nodded at her chest. "When you fight. I hadn't even thought of that."

"And you should not be thinking of it now." She tried to pull out of his grasp.

The music struck up again, this time in the far livelier tempo of a galliard. He pulled her close and guided her into the strident six-beat rhythm of the dance. His arm curved around her waist as he lifted her slightly off the floor for the required two beats, and then put her down.

"Are you and your groom lovers?"

She almost stumbled. "That is none of your concern."

He frowned. "He is of your faith and of the right age."

"And you are insufferably rude."

"That is because I'm distracted by your beauty." He lifted her again, his easy strength making the motion effortless and fluid. "I have been wondering if you have bewitched me."

She looked up at him, but this time he wasn't smiling. "Bewitched you? How on earth would I do that?"

"Druid women lack a certain purity or piety, and they *are* known to dabble in the pagan arts."

She deliberately missed her step and trod hard on his foot. He winced and she smiled. "Why would I waste my time trying to bespell you when I have a perfectly good man in my *impure* bed already?"

"So you are lovers?"

The music grew louder and he adjusted his grip and lifted her high in the air in the slow circle of the volta. As she revolved, she stared down into his fathomless blue eyes and couldn't look away. The lift went on forever, and still she held his gaze. It felt as if they were the only people on the dance floor, the only people in the kingdom . . .

When he finally set her on her feet, she was dizzy and breathless and had to grab on to his arm. The dance seemed too long, her reactions to being held in his arms far too intense. She wished she was somewhere less complicated, like in a fight to the death with a Vampire. Fighting her unwilling attraction to Sir Christopher on the dance floor was far more difficult than she had anticipated.

"Bewitched or no, what are we going to do about these unnatural feelings between us?"

She managed a superior smile. "Unnatural, sir? Surely even your kind finds lust natural, else your family would've died out long ago."

"That is true, my lady, although not lust for a Druid, more's the pity, or our feud would surely be over now. We'd either have wiped each other out or be living happily in perpetual married bliss."

"Then it's lucky that I feel nothing for you, isn't it?" Rosalind asked. "I'd hate to see the end of my race, *or* your face on the pillow next to mine."

She gasped as he lifted her high into the volta again and slowly spun her around. His long fingers encircled her narrow waist and his thumbs almost met in the middle. It was only when he put her down that she realized he had walked them right off the dance floor and into the shadows at the back of the hall. He drew her around another corner and suddenly they were alone. He backed her up against a tapestry depicting the fall of Troy and leaned into her, his hands braced on the wall, his mouth a fraction away from hers.

Before she could protest, he kissed her, his lips warm and firm. The flick of his tongue against the seam of her tightly closed lips was an enticement that sent heat quivering through her entire body. She had to breathe, had to push him away. His teeth tugged at her bottom lip and then sucked it. With a gasp she opened her mouth, and his tongue slid deep, possessing her completely, both demanding and cajoling a response from her.

She closed her eyes and fisted her hands by her sides to stop herself from touching him, gave him only her mouth and yet felt as if she gave him everything.

When he raised his head, she made herself look at him. He licked his lips as if her taste pleased him.

"Have you finished?" She was surprised she sounded so calm.

"Not yet." His mouth descended again and this time she kissed him back, slid her hand into his thick black hair, and explored the curve of his skull with her fingers.

"You want me as much as I want you," he murmured, his teeth nipping at her lower lip, his tongue dueling with hers. "You fight the same demons I'm fighting."

This time she managed to wrench her head away from his, and to push him backward. He didn't stop her, and he didn't move far, but it was enough for her to gather her scattered wits. She wiped a shaking hand across her now sensitive lips.

"I was going to agree that we work together to find the rogue Vampire, but now I'm not so sure."

"Why not?" He frowned at her, all evidence of his passion immediately erased from his face.

"Because if you are unable to restrain your lust, sir, I would fear for both my reputation and, in certain circumstances, for the continuation of my life."

He smiled. "I'm quite capable of separating business from pleasure, my lady. I can assure you that I'll never leave you unprotected or in danger."

"And that's another thing." She closed the gap between them again. "If I agree, it will be to work as equal partners. I do not wish you to protect or coddle me. I'm quite capable of looking after myself."

He bowed extravagantly. "You've already told me that on countless occasions."

"I mean it." She held his gaze. "If you cannot agree to treat me as a partner, I won't help you."

He regarded her steadily for a long moment. "Does that include my partner in pleasure as well?"

"No!"

"Because you already have Rhys Williams."

She glared at him. "Because I do not wish to bed *you*."

He shrugged. "I've heard that Druid women enjoy many lovers, particularly at festival times. Is that not true?"

Anger stirred in her stomach, drowning the awakening lust. "Are you suggesting that I would merrily swive any man who asked me?"

"I'm not suggesting anything other than perhaps we should scratch this itch before it becomes bothersome."

She stared pointedly at the black codpiece that covered his groin. "I suggest you scratch it yourself. I'm sure you are more than capable," Rosalind said. "Now please leave me alone."

His face sobered. "We need to catch this Vampire."

"I know!" She walked past him and then looked back. "That's the only reason I'm willing to be within a sword's length of you."

"The only reason you will admit to, anyway."

Rosalind bared her teeth at him. "You are impossible."

"So I've been told." He bowed. "Why don't you go back and enjoy the masque? I have an appointment with Elias Warner at midnight. I'll keep you informed."

Her smile this time was full of satisfaction. "I have the same appointment. He obviously considers me just as important as you."

He frowned. "I don't need to warn you about him, do

I? He likes to play games and he will not hesitate to kill to achieve his grisly ambitions."

"He's a Vampire. Of course I know that."

"Not all Vampires are the same."

She hesitated as she recognized something like pain in his voice. "Why do you care so much about a blood-sucking race devoid of humanity?"

His mouth thinned. "Why do you care about yours?"

She sighed. Standing here exchanging kisses and insults with Sir Christopher wouldn't help her catch a Vampire. He was a temptation she must resist. She curt-sied. "Good night, sir."

Rosalind headed back into the main hall. The danc-ing had stopped and the floor was now occupied by a group of tumblers and acrobats.

Soon it would be May Day, she realized, and com-moners and courtiers alike would erect maypoles and celebrate the old festival of Beltaine. Morris dancers would replace the tumblers and fools, if only for a day, and the pagan festival that the Christian Church had tried to bend to its own use would be upon them again.

Rosalind smiled to herself as she threaded her way through the throng. She was eager to celebrate Beltaine in the traditional way of the Druids, to reunite with her kin, and to be reminded exactly why joining her fate to Sir Christopher's was a very bad idea indeed.

Chapter 7

Twelve faint bells sounded from the king's chapel as Christopher made his way to the meeting place behind the stables that Elias Warner had suggested. He'd changed out of his elaborate finery into simpler black clothing, supple thigh-length leather boots, and a variety of weapons that served more than an ornamental purpose.

His dark mood matched his clothing. If Rosalind Llewellyn wasn't bespelling him, what was wrong with him? He'd never been attracted to a Druid before, and he was definitely attracted to her. His prick throbbed like a nagging toothache. Before leaving for the rendezvous, he'd had to break the ice on his water jug and splash his torso with freezing cold water or risk embarrassing himself by grabbing Rosalind's hand and suggesting she aid him.

He smoothed an impatient hand over his loins as his body responded with enthusiasm to the mere thought of Rosalind touching him. He needed to calm down. Elias Warner was far too astute not to notice his strange reaction to Rosalind. And if Elias could, he'd use that knowledge for his own ends. Dagger in hand, Christopher slipped around the corner of the abandoned brick building and stopped to survey the scene. In front of him sat Elias and Rosalind, their expressions as wary as his own, their weapons on display. Elias still wore his fine coat with the gold lace, but Rosalind had changed out of her red kirtle into her boy's clothes.

He nodded at them both, and settled between them on an old stack of hacked-off stone.

Elias cleared his throat. "I have a message from the Vampire Council." He paused to study them. "They have decided to allow you to work together to defeat this Vampire."

Christopher let out his breath. "That is very ... generous of them."

Rosalind shrugged. "That's all very well, but I'm not under their jurisdiction. They can't tell me what to do."

Christopher tensed as Elias's gaze went stony, and he hastened to intervene. "They can, however, warn other Vampires not to kill you on sight while you are working with us. Surely that warrants some appreciation?"

She turned to him, her brown eyes thoughtful and the contours of her arresting face enhanced by the moonlight. "I suppose that will make my task easier."

"*Our* task." By God's teeth, she was an irritating wench sometimes. "We will work together, aye?"

She folded her hands together on her lap. "I must wait for word from my grandfather."

"By the time you hear from him, Lady Rosalind, half the court could be dead, as well as the king," Christopher said. "Doesn't your grandfather trust you to make your own decisions?"

"Doesn't yours? Or do you always meekly do whatever the Vampire Council tells you?" Anger flashed across her face, leaving her cheeks flushed.

"My uncle trusts me. I have his full support." Christopher hoped he sounded more confident than he felt. His uncle could be a difficult man and he found it hard to believe that Edward had agreed to this unlikely pact. Allying himself with a Druid would probably be anathema to his guardian whatever the consequences to his race.

"If I might have your attention?" Elias asked. "The Vampire Council has spoken to both your families, and both have consented."

"Are you sure?" Christopher and Rosalind asked the question at the same time.

Elias looked pained. "This isn't the first time your families have worked together to overthrow a threat. And this threat is unusual. It has been foretold both by the Vampire book of prophecies as well as the Druids'."

"Long ago our priests prophesied a dark, bloody time for the Tudors and that we would be needed," Rosalind said slowly. "But I did not know that Vampires believed in prophecy as well."

Elias stirred and recited softly.

> *"The kiss of the rose is death to kin*
> *And three will stand alone.*
> *The bonds of blood will reunite*
> *And enemies become one."*

"How peculiar. That's exactly the same wording as our prophecy." Rosalind frowned as if the idea that the three of them might share anything other than the air they breathed troubled her.

"Not so peculiar, Lady Rosalind, if you consider that Vampires and Druids are descended from the same stock. It's hardly surprising we share some of the same ancient texts," Elias reminded them, his silver gaze resting curiously on Rosalind. "Surely, what is more interesting is how we should interpret the prophecy." He turned to Christopher. "Does not the wording suggest that Lady Rosalind is at the very heart of the matter?"

Rosalind made a face. "Hardly, Master Warner. Surely the prophecy speaks of the Tudor rose and the possibility of the king's death."

"Elias could be right, my lady. It might explain why you were called back to court." Christopher saw that Elias was nodding and went on. "And then there are the three who will stand alone."

"I suppose you think that refers to you, me, and Elias," Rosalind replied.

"Or, if you are indeed the center of the prophecy, the three might include Rhys Williams. That seems to make more sense."

Rosalind fiddled with her braid as if impatient for the conversation to be over with. "None of it makes sense. We have no bonds of blood!"

Elias stood. "Just as the Vampires and Druids share the same prophecies, we certainly share the same ancient blood. It will be intriguing to see what Sir Christopher adds to the equation." Elias gave Christopher a sidelong glance. "Whatever happens, I am pleased to offer you my assistance in your efforts to trap the rogue Vampire."

"Thank you." Christopher managed to be courteous even as his unease grew. He did not like the Vampire's insinuation about blood bonds—or his apparent fascination with Rosalind. "We might need your help."

Rosalind stood up and brushed at the grass on her knees. "Is there anything else, Master Warner?"

Elias bowed. "No, my lady."

Christopher rose as well. "There is something I'd like to ask you, Elias. Is it possible that Lady Rosalind can use magic?"

"All Druids use magic. What particular kind?" Elias asked, one eyebrow raised.

Christopher grimaced. "The kind that makes a man behave like a rutting fool."

"It's possible, I suppose. Druids use magic in their sacred ceremonies. Outside of that, they tend to leave such spells to their wise women. Lady Rosalind could have obtained a love potion . . ." He paused to study Christopher's face, a sudden stark interest dawning on his own. "Do you think you have been bewitched?"

"I'm not sure."

Rosalind gave Christopher a small complacent smile. "On my honor, I would hardly bother to go to all that trouble to bewitch *you*. And how on earth would I gain access to your vittles to add a potion? As I said, Sir Christopher, the problem is all of your own making."

"Hardly that, Lady Rosalind."

She narrowed her eyes at him. "We shall have to agree to disagree on this matter, sir."

"And both strive to restrain our unruly appetites."

"I'll leave that to you." She nodded at Elias and headed for the crumbling archway that connected the deserted building to the stables.

Christopher caught up to her in less than a moment. "Where are you going?"

She sighed. "Just because we have the Vampire Council's consent to work together doesn't mean that we have to do everything together."

He barred her way with his arm. "Aye, it does."

"I'm going to see if Rhys has returned from London, and then I'm going to bed."

"Whose bed would that be, my lady?"

She pushed past his arm and kept walking, her long legs taking her away from him, her braided hair bumping against the back of her blue woolen jerkin. He called after her, his voice low, but easily audible in the vibrant stillness of the night.

"Are you going to tell him you kissed me?"

She stopped walking and he found himself tensing with anticipation as she spun around. It was almost too easy to bait her, and yet he couldn't seem to stop.

"Of course I'll tell him."

"Even if he comes after me with his sword? The Vampire Council won't be pleased if he skewers me."

She met his gaze, her brown eyes clear. "I tell him *everything*."

"Then he is a lucky man." He wondered how that might feel, to have someone you could let down your guard with, someone who truly cared about you, and loved you just the way you were. He had no family except his uncle. The rest had been killed serving the Council, or in the bloody disputes common in the Vampire community.

His smile disappeared and he resumed walking until he joined Rosalind at the door leading up to the sleeping quarters above the stables. "I'll wait here for you while you check on Rhys."

She glanced up the rickety dark staircase. The smell of horse dung and sweat curled around them. "I'm not going up there. It's full of men." She stuck two fingers in her mouth and whistled softly, but there was no reply. She whistled once more, and then sighed. "I didn't think he'd be back yet, anyway."

Christopher bowed. "Then *I'll* escort you to bed. Which would you prefer? Yours or mine?"

She didn't answer, her expression troubled, as if her mind was still with her lover rather than on him. "I'm not going to bed yet. I have to check on the queen."

"I'll come with you." He took up a position behind her and to her right, so as not to impede his sword arm. "Are you worried about the queen?"

"I am concerned because she has lost the king's favor." She frowned, her voice quiet. "He never visits her, and her court has dwindled to a mere handful of loyal servants."

"She is growing old."

"I know."

"And as she can no longer give the king an heir, I fear he has grown increasingly dissatisfied with her." He leaned closer. "It is said that Cardinal Wolsey is seeking the pope's help to annul the marriage."

She turned her face up to his, her expression shocked. "How can he do that when it was the pope who gave him dispensation to marry his brother's widow in the *first* place?"

"A different pope and a different political climate. The king needs an heir. That is an inescapable fact."

"He has an heir, the princess Mary."

He shrugged. "A girl."

"And what, pray, is wrong with that?"

"The last time a woman claimed the throne of England, it threw the country into civil war."

"Only because her cousin Stephen decided he should rule in her stead. Matilda rightly should have been queen."

"Perhaps, but she was the one who gave up and ran back to France, wasn't she?"

"And you assume all women would do that?"

He glanced sideways at her. "Well, they are the weaker sex."

She tossed her braid back over her shoulder and muttered something he assumed was uncomplimentary before fixing her attention on the two guards on duty outside the queen's private chambers.

"Do they know you, Sir Christopher?"

He traced the line of her cheekbone with his finger. "There's no need to be so formal now that we've kissed. You may call me Christopher."

She opened her eyes wide at him. "Do they know you?"

"Of course they do."

"Then can you get us in?"

He pretended to hesitate. "You are asking for my help?"

"Yes."

"You can't get in there alone?"

"Not in these clothes." She grimaced and made as if to turn away from him. "Don't trouble yourself. I knew you would enjoy this far too much."

He caught her hand. "What were you going to do if I wasn't here?"

"Go to my chamber and change into a dress before coming down again. This would be faster, that is all."

He stared down at her, enjoying the sense of power that came over him, enjoying her need for him, if he was perfectly honest. "Get behind me."

They approached the two guards, and Christopher cleared his throat. There was no reaction from the men, who continued to stare straight ahead. Christopher pulled out his dagger. "Something's wrong."

Rosalind came around his shoulder, stepped right in front of one of the guards, and waved her hand in front of his face. "I can see that. They appear to be in a trance."

Their gazes met and without further discussion they headed into the queen's private chambers. Silence greeted them, and Christopher motioned Rosalind behind him. She ignored his gesture, and crept along the passageway checking the receiving rooms on her side of the hall as he checked those he passed.

A sudden chill enveloped Christopher and he stiffened. Glancing at Rosalind, he saw that she had done the same. Before either of them could move, a black shape flew toward them and knocked them both to the floor. When he hit the floor, Christopher's dagger skidded out of his reach across the tile and he had to crawl after it.

As the blackness above them hovered and swirled, it felt as if his head was about to cave in. He tasted blood in his mouth, but it wasn't his, the flavor so intense that he wanted to lick his lips and savor it. Was this how a Vampire felt when he fed, this sense of power and strength flooding through him? What in God's name was wrong? He gathered every piece of energy he possessed, and kept moving forward, strove to fight the Vampire's compulsion and make it across the narrow hallway to his weapon and Rosalind.

He swallowed hard to dislodge the taste of blood and focused on Rosalind. To his horror, she was trying to stand and face the apparition, her face lifted toward the creature as if she was seeking something. He opened his mouth to shout at her and couldn't speak, could only inch his way toward her at the speed of a snail.

With a cry, she threw her dagger at the center of the mass, and then collapsed back onto her knees. The Vampire, or whatever the Vampire had created, moved off as quickly as it had appeared.

Christopher stretched out a shaking hand and connected with Rosalind's knee. He hauled himself up until he could see her face.

"It's a female," she whispered.

"What?" He frowned as he checked her for any visible injuries.

"The Vampire." She swallowed hard. "She smells like decayed orange blossom."

He paused to study her dazed face. "Are you all right?"

"She is old and has great power." She shivered and wrapped her arms tightly around her chest.

Without thinking, Christopher picked her up, sat her in his lap, and held her close. For once, she didn't protest. He soon realized why, for her body continued to shake as if she had an ague. He smoothed his hands down from her shoulders to her wrists, then over her back and kept it up until she began to warm under his touch.

He swallowed hard and remembered the rich, seductive taste of blood in his mouth. "Did you get a sense that the Vampire had killed tonight?"

"No. Did you?"

He shrugged. "I'm not a Druid." He wasn't going to tell her that for a horrifying moment he'd felt as if the Vampire had somehow been inside his mind. "But the Vampire must have come here for a reason." He reluctantly released her. "We should make sure that all is well with the queen."

He extended his hand to help her to her feet. Her face was still too pale for his liking, her eyes huge. He wanted to ask whether she'd felt that strange connection to the Vampire, but was unwilling to raise her suspicions and risk her questions when he wasn't even sure what he'd felt himself.

They advanced down the hallway, pausing at every door to listen, checking for the signs of a Vampire kill, but there was nothing.

"I smell blood," Rosalind whispered.

Christopher paused at the open door of the small antechamber that led directly to the queen's bedchamber beyond. There were no guards posted there at all.

"Look." Rosalind pointed at the far door. "What is that?"

Christopher edged forward, bringing one of the lighted candles from the prie-dieu with him to dispel the gloom. Nailed to the door of the queen's bedchamber was an elegant long-sleeved lace-trimmed glove. The fingers pointed downward and dripped blood onto the wooden floor. Rosalind's breath hitched as she looked over his shoulder.

"That is one of the queen's favorite gloves."

"How can you tell when it's covered in blood?"

She pointed at the gilded lace. "It's embroidered with pomegranates, which is her emblem, entwined with roses, which is the king's. I believe he gave her this particular pair of gloves after Princess Mary was born."

Rosalind glanced at the door. "I have to make sure the queen is all right."

He nodded his assent and stepped back as she slowly opened the door to the bedchamber and slipped inside. She was back a mere moment later, which was when Christopher realized he'd been holding his breath.

"She's sleeping soundly," Rosalind whispered. "Three of her waiting women are also in there. I didn't want to disturb them."

With a resigned sigh, Christopher stripped off his favorite leather doublet and used it to cover his hand as he pulled out the nail, bringing the glove with it. Then he folded the doublet around the glove and looked around for something to clean the floor with. Rosalind was already checking the row of chests beneath the small diamond-paned window. She returned with an old woolen petticoat, which she used to mop up the rest of the blood.

When she'd finished, she unceremoniously stuffed the stained petticoat into the folds of Christopher's already ruined doublet. He jerked his head in the direction of the door. Rosalind followed him out and then touched his arm to lead him through another maze of passages that led to the rear of the building and the gardens beyond. He was surprised to see that it was still dark outside, and that over in the great banqueting hall, lights glowed and the faint sound of music reverberated in the air.

"We have to bury this glove," Christopher said.

"Are you sure?" Rosalind frowned. "I'm certain the queen will miss it."

Christopher crouched down and carefully opened his doublet to reveal the glove. Rosalind knelt next to him and peered at the bloodied object before recoiling. "You're right. It smells odd. It might be poisoned or bespelled."

It didn't smell of anything much to Christopher, but for once, he was willing to concede that a Druid might know better. "I'll take care of it."

He wanted to show the glove to Elias, to get his thoughts on exactly *whose* blood stained the soft leather. "If you permit, of course." He covered up the glove again and tucked the well-folded doublet under his arm. Rosalind remained kneeling beside him. He shivered as the wind ruffled the exposed black lawn sleeves of his undershirt. "We should get back."

Rosalind stared at him, her brown eyes fixed on his. "Why didn't she kill the queen? There was nothing to stop her. Even we would have been too late."

"Some Vampires like to play games. Mayhap she simply wished to prove she can get as close to the queen as she likes?"

She bit her lip. "Or mayhap her true target is the king." She struggled to her feet. "Come on!"

Chapter 8

Rosalind turned and ran as quickly as she could toward the wing of the palace the king and his household occupied. She kept low, stumbling over tree roots and avoiding overhanging branches that threatened to slap her in the face. Christopher kept pace beside her, his dagger out, his breathing far less labored than her own. With Rhys gone, she was actually glad for both his company and his strength.

She paused at the edge of the copse of oak that overlooked the front of the building. In contrast to the queen's apartments, the entrance to the king's suite was ablaze with lights, as a constant stream of servants and courtiers entered and left the building. Guards were stationed at all the doors. They seemed untouched by any Vampire spells and unaware of impending danger.

Rosalind bent forward at the waist to try to catch her breath. She was aware of Christopher at her shoulder, his keen gaze trained on the guards.

"The guards seem alert. Do you think we need to go in and check that the king is unharmed?" she panted.

"I will go," he responded quickly.

"Without me?"

He glanced down at her. "You are scarcely dressed to meet the king."

She tried to stand up straight. "I look like a boy. No one would recognize me."

He caught her braid in his fingers and wrapped it around his hand, bringing her face perilously close to his. "You look like a girl playing dress-up in her brother's clothing. I'll go. I promise I'll come back." He brushed a kiss on her lips and released her braid. "Stay here."

She watched him walk away, his doublet clutched securely in his left hand. She was caught between annoyance at his superior air and a suspicion that he was right. Her male attire wouldn't pass muster in the bright light of the king's chambers. She couldn't afford to lose her reputation and be sent home in disgrace.

To her relief, Christopher returned quickly and headed toward the tree behind which she was hiding.

"Everything looked well. I wasn't allowed into the king's bedchamber, of course, but I got as close as I could."

"Let's hope this was just a warning, then." Rosalind sighed. "I'll ask the king if you can have greater access to his person."

A smile flickered on his face. "*You'll* ask the king?"

She raised her chin. "Yes, he is bound by oath to listen to my family."

"Verily, is that so?" He regarded her solemnly. "I'd heard rumors that the Tudors had formed a pact with the Druids, but I didn't really believe them."

Rosalind winced as she wondered what her family would think of her revealing her secrets to a Druid killer like Christopher Ellis. But what else was she to do? She had to take him into her confidence, or else the Vampire would succeed in killing the king.

She sheathed her dagger. "I think it's time to go to bed."

He grinned at her and carefully placed his burden on the ground at his feet. "It has certainly been an adventurous evening. Have you decided where you will sleep tonight?"

"Not with you."

He grasped her chin in his hand, his intense blue eyes trained on hers. "I want you. I don't understand why, but I do."

"Stop wanting me. I'm sure there are many women willing to be seduced by your fine eyes and comely face."

"You think me handsome?"

She shrugged. "Some women might think so."

"But not you, because you prefer auburn hair and milk white skin." His smile disappeared. "Or are you simply too afraid to admit that you desire me?"

She pulled away from him and presented him with her back. "I cannot desire you. You are my enemy."

"Do you always kiss your enemies?"

"I don't want you." She swung around, her hands clenched into fists. "I don't want *any* of this."

He raised his eyebrows. "And you think that I do?"

"You are always the one who brings it up."

"And it makes you uncomfortable."

"Yes!"

He held her gaze, his gaze intent. "You heard the prophecy."

Rosalind brought her hand to her cheek and pushed back the strands of hair stuck to her face. "What does that have to do with anything?"

"I've been thinking about it."

"And?"

"And I believe it is very relevant to us indeed."

"That's ridiculous."

"Are you sure?" He advanced until he was standing right in front of her. "I'm beginning to wonder. *The kiss of the rose is death to kin, and three will stand alone....* Perhaps Elias is right and the rose is *you*, Rosalind, rather than the Tudor emblem. Perhaps you are destined to destroy me and my kin by binding me to you with lust."

"That is absurd. I'm not that powerful."

His smile was both rueful and desperate. "Your power seems very apparent to me."

She took two stumbling steps away from him. "I'm going to see if Rhys has returned."

He grabbed her hand and brought her crashing against his chest. She refused to look up at him. Instead, she stared blindly at the black fabric of his shirt, the laces that closed the neckline, the rapid rise and fall of his chest.

"Does he please you in bed?"

She shuddered as he traced the curve of her jaw with one fingertip.

"Does he kiss your mouth until you can't think, or breathe; does he suckle at your breasts until your nipples are as hard and needy as his cock"

She stood still as his hand traveled lower to curve around her back and settle over her bound breasts. Could he feel the tight bud of her nipple through the binding? She wanted him to.

"Does he slide his fingers inside you until you open for him as succulently as a flower for a honey bee, and then does he use his mouth to suck you dry?"

His hands drifted lower, to her buttocks. He cupped them until she gasped and rose on tiptoe. With easy strength, he dragged her up his body until the juncture at her thighs met the fullness between his. He wore no codpiece, just the soft buckskin of his hose that covered something harder and hotter. She fought an urge to wrap her legs around his hips, to allow his heat and thickness to rub against her quim, to ask him for what her body demanded. She couldn't seem to move away, his soft, beguiling voice detailing pleasures of the flesh that he made sound more alluring than she had ever imagined.

"Does he bring you pleasure, Rosalind?" She heard herself moan as his mouth settled on the sensitive skin behind her ear and he kissed his way down to her shoulders. "Or does he simply slake his need on you and leave you wanting?"

She finally found the strength to push him away, to slide down his body and stand on her own, admittedly shaky, legs. He didn't stop her, allowed her to see the desire in his eyes, the heat and need coursing through his strong frame, the huge bulge in his hose.

Rosalind licked her lips and backed away from him. She'd never understood lust before, never imagined this raging need, this ridiculous urge to throw herself back into his arms and take what he offered, and the consequences be damned.

She shook her head to clear it of the fog of lust. "Stop it."

A muscle flicked in his cheek. "I know you don't believe me, but I cannot stop. I wish I could."

"I can't . . ." Goodness, was that her voice? So shaken, so vulnerable, so . . . afraid. She was never afraid; she couldn't afford to be in the man's world she inhabited.

"I could give you pleasure," he said softly, and held out his hand. "Let me show you."

She retreated two more steps. "Pleasure is fleeting. No woman wants to be bedded and forgotten the next day."

"I don't think I'd ever be able to forget you." His gaze drifted down and came to rest on her hips. "I suspect I'd never want to leave your body."

An image of them entwined naked on her bed flashed

through Rosalind's mind, and she immediately banished it. "I'm going to bed."

He bowed. "As you wish, my lady."

"Alone." She clarified, just in case he was still harboring any salacious thoughts of joining her.

"I understood that."

"I'll let you know when I hear from my grandfather."

He shrugged. "If you feel that it is necessary."

"Or if anything untoward happens."

"Naturally."

She paused to stare at him. Was she hoping he'd ignore her request to stay away, and take matters into his own hands? As she walked back toward the stables, she cringed at her own indecision and barely managed to whistle for Rhys.

He appeared in front of her so suddenly she almost gasped. He was still dressed for travel, his clothes dusty and his hat in his hand. His faint smile dimmed as he studied her. He put his hand on her shoulder and drew her back into the shadows of the nearest wall.

"Are you all right?"

She grimaced. "We were attacked by the Vampire in the queen's apartments."

"We?"

"Sir Christopher and I."

He scowled. "Trust the Druid slayer to be in the thick of things. He stalks you like Vampire prey."

"Rhys, he simply came with me when I went to check on the queen. Her guards had been bewitched."

"The queen was unharmed, though?" Rhys crossed himself. "That is good."

"Yes." Rosalind repressed a shudder. "Although no thanks to us. The Vampire was there, in her chamber, but chose not to attack her."

Rhys frowned. "That's odd. Although we've always

believed the target is the king, why would the Vampire go to the queen in the middle of the night and *not* attack? Did you find out anything else?"

"The Vampire is female and old. She smelled like orange blossom."

He nodded. "Excellent. At least you'll be able to recognize her scent next time you come across her. Although even I know that orange blossom is a commonly used perfume these days at court."

Rosalind sighed. "And she is powerful enough to conceal herself even from her own kind. We also met with Elias Warner tonight, and he said the Vampire Council agrees that Sir Christopher and I should work together."

"I'm sure they did." Rhys's expression cooled. "They'd be quite happy for you to die for them."

"I don't see that I have a choice."

Rhys met her gaze, his own somber. "Unfortunately, neither do I."

Rosalind took his gloved hand. "How was your journey?"

"Far less eventful than your evening, it seems. Your letter is on its way to Wales and your grandfather."

"Thank you." She squeezed his fingers. "You are far too good to me."

His smile was guarded. "I was only doing my duty." He let go of her hand and nodded in the direction of the nearest stall. "I was just settling Geithin and then I was going to bed."

"I'm glad you're back." Impulsively she threw her arms around him, and kissed him on the lips. She felt him stiffen, and held on to him even tighter. Didn't he understand that she needed him now, needed him to replace the traces of Sir Christopher that lingered? The taste and texture that threatened to overwhelm her senses?

His mouth came down over hers and he kissed her, his hands all over her, his tongue plundering hers. After a moment, though, he raised his head and stepped out of her arms. He slowly wiped his lips with the back of his hand. "Don't do that to me."

She swallowed hard. "Do what?"

"Kiss me when you still taste of another man."

Briefly she closed her eyes, ashamed beyond measure. "I'm sorry I did not mean for it to happen. I want to forget all about him—"

"No, you don't." For the first time in her life, she was afraid of Rhys, and of what she had roused. "I saw the way he looked at you—and the way you looked back."

"But I don't want to feel like that, and neither does he!"

Rhys regarded her steadily, all signs of emotion now stripped from his face. "Whatever he said to you, Rosalind, he wants you, and I suspect he'll do anything necessary to bind you to him. And, in the heat of battle, remember, we cannot always help what we feel." He slid his hand inside his coat and brought out a folded parchment. "This is for you."

"From my grandfather? Why would he be writing to me so soon?"

"Perhaps he received new information after we'd left."

"Do you know what it says?"

He arched an eyebrow at her. "Despite my jealousy, I haven't taken to reading your private correspondence, Rosalind."

She sighed. "I didn't mean that. I just wondered if he had communicated with you as well."

"He did."

"And?"

His smile was wry. "And we'll discuss it after you've read your own letter." He turned toward the sleeping quarters, one hand shoving back his thick auburn hair. "I'm weary, my lady. Good night."

Rosalind bit down on her lip. "I'm sorry, Rhys," she whispered.

He stopped at the bottom of the stairs and looked over his shoulder at her. "It's all right."

"No, it isn't." She tried to stop her voice from trembling. "I've hurt you."

With a soft sound, he swung around and enfolded her in his arms. "No, *cariad*, it's not you. It's this whole cursed situation." He kissed the top of her head. "You're as tired as I am. Go to bed. We'll discuss this in the morning."

She lifted her head to look him in the eye. He'd called her his darling in Welsh. "You're sure you're not angry with me? I couldn't bear that."

He smiled, even though it seemed forced. "Let's talk in the morning, aye? Now, good night."

She watched him disappear up the stairs and then she headed back toward the queen's quarters, her thoughts in turmoil. How could she lust after Christopher when she was practically promised to Rhys? And she *was* as good as promised to him, even though he'd told her he would wait for her and never force his claim.

Her steps slowed. Perhaps her attraction to Christopher was because of the danger they'd faced together rather than any true emotion. Her relationship with Rhys felt safer and far more grounded in reality. Rhys might not be able to offer her the delights Sir Christopher promised, but he certainly wouldn't bring her to her knees either. . . . But did she want to be safe? Had she ever wanted that? She couldn't even begin to think about Christopher's pointed comments about the prophecy. Could it really refer to her? Was that why her grandfather had insisted she be the one sent to court as the representative of the Druids, despite being female?

Yet the prophecy mentioned three who would stand

alone. Was she inextricably linked with Christopher and Rhys or, even worse, with the Vampire, Elias Warner? Rosalind almost turned back to the stables. Rhys would know where to find an elder of their race she could speak to about the prophecy. Or she could wait for Beltaine and seek out a Druid priest there.

Her eyes strained to catch the faint rays of the sun that now tinted the horizon. She was far too tired to think anymore and could only pray that the morning would bring her better counsel.

Christopher waited until Rosalind disappeared into the gloom, and then checked his bloodied bundle again. The second glove he'd retrieved from the king's apartments lay on top of the first and matched it completely. He wasn't sure why he hadn't shown the glove to Rosalind on his return. Had he been concerned she would storm the king's chambers, dagger raised to defend the sovereign, or had he been trying to protect her again?

Perhaps both. Whatever the Vampire had intended, the king's apartments were far too busy and well guarded for the creature to get as close to the king as she had gotten to the queen without causing a huge uproar.

He grimaced. All he knew was that Rosalind wouldn't appreciate him concealing anything from her at all. He headed back toward the ruined building behind the stables and found Elias seated in the same spot he had occupied earlier. He was not alone. His head was bent forward at an angle as if he was whispering something to the young woman kneeling between his thighs. After a moment, Elias sat back. He smiled at Christopher; his long fangs were still extended.

"It's all right." He beckoned Christopher forward. "I've just fed from her. She's in a trance."

Christopher could sense it now—that elusive hint of blood and magic that a Vampire feeding always evoked in his mind.

"Would you like to drink from her? She is free of infection."

Christopher recoiled. "I am not a Vampire."

Elias considered him, his head to one side, his immaculate gilded curls barely stirred by the cold wind. "Yet you have Vampire blood in your family."

"Who told you that?"

"I have known your family for almost three hundred years. Do you think I am not privy to their secrets . . . such as why you, in particular, hold to the ancient vows of Mithras?" The Vampire's smile was pitying. "Even those secrets you try so hard to bury with your dead."

Christopher set his jaw. "I am *not* a Vampire."

"If you insist." Elias returned his attention to the young woman whose clothing showed her to be a dairymaid. "My dear, you must leave this place and go to bed. Sleep until dawn and forget everything that has passed between us this night."

Obediently, the woman stood up, bobbed Elias a curtsy, and headed out of the ruined building, her eyes still glassy and her footsteps uncertain.

Christopher glanced at her as she passed him; the two puncture marks on her neck were still visible. "Will she be all right?"

As Elias's fangs retracted, he licked a tiny speck of blood from the corner of his newly reddened lips. "Certainly. She's young and healthy and I took very little from her."

Christopher tried not to react to Elias's casual air. Despite all his years among the Vampire kind, he'd never enjoyed watching a Vampire suck blood from another human. He'd told himself that the Druids did much worse, that the Vampires rarely killed and only occasionally made more of their own kind, whereas the Druids practiced ungodly rites, like human sacrifice. But if Rosalind spoke the truth, they no longer practiced that perversion anymore. . . .

"What do you want of me, Sir Christopher?"

Christopher knelt and placed his doublet on the ground, unfolding it to reveal the gloves. Elias leaned forward, his neutral expression dissolving as he inhaled the scent of dried blood.

"What exactly do you have here?"

"A pair of the queen's favorite gloves. One was nailed to the door of the queen's bedchamber, the other to the outer door of the king's inner chambers."

Elias's breath hissed out in a vicious curse. He stared at Christopher. "This is intolerable. The Vampire is playing with us all."

"Are you afraid?"

Elias shuddered. "Of course I am. This Vampire is so powerful it could kill me with a thought."

"Then why hasn't it simply gone ahead and killed the king?"

"I don't think this Vampire is acting in a rational manner, do you? Its aims are illogical and unclear, and that is why the Vampire Council cannot dispatch the problem quietly." He gestured at the gloves. "These gloves simply illustrate my point."

"In what way?"

"That isn't human blood."

"Then what is it?"

"Vampire. Old Vampire. From the one we seek, I suspect. Can't you smell it?"

Christopher cautiously inhaled. "It smells like old leather and orange blossom to me."

Pure speculation flashed in Elias's silver eyes. "Why, you underestimate your talents, Sir Christopher. Your sense of smell is like a Druid's." He fingered the glove. "The Vampire leaves his blood like a dog his piss, to warn others off. This is a challenge." He paused. "Mayhap your infatuation with Rosalind Llewellyn has affected your senses more than you realize."

"My sense of smell is nothing like Rosalind's and I'm not infatuated with her."

"She seems to think you are."

Christopher sighed. "There is more to it than that."

"You're in *love* with her?" Elias smiled. "How charming."

Christopher didn't smile in return. "I'm not stupid, Elias. I've suspected all along there was a reason I of all people was chosen for this task. No one would care if I died to stop this prophecy coming true." He watched Elias's face carefully, but there was no sign of a reaction. "I believe I was sent here just as deliberately as Rosalind Llewellyn was."

"That's a very interesting thought, Sir Christopher."

"You heard the prophecy."

Elias blinked very slowly. "It refers to a group of three."

Christopher tried to force the issue. "And you have your own ideas as to why I might be included in this unlikely group. It might also explain why I have this unholy attraction to Rosalind Llewellyn. What say you?"

"I'm saying naught, Sir Christopher." Elias's smile wasn't meant to reassure. "I'll leave such wild speculation up to you." He rose and bowed. "Good night."

Christopher didn't try to stop the Vampire leaving. There was no point. He'd said his piece and nothing had changed. He hadn't really expected it to. Unease settled in his gut. Vampires were notoriously closemouthed, but it was quite possible that Elias knew about Christopher's tangled, bloody history. Christopher sighed and set about thinking of a place to bury his ruined doublet. He hoped nothing turned up in his bedchamber tonight. He desperately needed his sleep—and a clear head for the morning.

Chapter 9

Rosalind slowed her horse. "Shall we dismount and walk a little?" she asked Rhys.

It was a clear morning with the kind of sharp brightness that promised much, and at this time of year, often delivered nothing. Rosalind had hardly slept at all, her thoughts tangled with Rhys, Christopher, and the disturbing letter from her grandfather. She'd dressed and come down to the stables at dawn, where Rhys was waiting as if he'd been expecting her.

He nodded and dismounted, caught her reins, and expertly hobbled the horses before reaching up to lift her down. He made no effort to kiss her this morning, and his expression was watchful rather than warm and relaxed. Had her grandfather given him the same instructions as he'd given her?

"I read Grandfather's letter."

He glanced down at her. "And?"

She took a deep breath. "My grandfather has discovered that Sir Christopher is at court, and he ordered me to become acquainted with him."

"*Acquainted with him*? That's not what he wrote me."

Her cheeks heated. She found herself staring at his serviceable brown woolen doublet rather than up at his face. "I did not want to upset you."

His laugh was harsh. "What exactly did he say?"

She twisted her riding gloves into a knot. It was difficult to talk of such delicate matters with a man who might one day become her husband. "He ordered me to become as intimate with Sir Christopher as I could."

Silence fell between them. All she could hear was the jingling of the horses' bridles and the uneven sound of her own breathing. She slowly looked up and found Rhys's gaze already waiting for her.

"I know. And he told me to aid you in every way possible." His mouth twisted. "Your grandfather thinks I'm so loyal to him that I'd willingly tie you up and dump you in that whoreson's bed."

Rosalind laid her hand on his sleeve. "He knows how you feel about me. He would never expect that." It seemed her grandfather would demand it of her, though, and the thought made her sick to her stomach.

Rhys didn't answer her, but she felt the tension vibrating through his muscular frame.

"I won't do it, Rosalind," he finally said. "I won't make it easy for Sir Christopher and I can't do that to you. I am sorry to say it but your grandfather has lost my respect."

"I don't expect you to go against your principles." Rosalind reached out to stroke his unshaven jaw. "In truth, I'd be hurt if you did."

He sighed and pushed her hand away from his face. "But this has to stop. I can't let you touch me."

"Can we not even be friends anymore? I'm only trying to offer you comfort."

"And I'm already hard." He swallowed. "The best I can offer you is my promise not to interfere with your . . . duty."

"I have no choice," Rosalind whispered. "My grandfather was most explicit."

His smile wasn't kind. "I'm sure you'll reconcile yourself to your fate, my lady."

"That's not fair. I told you I didn't want to have feelings for Sir Christopher. That it's all wrong!"

He started back toward the horses, jerking his gloves on as he walked. "Has it occurred to you that your grandfather anticipated this when he sent you here?"

The shock of such wounding words coming from her staunchest ally resonated through her, but she drew herself up to her full height and said calmly, "I assumed I was sent because I am marked with the sign of Awen and that I've trained to fight Vampires since birth."

He swung back toward her. "Aye, but there are other Vampire hunters, more experienced ones. *And against you* the Ellis family sends Sir Christopher, a relatively untried Druid hunter—a handsome young man who would appreciate your charms."

Rosalind lifted her chin. "Are you suggesting that there is a conspiracy to create an attachment between myself and Sir Christopher? To what end?"

"I don't know. Possibly to distract you from your investigation of the murders while the Vampires achieve their nefarious aims."

"If that were so, why would my grandfather agree?"

"Mayhap this has something to do with that cursed prophecy."

"Why ever would you think that?" Rosalind fought to keep the alarm from her face. It was bad enough that Sir Christopher thought she was involved in the prophecy. Why did Rhys have to mention it as well?

He studied her closely. "It seems rather . . . fitting, does it not?"

Rosalind met his gaze. "Nothing is certain. The rogue Vampire has likely manipulated the situation for her own ends." She grabbed her horse's reins. "I think we should return to the palace."

"Of course, my lady." Rhys boosted her into the saddle and mounted his own horse.

Rosalind bit her lip and sought his gaze. "You won't leave me, will you?"

"For something your grandfather has done? Nay, I won't desert you."

"Thank you," she whispered, but he'd already turned away, his features set in an unusually solemn cast, his horse picking up speed. Rosalind followed him as quickly as she could, her thoughts even more confused than they had been on the previous night. Her own grandfather, that stalwart hater of all things Vampire, had suggested—nay, *commanded*—that she seduce Sir Christopher Ellis.

She stared blindly at the fast-approaching walls of the palace. Would her father have ordered her to do the same thing? Would he have betrayed her like that? And why was it even necessary for her to seduce Christopher? Surely gaining his confidence, even making him fall in love with her, would be enough to compromise his position and distract him. Was it something to do with the prophecy? Did her grandfather truly expect her to "become one" with her enemy?

All her old uncertainties about her acceptance as a Vampire slayer had returned. Had her grandfather allowed her to train only for this aim, that she act as bait to lure Christopher to his doom? The implications were horrifying. She realized she didn't want Christopher dead. Would, in truth, do anything to prevent it.

Rhys pulled up alongside her. "I assume you'll want to speak to Sir Christopher. Do you want me to find him?"

Rosalind glanced uncertainly at the palace. "I'm not sure where he'll be."

"I'll bring him to the chapel. You can help take care of the horses while I'm gone and then meet us there."

Obediently, she followed Rhys to the stables, waited while he removed their cumbersome saddles and tack and drove the horses back into their stalls. She took over the task of brushing them and making sure they had clean water and food. At least the mundane everyday job soothed her, made it easier for her to calm down and plan how she would tell Christopher that everyone was far too willing for them to work together.

When she'd finished, Rosalind picked up the dusty skirts of her green riding habit and headed slowly up to the chapel. Why was it so much easier to face Sir Christopher at night when she was hunting Vampires than in the light of day? He and Rhys were already waiting outside for her. Sir Christopher swept her a low bow.

"Good morning, Lady Rosalind."

"Good morning, Sir Christopher." She looked at Rhys, whose expression was anything but helpful. "Is this a safe place for us to talk?"

Rhys shrugged. "If we wish to avoid any Vampires, the chapel is ideal. Mass isn't due to start for a while."

In the small entranceway to the church, Rosalind turned to the men. Sir Christopher's gaze lingered on her face, and he frowned. "You look tired, my lady."

"I'm tired because I can hardly sleep with worrying about all this. Surely you must feel the same?"

"Indeed. It preys heavily on my mind." He shifted his stance until he leaned against the wall, his dark blue silk doublet and black jerkin in stark contrast to the lime-washed stone.

Rosalind took a steadying breath. "Do you really be-. lieve we are somehow involved in the prophecy?"

"It is hard to escape the notion that we are." His gaze moved between Rosalind and Rhys. "All of us, and that includes you, Rhys."

Rhys nodded. "I wondered about that too. I expect that's one of the reasons why the lady's grandfather sent me back to court with her." He glowered at Christopher. "I'm not sure what any of this has to do with you, though, Ellis."

Rosalind tensed, but Christopher didn't react to Rhys's challenge. "In all honesty, I was surprised to be sent in my uncle's stead."

Rhys stirred beside her. "Aye, for you are not a well-known Druid killer, are you?"

"Not in England. I have lived most of my life in Aragon and Brittany."

"Your family isn't English?" Rosalind asked.

He frowned as if the question was an insult. "My father was English, my mother, Spanish."

"Which is why you are such a favorite of the queen?"

"She enjoys speaking the language of her childhood."

Rosalind glanced up at Rhys, but he was steadfastly ignoring her. She remembered his vow not to interfere with her relationship with Christopher, and silently groaned. Despite the fact that she was standing between them and that Rhys had sworn not to overreact, she could feel the tension in both of them, the sensation that she was like a meaty bone cast between two snarling dogs. She attempted to redirect the conversation back to the prophecy and away from the competitive instincts of the two men.

"Sir Christopher, do you think I am central to the prophecy?"

Christopher studied her for a moment and then nodded. His gaze returned to Rhys. "Isn't it strange that so many races and religions hold by the power of three? The three rays of the Awen, the Holy Trinity of the Christians, and the Three Lords of the Vampire world . . ."

"What are you trying to say, Sir Christopher?" Rosalind asked.

He sighed. "I'm simply trying to understand. Why would all your prophets agree on the same thing happening at the same time? And why did they choose us to fight this particular Vampire?"

"Well, I am not convinced there is a conspiracy behind our being here. Prophecies are notoriously vague. I'd warrant the scholars themselves don't know exactly what will happen," Rosalind answered.

"That's one possibility." Sir Christopher grimaced. "It makes my skin crawl to think I've been prepared and trained for this moment from birth, shaped by forces beyond me and used as an unwilling pawn."

Rosalind stared at him as his words crystallized her own feelings. Was that why she'd been taught to fight as well? Simply to play out her part in this mystery, rather than because she deserved it?

"It doesn't matter how we got here. We still have to find and kill that Vampire," Rosalind said.

"That's true, and I'm sure you and your manservant will do your best to aid me on my quest."

"*Our* quest," she reminded him sharply, and he smiled at her for the first time. "How do you suggest we proceed?"

"Although we have assumed the target is the king, I believe the queen is at risk." He stroked his chin in thought. "Because she is out of favor with the king, she is less than well protected and an easier target."

"And, as the Vampire we seek appears to be a woman, it is more likely that she resides in the queen's court."

"Then we should concentrate our efforts there. We both have access to the queen's inner circle. I suggest we spend our daylight hours trying to puzzle out which of her court is the Vampire, and our nights, when the king is more vulnerable and the Vampire is more powerful, making sure he is equally well protected."

"And what exactly do you expect me to do while you two gallivant about the court?" Rhys asked, his attention focused on Sir Christopher.

Rosalind tensed as Christopher turned toward Rhys and slowly studied him. "Do whatever servants do. You are able to pass unnoticed. I suggest you use that ability to aid us as best you can."

Rhys made a sudden movement forward until he was toe-to-toe with Christopher. "I'm no more a servant than you are, *sir*. I'm only tolerating your presence because of my lady."

"I understand, and do not mistake me. I have great respect for your fighting skills. My uncle speaks very highly of you indeed."

"He should, because prophecy or no prophecy, if you harm my lady, I will separate you from your head."

"You can certainly try."

Luckily Rosalind was able to slip between the two much taller men again and shove them apart. She hated having to look up at them both. "After Mass, I'll take Sir Christopher to visit the king, and secure him greater access to the king's personal chambers."

Rhys finally stopped glaring at Christopher and nodded at her. "That's an excellent idea." He bowed. "I must see to the horses. Until tonight."

Rosalind watched him leave, his back stiff, his stride eating up the ground as if he couldn't wait to be away from her. She sighed and then went still as she realized Christopher was watching her closely.

"I see Rhys is the jealous sort."

She opened her eyes wide at him. "Jealous of what?"

"Of you and me."

"There is no 'you and me.'"

His smile widened and he gently traced the curve of her lower lip with his gloved finger. "Aye, there is."

She jerked her head away. "Rhys will do what my grandfather tells him to do."

"Poor man."

"You are in a far worse position. You serve two masters, the Vampires and your family."

His gaze sobered. "Verily, but I don't have to stand back and watch my lover with another man."

Rosalind bit down on the retort that sprang to her lips. Her grandfather had ordered her to be nice to Christopher, not bait him at every turn. He frowned and stepped closer, angling her back against the wall of the chapel until there was nowhere else for her to go. "Now I am concerned."

"Why?"

"Because instead of spitting out some caustic retort, you stand there like a wooden quintain waiting to be whacked by my lance."

Eagerly, Rosalind clutched at the chance to change the subject. "You joust, sir?"

His smile was wary. "Of course. I'm considered quite proficient. You should come down to the lists one day and watch me."

"And will you ask me for my favor to carry with you into battle?"

"Naturally." His gaze swept over her, settled on her mouth. "I'd be honored to be your champion."

Rosalind licked her lips and his blue eyes narrowed. He braced one arm over her head and leaned into her. "Yet again you hesitate to bait me. Is there something I should know? Have your feelings toward me changed for the better?"

She tried for a light, teasing tone. "My feelings are my own business, sir."

He closed the space between them, his mouth brushing hers, his breath soft on her cheek. His finger traced the stiff lace ruff at her neck, and then dipped lower to stroke the hollow at the base of her throat. "Indeed they are, and mine too, if you would let me cherish you as I wish."

Rosalind closed her eyes and inhaled his spicy scent. It would be so easy to capitulate, to melt into his embrace and allow him to believe he had conquered her affections, but she couldn't quite bring herself to do it. She sensed he wasn't the sort of man who loved easily. He would demand things of her she wasn't yet prepared to give.

She unclenched her fist and shoved at his shoulder, but found no give in his rigid stance. At her back, the wall vibrated as the single bell in the tower called the faithful to Mass. "Sir Christopher, we are in the chapel. This is scarcely the place for declarations of love."

"On the contrary," he whispered. "Isn't this the perfect spot for you to plight your troth to me?"

"You wish to marry me?"

He went still and eased a little away from her. "I didn't quite mean that."

"Of course! You only wish to use my body to rid yourself of your annoying itch. You should be careful that God doesn't strike you down for displaying such immorality in His very church."

He sighed and shook his head. "Rosalind, you are incorrigible." The door opened behind him and several people entered. He took her hand and placed it on his arm. "Let's find somewhere to stand."

"Are you sure that you don't need to visit your confessor first?"

He winked at her. "My confessor is well aware of my sins. What about yours?"

Rosalind chose not to answer, and swept past him into the nave of the church. She hoped the heat from the banked candles would disguise the source of her blushes, but doubted the man at her side would be fooled. Beneath his easy charm was a far more complex and determined man than she had anticipated. The thought of entangling herself with him made her simultaneously curious and repelled. In some ways, he reminded her of her Vampire foes, but then, there was that annoying protective streak he sometimes showed, which unfortunately made him all too human.

With a sigh, she sank to her knees and crossed herself. Her grandfather always insisted that temptation came in many disguises. Until she'd met Christopher Ellis, she'd always believed she had the strength to defeat anything. Now she was no longer sure. He was her enemy, her reluctant partner, *and* the man she was supposed to seduce. Her task wouldn't be easy. He'd already demonstrated that he was far too sharp not to notice her changing moods. Any attempt to fool him would probably be doomed to failure.

Rosalind bent her head as the queen and her ladies hurried down the aisle to the front of the church and the bell rang to begin the Mass. She started to rise and Christopher's strong fingers closed around her elbow and brought her to her feet. Even through the thick cloth of her riding habit, she could feel the heat from his body, the subtle strength within his deceptively slender frame.

Not an easy man to deceive at all . . . She stared at the priest and tried to turn her thoughts to more spiritual matters. All she had to do was let her unfortunate inclination to lust after Sir Christopher follow its natural path. Surely it was not so complicated? Rosalind tried to relax as she contemplated the days ahead. If she could behead a Vampire, she could certainly ensnare a lover.

Christopher watched Rosalind walking back to the palace surrounded by the queen's ladies. She'd introduced him to the king and he'd been granted far greater access to the royal personage than he could ever have dreamed possible. The Vampire legend about the Llewellyns' pact with the Tudors was obviously far from fiction. He must remember to tell his uncle about it.

At that thought, he grimaced and increased his pace. He would've preferred to stay close to Rosalind, but he had far more pressing business to attend to. Uncle Edward had arrived at court, and he wasn't the kind of man who appreciated being kept waiting. Mindful of his uncle's preference for security, Christopher had arranged to meet him in a private chamber procured by Elias Warner far away from the prying eyes of the court.

He nodded at Warner, who stood guard outside the door, and went in, pausing at the doorway to try to judge his uncle's mood before he had to speak. It was an old habit, painfully learned in childhood . . . and a pointless task. His uncle had made no secret of his distaste for rearing his brother's cursed son. Sometimes, when he looked into those cold blue eyes that were so like his own, Christopher thought it was a miracle he'd survived at all.

"Good morning, sir."

"Good morning, Christopher." His uncle's critical gaze swept over him and found him wanting as usual. Christopher straightened his spine. His uncle was dressed in rich brown and gold clothing that suited his tall, angular frame and pure white hair. "I suppose you are wondering why I bothered to come and seek you out."

"It is an unexpected pleasure, sir." Christopher kept his tone and his expression agreeable. He'd learned early in life to present an amicable face to the world. No one looking at him would ever have guessed the boyish fear lurking behind his every action. Fear that he would be found wanting, unworthy of the Ellis name, that his tainted blood would somehow show through and that his uncle would have him killed.

"Scarcely a pleasure, nephew." Uncle Edward grunted. "You don't like me any more than I like you."

"And with good reason, sir. You've always treated me with the deepest suspicion."

"Yet, until now, you've done quite well for yourself."

Christopher frowned. "Until now?"

"Aye, I sent you to court to aid the Vampires, and so far you haven't done a damned thing."

"You know the situation is complicated. We must act with the utmost discretion. While we deal with the threat, we must ensure that there is no panic at court."

Uncle Edward took the high-backed chair beside the fireplace and sat down. "When you say 'we,' are you referring to that Druid spawn Rosalind Llewellyn?"

"Yes, and Elias Warner," Christopher said evenly. "You know that. You gave the Vampire Council your blessing."

"I know it, but I don't like it." Uncle Edward shot Christopher a glare. "You with your mother's *beauty*. You've always been too comely. I expected by now you would have that girl eating out of your hand." He chuckled. "Or any other part of you she fancied nibbling. Those Druid women are notorious wantons."

Christopher's fingers flexed in an instinctive desire to wrap themselves around his uncle's neck. "Are you saying you wish me to seduce her?"

"I'm telling you that she needs to be contained and nullified. Put her on her back, keep her well satisfied in bed, and she'll give you no trouble."

"Why would you want me to contain her when you have already agreed to her working with me to catch this rogue Vampire?"

"What I agree to and what I expect you to do are completely different matters."

"Are you saying that you lied to the Vampire Council when you agreed to this arrangement?"

"Certainly not, nephew. I'm just suggesting that you take the upper hand with the Llewellyn wench and make sure she has little to do with the whole business."

"Have you met Lady Rosalind, uncle?"

"Of course not."

"Then I pray you never do. She'd probably slit your throat in an instant."

Uncle Edward half rose from his chair, his complexion coloring. "Are you suggesting I'm too weak to fight a woman?"

"No, I'm suggesting Lady Rosalind is as well trained as any man, and twice as brave. She also has certain skills I do not possess that will help me catch this Vampire." He held his uncle's gaze until the man subsided back into his chair again. "I need her help. If you don't believe me, ask Elias Warner. You probably trust him more than you trust me."

"I don't trust anyone."

"Obviously, sir." Christopher inclined his head and turned toward the door. "If you have finished telling me how to manage my business, I'll take my leave of you."

"Don't be insolent!"

Christopher swung back round. "By God's blood, just tell me the truth! If you didn't think me capable of handling this task, why give it to me? Why not deal with it yourself?"

His uncle's smile wasn't pleasant. "As I said, nephew, your visage is far more pleasing than mine."

"You chose me because I am handsome?"

"Partly."

Christopher barely hung on to the remnants of his temper. "I have fought well against the Druids and, when necessary, the Vampires. I refuse to allow you to belittle me."

"Why so offended, Christopher? Don't you think the Druids selected Lady Rosalind for exactly the same reason, to entice you?"

Christopher let out his breath. "So this does have something to do with the prophecy after all."

"Of course. You're not without wits, my boy. I knew you'd work it out."

Christopher strode back to the fireplace to tower over his uncle. "I'm not sure I appreciate being used in this fashion. The prophecy speaks of death. Am I so expendable?"

"You are serving your family's best interests. A family that took you in despite the circumstances of your birth." Uncle Edward lowered his voice. "Do not forget your sacred vows to Mithras and to me. Don't you owe us everything?"

Inside Christopher, old loyalties and new emotions fought an unceasing battle. Since ancient times, every member of the Mithraic cult had vowed to annihilate the Druids, though recently the sect had spent as much time cultivating its links with the Vampires as chasing after the few remaining Druids. After his initial youthful euphoria at being deemed worthy to join, Christopher had come to realize he had no stomach for the slaughtering of innocents, whatever religion they might practice.

The doubts he'd been having had only doubled since he'd met Rosalind. He hoped his distaste didn't show too plainly on his face.

"I am loyal to you, sir. Don't ever doubt that."

His uncle sat back. "Then you will do as I say. Get rid of Rosalind Llewellyn. Swive her into loving submission and then abandon her or kill her—I care not. But the Vampire must die."

"The Vampire will die, Uncle." Christopher hesitated. "May I ask why the Council is so afraid of this particular Vampire?"

His uncle's blue gaze flicked away from him. "Because the Council is made up of weak fools who can no longer control their own race."

"You sound almost contemptuous, sir. I thought the Vampires were our allies."

A flicker of distaste crossed his uncle's fine features. "They are what they are."

"You don't respect the old alliance anymore?"

"I didn't say that, nephew. As long as the Vampires exist, we will protect them. That is all that concerns you." He waved his hand in dismissal.

Christopher inclined his head. "Good-bye, Uncle." He swung open the door and started back toward the queen's chambers, rage churning in his gut, his vision tinted red. It wasn't until he was well on his way that he realized Elias was walking beside him.

"Your uncle is a hard, difficult man, Sir Christopher."

"He is indeed."

"And yet he allowed you to take on this Vampire alone."

"Hardly alone. I have you and Lady Rosalind to help me."

"But why did he send you?"

Christopher sighed. "You were listening to our conversation, were you not?"

Elias shrugged. "I might have caught the odd word."

"Then you know why he chose me, because he thinks I will be able to seduce Lady Rosalind from her cause."

Elias cocked his head to one side, an amused glint in his eyes. "And you believed him?"

"Why wouldn't I? My uncle has no compunction about speaking the truth as he sees it."

Elias's smile was full of sly amusement. "You're probably right. After all, your handsome visage does seem to have a decidedly promising effect on the lady in question, does it not?"

Christopher scowled and walked away, his step slowing as he considered his uncle's words. It was interesting that Edward seemed to have doubts about the Vampire Council. Was it possible that the Ellis family sought to extricate itself from the old ties? A flicker of hope awakened in Christopher's soul. He realized he would be more than willing to relinquish his bloody vows, especially those to the Cult of Mithras.

His moment of optimism faded. Even if his uncle was tiring of his responsibilities to the Vampires, he was unlikely to challenge them, or tell Christopher if he did. It would be better to consider the problem at hand rather than worry about the future. He'd just been given permission to seduce the object of his desire, and yet he couldn't enjoy it at all.

Chapter 10

Rosalind sighed and moved closer until her thigh was aligned with Christopher's. He seemed less self-assured than usual, and far less charming. Tension sang through his entire frame, making Rosalind ill at ease. She really had no idea how to go about enticing him.

"Stop wiggling," Christopher murmured.

"I'm not. It's just that this is a small space."

Rosalind fixed her gaze on the entrance to the queen's chambers. She and Christopher were situated within a small copse close to the main door. A ragged tangle of pruned rosebushes and bushy sage covered the ground in front of them, offering even more protection.

"I'm still not sure why I have to spend my nights out here with you in the cold, when I could guard the queen quite adequately from the warmth of her private chamber."

"Because we want to apprehend the Vampire *before* she reaches the queen, and the queen might grow suspicious if you always want to stay with her at night. Didn't they teach you anything when you trained as a slayer?"

Rosalind pivoted and pressed the tip of her dagger to his lower lip. "Enough to cut out your tongue."

He cursed as the sharp blade caressed his skin and knocked her hand away. "God help the man who marries you, Rosalind. He had better guard his prick with his life."

She glanced down at the shadows of his groin. "You are right, sir. Should I be displeased with a man, there is apt to be a terrible accident."

He flinched and drew his knees tightly together. "Perhaps it *would* be better for you to be inside the palace. Then we would have two separate vantage points."

Rosalind glowered at his averted profile. Here she was, trying to think of ways to allow herself to be seduced, and he was trying to get *rid* of her. "There's a reversal indeed. You don't usually want me to go."

His quick smile was strained. "I know. I'm not quite sure what's come over me."

"You no longer find me to your liking?"

His only response was a muttered curse and she poked his upper arm. "It's not like you to be silent. Is something wrong?"

He finally turned to look at her, his teeth bared, his eyes a vivid blue. "Nothing that a night of fornication wouldn't cure."

"Don't let me stop you!" She tried to make her laugh sound genuine. "I'm quite capable of defeating this Vampire by myself while you go and fornicate."

He moved so quickly that she could only gasp as his hand cupped the back of her head and his mouth covered hers. He kissed her hard, his tongue voracious, and she kissed him back, wrapping her left arm around his neck to keep him close.

He pulled her into his lap so that she straddled him. One of his hands dropped from her waist to curve over her buttocks and pressed her into the driving rhythm of his kiss. Heat gathered in her lower belly as his leather codpiece notched against the soft mound between her legs.

She dragged her mouth away from his. "We're supposed to be watching for the Vampire!"

His answer was a growl as his mouth descended once more and he licked and nipped his way down her throat. She moaned as he undid the top three buttons of her old doublet and shoved his hand deep to cup her breast. His fingers brushed over her bound nipple. It hardened into a tight, thrusting bud that ached for his touch.

His teeth grazed the soft skin of her throat, and then he licked her ear and bit down on the lobe. Her body was on fire, her hips moving in helpless circles trying to merge with the hardness she sensed behind his clothing. She wanted to rip off his hose and—

When he drew back, she was panting and so was he. She bit back a protest when he set her firmly away and scowled down at her. "I'm sure it will amuse you greatly to hear that I am not interested in fornicating with any other woman. The only wench I want naked and writhing under me is you."

Rosalind pictured that and shivered.

He frowned at her. "Don't do that."

"What?"

"Look as though you quite like the idea."

Rosalind hesitated for only a moment before reaching her arms out to him. He shot to his feet, all thought of remaining hidden gone. "You were right. You should spend the night in the queen's chambers."

"What? Why?"

He looked grim. "Because I'm a fool."

Now he was making no sense at all, Rosalind thought as she set her clothing to rights. "You *want* me to leave?"

"Aye. The sooner the better."

Rosalind scrambled to her feet. "There's no need to be unpleasant, Sir Christopher."

He towered over her, his expression furious. "By God's teeth, there is. Now go inside!"

She stared up at him for a long moment. "Elias told me that you met with your uncle this morning. Whatever did he say to put you in such a bad temper?"

"Do you really want to know?"

"Of course I do."

A muscle flicked in his cheek. "He told me to seduce you."

A hysterical desire to laugh bubbled in Rosalind's chest. "How strange. That's exactly what my grandfather told me to do to you." She bobbed a curtsy. "Good night, Sir Christopher."

His hand shot out and he took hold of her upper arm. "He told you to do *what*?"

"You heard me, sir."

"Then why the devil are we standing here instead of enjoying each other in my bed?"

Rosalind swallowed hard. "Because neither of us likes being told what to do?"

His breath hissed out and coalesced in the rapidly freezing night air. "By all the saints, I want you, Rosalind."

She couldn't help herself. "And I want you."

His eyes glinted with satisfaction as he slid his fingers down her arm and took her hand instead. "I would like to say I told you so, but I fear for my tongue."

"You fear nothing." She gazed up at him wonderingly. "You have already proved that you are capable of overpowering me. Why do you not push me to the ground and take what you desire?"

He brought her hand to his lips and kissed her fingertips. "The same thing that stops you, I imagine. The desire to be freely welcomed into a lover's arms without artifice or deceit."

Rosalind studied their clasped hands. "And I cannot offer you that, because our families and the Vampires have manipulated us both. How can we know if we truly desire each other when we are trapped together in a web of deceit?"

His smile was wry. "Exactly." He let go of her hand. "You should go."

She grabbed his hand and kissed his knuckles, almost afraid to speak because of the emotion rising inside her.

He pulled gently out of her grasp and turned away from her. "Sleep well, my lady, and God keep you safe."

"And you, sir."

She whispered the words as she ran toward the palace. She was a fool. She should be taking his hand and following him to bed rather than keeping watch on the queen. Her body throbbed a lament that echoed the numbness in her mind. She'd done the right thing and so had he, but it felt like a double betrayal.

She paused at the bottom of the stairs, and wrapped her arms around herself as if she'd been injured. Walking away from the lustful promise in Christopher's blue eyes hurt more than any physical wound ever had. Did he feel the same, or would he salve his hurt in another woman's bed? He said he only wanted her. . . . She fingered her dagger and hoped he had spoken the truth.

When she reached the door to her chamber, she paused and took off her boots. There was no need to awaken Margaret, who was spending her last night with Rosalind before her husband's return.

What on earth would she tell her grandfather? If she refused to seduce Christopher, would he demand her instant return and instruct Rhys to take over her mission? Although he wasn't a Llewellyn and didn't have her access to the king, Rhys was more than capable of killing the Vampire. But then there was the matter of the prophecy. . . .

Rosalind stared into the darkness and listened to Margaret's slow, even breathing. If she was clever, perhaps they would be able to find a way to kill the Vampire . . . before they succumbed to the temptation to bed each other after all.

Christopher brushed the dirt and dried rose petals from the knees of his hose and stood back against the nearest tree trunk. At least, with the temptation of Rosalind removed, he stood a chance of keeping his mind on his mission. He licked his lips and tasted her sweetness. Then he imagined her mouth on his chest, his belly, his prick . . .

A whisper of sensation above him set all his instincts clamoring and he looked around, behind him, and up at the leafy branches above him. Something as gossamer-light as spider silk brushed his neck, and he went still. He knew there was no one there, but he also knew he wasn't alone. He inhaled the scent of orange blossom and inched his fingers toward the sheath of his dagger.

"Canst thou hear me, blood of my blood?"

The chilling whisper echoed inside his head, but went no further. Christopher closed his eyes, and concentrated on the strangely familiar accent. "Yes," he murmured hesitantly. "I can hear you."

A sense of gloating satisfaction flowed through his mind. *"Why dost thou hunt me?"*

"I have no choice. You have violated the rules set out by the Vampire Council."

"But thou dost not wish to harm me."

"How can that be true?" he whispered. "I don't know who you are."

Soft laughter stirred the hairs on the back of his neck. *"Thou knowest me. We are kin."*

He spun around, but there was nothing there—only the echo of her laughter in his head. He was shivering, and perspiration had broken out on his forehead. What in the name of all the saints was happening to him?

With a groan, he fell to his knees and pounded the ground with his fists. The Vampire had spoken to him, and she'd sounded as familiar as his soul. Her voice carried the same soft cadences as his Spanish childhood, of his mother . . .

Christopher looked back at the queen's chambers, then reached out to pick up his dagger, which lay abandoned on the ground. He had no idea how it had gotten there—not that the blade would've been much use to him. It wasn't as if he could cut out his own ability to think.

His childish terror threatened to break through the iron bands of his memory. He'd feared something like this his whole life, and now it was finally upon him. But he was a man now, not a child, and it was up to him whether he used the truth wisely, or continued to run from it.

Christopher began to pray, his words stumbling at first but then stronger, and more comforting than he could ever have imagined.

Chapter 11

"Someone's out early and is in a hurry."

At Rhys's laconic words, Rosalind glanced up to see another rider emerge from the mist that enclosed the ancient forest and head straight for them. It was shortly before the sun was due to rise. The ground was hard and laced with frost as was the very air they struggled to breathe. Rhys drew his dagger and Rosalind did the same. She brought her horse around to face the threat more directly, and then relaxed.

"It's Sir Christopher."

"Aye," replied Rhys. "He can't seem to leave us in peace, can he?"

When he drew closer, Christopher doffed his black cap to them and dropped his horse into a walk. "Good morning to you both. I apologize for disturbing your ride, but there is something important I need to tell you."

Rhys glanced at Rosalind and then nodded. "We can dismount by the edge of that field and talk there. I doubt we will be seen through all this mist."

Rosalind stole another quick look at Christopher's expression. She found it hard to reconcile this hard-faced man with the smiling charmer who had danced with her in the Great Hall. He concealed his abilities almost as well as she did, hid both his strength and vulnerability behind a gracious social mask.

She swung her leg over the saddle and paused as both men strode toward her to help her dismount. She tried not to sigh at their ridiculous male posturing as Christopher deliberately shouldered Rhys out of the way and brought her down to the ground himself.

"Thank you."

"You are welcome, my lady." Christopher was slow to release his grip on her waist and step back.

Rhys's low, musical voice intruded on her growing exasperation. "Now, what did you wish to tell us, Sir Christopher?"

Christopher sighed. "I fear you will think me mad. But on my oath I am telling the truth."

"We are both accustomed to the strange and unusual, sir," Rosalind said.

"Verily, I know that, but this . . ." Christopher shook his head. "This is like a fairy tale to frighten children." He swallowed hard. "Last night, while I was watching the queen's apartments, the Vampire spoke to me."

"What do you mean, spoke to you?"

Rhys cut off Rosalind's words with a disgusted sound. "Why didn't you kill the thing?"

"Because I didn't actually see it. I'm not even sure if she was there or not."

Rosalind frowned as Christopher shifted his stance yet again.

"She spoke to me, in my mind."

"You could hear her thoughts?"

"Aye." He shivered. "It was the most peculiar sensation. I hope I never have to experience it again."

Rosalind touched his arm. "But what did she say?"

"She said we were of the same blood and I should not be hunting her."

"That makes no sense at all." Rosalind frowned. "You are not a Vampire."

Rhys stepped forward, his dagger drawn. "It makes perfect sense—is that not so, Sir Christopher?"

Rosalind stepped between the two men and placed her palm on Rhys's broad chest. "What are you talking about?"

Rhys didn't look down at her, his gaze still locked with Christopher's. "I've heard it said that this Druid slayer is not of pure human blood."

Something fierce shifted and deepened in Christopher's stark blue eyes and Rosalind shoved at Rhys's chest. "That is a vicious thing to say."

"No, my lady. It's all right. It pains me greatly to say so, but there is some doubt—that is, my branch of the Ellis family may have been infected with Vampire blood." Christopher held up his hand. "I do not know if it is true. By all that's Holy, the Vampire did sound familiar." He hesitated and then continued. "She spoke to me in the language of my family in Aragon."

Rosalind tried to hide the instinctive shiver of revulsion his words conjured. Was it possible that she was falling in love with a Vampire? She struggled to speak normally. "Then you think she is indeed related to you somehow?"

He shrugged, his gaze evasive. "I fear it may be so. The fact that she could enter my thoughts suggests she is. It is the custom of Vampires who have a familial link."

Rosalind nodded and tried to concentrate on the practical aspects of Christopher's revelation rather than her confused emotions. "That is why we sometimes lose our prey or find ourselves facing twenty Vampires when we started off chasing only one."

Rhys stepped back, his expression thoughtful. "Could you talk back to her?"

"In my mind? I do not know. When she asked me a question, I answered her aloud."

"Why do you ask, Rhys?" Rosalind looked at him even as he continued to stare speculatively at Christopher.

"Because if the Vampire can communicate with him, she may also be able to read his mind."

Christopher groaned. "Then she will know whatever plans we make against her!"

"Yes," Rhys answered. "But we could also use that in our favor, by giving her the wrong information."

"So you imagine I could conceal my *true* thoughts from her yet communicate false ones! Alas, I do not think you understand what power she has over me." An expression of revulsion flooded Christopher's face. "You have no idea how it felt to have that creature in my head."

"Actually, we do." Rosalind went toward him and took his hand again. At least, she could help him with this. To his credit, he seemed as horrified at the thought of becoming a Vampire as she would be. "We're taught from an early age how to protect our minds from Vampire spells, but even a good hunter can be deceived. I know it must have been more than unpleasant to have that monster inside your head."

His smile was forced. "I'm sorry for being such a coward."

"We can show you how to shield your thoughts from the Vampire, and we don't think that you are a coward, do we, Rhys?" She glared at Rhys, who merely looked skeptical. "No one would enjoy being in the power of that rogue Vampire."

"But I'll have to endure it if we are to understand the creature better." Christopher paused. "I'll ask Elias if a Vampire can form a bond with a human."

"We'll both speak to Elias." Rosalind paused as another thought struck her. "I wonder if the Vampire would speak to *me* if I let down my shields and allowed her in."

"No."

Both men spoke at the same time and Rosalind felt her cheeks heat up. She raised her chin. "I don't believe either of you has the authority to tell me what I can or cannot do."

Christopher turned until he stood shoulder to shoulder with Rhys. "At least we are in agreement about something. Lady Rosalind has to be protected."

"Aye, if she is the key to the prophecy, she cannot be allowed to do anything rash."

Rosalind picked up her skirts and stomped back toward her horse. Not allowed to do *anything rash* . . . She clamped her teeth together so firmly that her jaw ached. Perhaps she should simply seek out Elias on her own and leave the two puffed-up peacocks to make their own way back to the palace.

"Lady Rosalind?" Rhys ran up behind her.

She refused to acknowledge him and returned her attention to her horse. Not for the first time, she cursed her long skirts, and the tight bodice of her riding gown that made it impossible for her to get on a horse without help.

Rhys tossed her into the saddle as if she were a sack of flour. He kept his hands firmly over hers, and leaned close. "Don't forget our original purpose for riding this way this morning. I must show you to the site of our Beltaine celebration tomorrow night."

"I had forgotten. But you shall be escorting me, so it's all right."

"Yes, if I am able. But I would prefer you know the way in case I am delayed."

Rosalind sighed. "I suppose we must let Sir Christopher talk to Elias alone."

Satisfaction flashed across his face. "Indeed, my lady. If you trust Sir Christopher as well as you say you do."

Rosalind met his gaze. "I do. Now stop this."

"Stop what?"

"This . . . display of possessiveness."

"I have no idea what you are talking about." Rhys turned away from her toward Christopher, who had appeared by his side. "My lady regrets to inform you that she cannot come with you to find Elias Warner."

"Thank you, Rhys. I am quite capable of speaking for myself." Rosalind clicked at her horse and moved forward to block Rhys and smile down at Christopher.

"You'll not come with me?" Now Christopher looked as insulted as Rhys.

"Let us meet in the queen's apartments after we've broken our fast to discuss what you have found out."

Christopher's brows drew together and he cast a wary glance at Rhys. Rosalind extended her hand, and Christopher brought it to his lips. "I shall count the hours, my lady."

To her relief, he released her gloved hand and stepped back with a bow. She imagined he might actually be relieved not to have to discuss his experience with the Vampire in front of her and Rhys. And Elias might be more forthcoming with Christopher, although he was hardly known for his frankness.

She watched Christopher mount his horse, his movements as graceful and assured as Rhys's. He nodded a farewell and trotted back toward the trees, the feather in his hat tangling in the breeze with the curling strands of his black hair.

"He rides well," Rosalind said musingly.

"He is a preening ass."

Rosalind glared at him. "Why must you speak of him so?"

"There's no need to poker up, my lady. He's quite capable of defending himself."

"Not when he's riding away from us."

His smile was fleeting. "And do you defend *my* honor when he insults me?"

"Of course I do."

"So he does insult me."

Rosalind fought a desire to scream. "Why are you so obsessed with each other? Are all males in rut the same?"

"I should imagine so." He sighed and his expression relaxed to reveal the old Rhys, the man she'd trusted and laughed and trained with. "I'm sorry, Rosalind. I promised not to interfere, didn't I?"

"You did." It made her uncomfortable to see Rhys getting angry on her behalf. She didn't deserve his trust and she sensed he was beginning to realize it too. In some ways he acted far more like her brother than her lover and she wasn't at all sure which she liked less. "Now, show me where this sacred site is so that I can find my way there tomorrow night after the court finishes celebrating."

Rhys pointed at another cluster of oak trees in the near distance. "It's not far. You could even walk there if you had to, although it would take a while."

Rosalind peered into the mist and urged her horse into a trot. She was sure they'd ridden this way before, but she hadn't sensed anything different about this particular group of trees. As they approached the thick circle, she noticed a change in the air, the indefinable hum of ancient magic calling to her from the very earth.

When she dismounted, she could hear the sound of rushing water above the slight, cutting wind and headed toward it. The ground started to slope downward, and she made her way more carefully. She was surprised to find herself in a substantial hidden valley. On the opposite side of the slope, a waterfall picked its way down the hill, glinted off gray and blue stone, foamed briefly, and then disappeared into the ground.

Rhys caught up with her, and pointed downward through the tangle of bushes. "Druids have worshipped in this spot for thousands of years. There was once a complete stone circle here, but much of it was taken away and used to build the palace and the chapels." Tangled ivy and vegetation marred the perfection of the remaining standing stones. They surged upward in two concentric circles, like jagged, uneven teeth.

Rosalind stood still and simply breathed in the atmosphere. She sensed the echoes of celebration, of blood spilled, of rebirth. Beltaine was the festival of fertility and new life, a time of hope and renewal, in contrast to the darker celebrations of Yule and Samhain. She had always enjoyed it the most.

"Do you think you will be able to find this place again?" Rhys asked.

"I think so. How many worshippers are expected?"

Rhys took her hand and helped her back up the steep slope of the valley. "I'm not sure how many of us are left in this area, but whosoever can will be here tomorrow night."

"It is a holy place."

He squeezed her fingers. "You feel it too? The excitement waiting to erupt when the fires are lit and the priests begin their ceremonies. Aye, it will be glorious."

Rosalind glanced sideways at Rhys. He sounded far more animated than usual. Despite all his protestations of neutrality, was he still hoping she'd jump through the Beltaine fire with him, and thus proclaim themselves a couple? The mood between them was so strained she couldn't think of a way to ask him.

She fixed her gaze on the top of the slope and continued to slog up the hill, her breathing now ragged. There was no point in asking for trouble. He'd said he would wait. . . . But was it fair to expect Rhys to wait until the Vampire was dead and her complicated feelings for Christopher were resolved?

Rosalind sighed. He'd always been a patient man. She tried to cheer herself with the thought of the night to come, the freedom to be herself, to worship the ancient gods with her own kind.

Her faint smile died. She wondered what Christopher thought of such pagan celebrations. Had he ever participated in a massacre of her people during one of their ceremonies, as his Roman forebears had done? Did he relish the thought of killing Druids during their sacred rites?

Rosalind found herself shivering. She'd heard horror stories about Druid slayers all her life, but she couldn't picture Christopher at the center of such violence. Still, she must take care not to reveal this location to him.

And hope that tomorrow night he would be too busy chasing the female Vampire to worry about her and her kind for a few hours.

Chapter 12

"Ah, there you are, Master Warner," Christopher said as he spied Elias in one of the bustling courtyards adjoining the royal palace. "I've been looking for you all day."

"I rarely rise before noon, and since then I've been busy arranging some musical entertainment for the queen and her May Day guests." Elias held up a lute, his golden eyes guileless. "You play and sing, do you not?"

"A little." Christopher glanced at the ornate instrument, and then at the crowd of courtiers who scurried back and forth between the wings of the palace like busy ants. Despite the sun streaming down on them, the enclosed stone courtyard was full of shadows. "But first, there is something I wanted to ask you."

Elias gave a long-suffering sigh and put down the lute he was holding. "Of course. How may I be of service to you?"

Christopher walked him over to a quieter corner and checked to see that they were alone. "The one we seek spoke to me last night."

"Spoke to you?"

"In my mind."

Elias's eyebrows rose and he studied Christopher intently. "But that's impossible."

"Why? Vampires often use magic to compel humans to give them blood."

"Did she feed from you?"

"No."

"Then it's not the same at all, is it?" Elias looked thoughtful. "It seems the Council was right to ask your uncle to send for you, after all."

"I don't understand."

"If you can hear the rogue Vampire's thoughts, you must be involved in the prophecy."

"In what way?"

"If you are connected to the rogue Vampire, you can help Rosalind Llewellyn track the Vampire down and defeat her before she succeeds in killing the king."

"I'm beginning to understand that part of it, but why might I have this connection?"

"The only explanation I can imagine is that she is somehow related to your family." Elias shrugged. "Did she sound familiar to you?"

"She sounded . . . Spanish."

"Ah, from your mother's side. That makes sense, although it scarcely narrows our search. At least a dozen of the queen's ladies and fifty of her servants come from Aragon."

Christopher sighed. "I suppose I can ask my uncle if I have any distant kin from Aragon serving at court, though he is reluctant to speak of my mother's family." And, in truth, he had always been reluctant to ask his uncle about them as well—or anything that might complicate his already precarious position within the Ellis family. At least with Elias he had no reason to pretend that everything was well between him and his uncle. As the Vampire had reminded him, Elias had lived long enough to know all the pitiful secrets of the Ellises. "But this is what I wished to ask you: If she can speak to me in my mind, can I do the same to her?"

"I have no idea. I've never heard of a Vampire communicating with a 'human' before."

Christopher picked up the lute and absentmindedly tried to tune it. "Then I'll have to try it and see what happens."

Elias laughed. "I wish you luck."

Christopher met his amused gaze head-on. "I shall need it."

"Then perhaps, if we are done, you could aid me in bringing these musical instruments to the queen's apartments?"

"Of course." Christopher accompanied Elias back to the pile of instruments the servants were unloading from a cart and picked up an exquisite psaltery and a harp to go with the lute he already carried. He brought his treasures carefully into the palace and through to the queen's private chambers.

The queen's rather somber expression lightened as he approached and bowed to her. She put down her embroidery.

"You will play for us, Sir Christopher?"

"Of course, Your Majesty."

She clapped her hands together and smiled, the pleasure on her face making her look younger than her forty-four years. "I am already looking forward to it. You play exquisitely."

Christopher bowed again, and as he backed away, he saw Rosalind and her friend Margaret appear in the doorway.

No doubt, Rosalind would be eager to hear what he had learned from Elias Warner, although the Vampire had been less than forthcoming. Christopher stopped walking. Why had his uncle insisted he had no part to play in the prophecy except to seduce Rosalind? Elias implied he was far more important than that and Christopher had to believe him. In truth, his ability to communicate with the Vampire might prove invaluable.

Christopher took up the lute the queen offered him. He sat down in the window seat and focused his attention on tuning the lute to the more accurate pitch of the flute Margaret was playing. He breathed in a now familiar fragrance of roses, and looked up to see Rosalind settling herself beside him. She'd replaced her old green riding habit with a brown-and-gold embroidered kirtle that matched her eyes.

He smiled at her. "Do you play, my lady?"

She shrugged, the motion drawing his attention to her breasts and the amber cross nestled between them. He wondered if anyone would notice if he leaned forward and licked a path down that soft valley. . . .

"I have no talent for any musical instrument, but I can sing a little."

He swept his hand over the strings of the lute in a melodious chord. "Shall we make sweet music together, then, my lady?"

She raised her chin at him. "I will sing as the queen commands me to, sir."

Christopher looked over at the queen, who was smiling and nodding in his direction. "Your Majesty? Would you like to start with a rousing song for May Day?"

"Indeed, Sir Christopher. Then we can all join in." The queen clapped her hands and the small court settled down in a circle around her, some seated on the floor, others leaning up against the walls. One man took up a set of drums and another the psaltery, and both looked at Christopher expectantly.

He struck a loud opening chord of an old familiar tune, and the other musicians joined in. Beside him, Rosalind took a deep breath and began to sing. He angled his head to hear her better, entranced by the purity of her voice, and the bell-like tones.

> "Unite, and unite, and let us all unite
> For summer is a-comin' today.
> And whither we are going we will all unite
> In the merry morning of May."

Christopher picked up the harmony and the rest of the court joined in. He studied the happy, laughing faces around him. Which one of these courtiers was the Vampire? He could get no sense of her now. He wondered if Rosalind could, but she seemed too intent on singing to be aware of anything else.

Even as he forced himself to seek that elusive, malevolent presence, he kept on playing. The quiet joy in the queen's dark eyes was reward enough for his efforts. Rosalind sang steadfastly alongside him, her voice blending effortlessly with his, her body leaning into him as she swayed in time to the music. At long last, the queen clapped her hands again.

"Thank you, Sir Christopher, and all of you. That was wonderful." She sighed. "May Day has always been a special time of year for me. It reminds me both of Our Blessed Virgin and my daughter, who is named for her." She glanced out of the window to the garden beyond where the preparations for the May Day celebrations continued. "Shall we venture outside and see if the Maypole has its ribbons yet?"

Most of the court got to their feet, their excited chatter almost drowning out the queen's quiet voice. When Rosalind attempted to rise, Christopher touched her sleeve and she hesitated.

"I have one more song to sing, my lady. Will you stay and listen to it?"

She bit her lush lower lip and slowly sat down again.

He retuned his lute and settled his fingers over the strings before looking into her eyes.

> "Heaven pictured in her face
> Doth promise joy and grace.
> Fair Rosalind's silver light
> That beats on running streams
> Compares not with her white,
> Whose eyes are all sunbeams.
> So bright my Nymph doth shine
> As day unto mine eyn.
> With this there is a red
> Exceeds the damask rose,
> Which in her cheeks is spread,
> Where every favor grows;
> In sky there is no star
> But she surmounts it far.
> When Phoebus from the bed
> Of Thetis does arise,
> The morning, blushing red
> In fair carnation-wise
> He shows in my Nymph's face
> As Queen of every grace."

Christopher let the last sweet notes fall away and found he still couldn't look away from Rosalind's gaze. He cleared his throat. "Did that please you?"

She nodded slowly, her brown eyes huge in her face. "It was beautiful."

He shrugged. "It needs a far more talented hand than mine to make it perfect."

"You wrote that?"

He inclined his head, and busied himself propping the lute up against the wall. He almost startled when she grabbed his hand and squeezed it hard. "It was perfect just as it was."

He was so used to his uncle's dismissive remarks about his interest in music that pretending her shy compliments meant nothing to him was extremely hard. He stood up and bowed.

"I'm glad my pitiful efforts met with your approval, my lady."

Rosalind remained in her seat, her head cocked to one side as she regarded him. "Did you write it for me?"

"Some of it. I'm sure you can guess which part."

She pouted. "And the rest of it was written for another of your conquests?"

"I believe the original, much shorter version, was addressed to a fair-haired lady called Cynthia."

"Cynthia." Rosalind stood up and he instinctively backed up a step. She dropped into a curtsy and gave him a blinding smile. "It was still beautiful, Christopher. Thank you for sharing it with me."

She turned on her heel and headed for the open door. He called after her, "You are the only person who has ever heard it."

She turned at the door and looked back at him. "You didn't play it for dear Cynthia?"

"No, she was a passing fancy—unlike you."

She looked at him for a long moment and then walked slowly back toward him. She stood on tiptoe, framed his face in her hands, and kissed his mouth. Before he could respond, she was gone again, her skirts flying out behind her along with the long tails of her hood. He brought his fingers to his lips and simply stood there like a half-wit until she disappeared from sight.

Rosalind swallowed hard as the fatty smell of roasting pig and lamb floated across from the fire pits where the king's cooks strove to satisfy the gluttonous appetites of the court and the villagers from the surrounding countryside. The sky was a calm blue that matched Christopher's eyes, and there were no clouds on the horizon.

Rosalind picked her way through the crowds watching the Morris dancers, and avoided those slurping ale. Sunlight glinted off the golden crown set atop the red-and-white-striped Maypole. The brightly colored ribbons swung gently in the breeze as they were untangled and readied for use.

On a high dais, set against the protection of the palace walls, sat the king and the queen attired in matching green and gold. Although their chairs were a scarce foot apart, the king ignored the queen, and chattered instead to his courtiers and a few chosen ladies. Rosalind felt a surge of anger on the queen's behalf, but could do nothing to help her.

"Lady Rosalind, you look very fetching in that silver and green gown."

Rosalind curtsied to Elias Warner, who was attired in sumptuous pale blue velvet and satin, a heavy silver chain around his neck. His matching hat and shoes were indigo blue and his hat sported a peacock's feather.

"Thank you, Master Warner. Are you enjoying the festivities?"

"I'd enjoy them a lot more if we could be rid of our little problem." He shivered extravagantly and glanced up at the sky. "Although I doubt she will draw attention to herself out in the open like this."

"Rhys, Sir Christopher, and I are keeping watch for anything unusual. I'm sure you will do the same."

"I will indeed." Elias bowed low. "Have you seen Sir Christopher today?"

"Not yet." Rosalind kept her smile in place as Elias moved in close.

"He is enamored of you."

"Is that so?"

"And despite your attempts to appear indifferent, you are interested in him as well."

"That is none of your concern."

His eyes went cold and flat. "Indeed it is. You were told to help Sir Christopher kill this Vampire."

"And I am."

He brought her palm to his lips and she flinched as the tips of his fangs pricked the soft skin at her wrist. Pain shot up her arm and she swayed.

"Let me go."

"When you taste so . . . alive?" His smile dimmed. "You are not trying hard enough."

"To do what?" Rosalind struggled to sound calm as her wrist pulsed to the frantic rhythm of her heart. She inhaled the scent of her own blood and Elias's voice took on a seductive note that beckoned and beguiled her senses.

"You know what is required."

"That I lie with Sir Christopher? That is nothing to do with you."

His grip tightened. "Untrue. Three are mentioned in the prophecy. If Sir Christopher is not to your 'taste,' I'd be happy to offer my services."

Rosalind wrenched her hand free of Elias's. "I will never bed a Vampire."

Elias's smile was mocking as he deliberately licked his fangs. "We'll have to see about that, won't we?" He bowed and walked away. Rosalind unclenched her hand where twin pinpricks of blood welled. She patted the wounds with her kerchief, but the blood kept coming.

"Are you all right, my lady?"

She looked up to see Rhys and Christopher bearing down on her, and unsuccessfully tried to hide her injured wrist. "I'm fine, thank you."

Rhys scowled and gently took her hand. "You're bleeding."

"It was just Elias Warner playing games." She allowed Rhys to dab at her skin with his kerchief and then snatched her hand back. "It will stop bleeding eventually. There is something in a Vampire's spittle that seems to keep blood flowing longer than it should."

"So I've heard," said Sir Christopher grimly. "I shall find Elias and remind him of his manners."

"We might need his help. There is no point in antagonizing him." Rosalind peered at the tiny puncture marks. "There, they seem to be healing up now. No harm done."

From the matching expressions on Rhys's and Christopher's faces, she realized they didn't quite agree with her. She folded her ruined kerchief and tucked it back into her hanging pocket. "Please, let's not let such a minor thing stop us from enjoying the day and watching over the king and queen."

Christopher's face relaxed a little, although Rhys still seemed grim. "You're right, of course, my lady." Christopher offered her his arm. "Would you care to promenade with me and enjoy the fair?"

Rhys rolled his eyes at Rosalind. "I'll be off, then. I'll take first watch on the king and queen and I'll see you later tonight."

Christopher waited at her side, his brow creased as Rhys disappeared. "Are you planning on spending your night hours with Rhys rather than guarding the king with me?"

Rosalind took a deep breath. On the day of such an important festival, it was fitting that she remind Christopher of what she was. "It is the feast of Beltaine."

"Beltaine?" Christopher went still and drew her down the darkened passageway between two of the vendors' tents. He dropped her arm and swung around to face her. "And what will you be doing?"

"What I wish."

"With Rhys?"

"With those who practice my faith."

He stared down at her, his blue gaze narrowed. "I've heard how you practice your 'faith.'"

"Indeed?"

"By fornicating in the fields."

She opened her eyes wide at him. "It *is* a fertility festival, Sir Christopher."

He snorted. "You deny me a place in your bed, and yet under the convenient blanket of your faith, you slake your lust with as many men as you wish."

She struggled to control the tremble in her voice lest he think she was upset rather than justifiably angry. "I would ask you not to speak of things of which you know little and respect not at all."

"By God's teeth!" He glared down at her, a muscle flicking in his cheek, and slowly let out his breath. "I cannot believe I'm jealous."

Rosalind gaped at him. "What did you say?"

"I'm jealous of any other man who gets to touch you." His laugh was short and harsh. "But considering what you are, that's ridiculous, isn't it?"

Rosalind drew herself up to her full height, her hands fisted by her side. "I do not owe you either an explanation or an apology for the way I choose to live my life. Your slurs on my character are based on nothing but your distorted hatred of my people."

"As are yours."

"No, I've seen the work of Vampires firsthand. As a slayer, I vowed to rid this world of those who prey on the weak and plot to destroy humanity. I have never understood why the Ellis family has to interfere. Haven't you killed enough of my people?" She shook her head. "By all that is holy, I should not have reminded you it is Beltaine."

"Why not?" Christopher scowled at her. "Do you

think I'm now sharpening my sword and licking my lips at the prospect of a gathering of Druids?"

"Your ancestors certainly did!"

"Well, I'm quite happy to leave you to your ridiculous posturing, as long as there is no human sacrifice involved."

"And who gave you permission to be judge and jury of my race?"

He shrugged. "Those who came before me."

Rosalind shook her head. "Thanks to your ancestors, there are so few of us left now that most people have no idea we even exist." She raised her head to meet his eyes. "I suppose that makes you proud."

He sighed. "Rosalind, I cannot speak for my ancestors. All I know is that for the last few hundred years we have only killed Druids when the Vampires have been threatened—Vampires who are as innocent as you or I, and are just trying to survive."

"And you expect me to feel sorry for them?"

He glared down at her. "If you expect me to change my opinion about your race, why shouldn't you change your opinion about mine?"

"Because you aren't a Vampire! You just do their bidding."

"It isn't as simple as that! I have made vows. I am just as bound to my cause as you are!"

Now he was as angry as she was, and she welcomed that. At least if she was fighting him, she could forget the hurt of his assuming she was a wanton. . . .

He took a deep breath and then let it out again. "My lady, I would appreciate it if you didn't celebrate Beltaine."

"Why, because you have changed your mind and intend to go on a killing spree after all?"

His teeth snapped together so hard that she heard the click. He stepped into her until their bodies were aligned from knee to forehead. He used his fingers to raise her chin. "Don't say another word, or I'll be sorely tempted to put you over my knee and spank you until you scream for mercy."

"I'll never scream for you."

He raised his eyebrows. "Never is a long time, Rosalind, so be careful what you say."

"I am going to celebrate Beltaine, whether you like it or not."

"I don't like it. I think I've made myself clear about that." His thumb shaped her jaw and then her earlobe.

She jerked her head away from his far too beguiling touch. "You have no claim on me."

"I know that, yet I am asking you to stay and guard the queen with me tonight."

"Why is it so important?"

"If the Vampire knows you and Rhys are absent, she might choose tonight to strike."

Rosalind stepped away from Christopher and almost bumped into the flimsy structure of the tent siding. She didn't want to belong to him in any way, so why was she disappointed that he had asked her for the queen's benefit rather than his own?

Rosalind gave him her sweetest smile. "I'm sure you'll do splendidly without me." She bobbed him a curtsy and ran for the exit of the narrow alley. She heard him curse behind her, but he let her go. She kept running until she was hidden by the crowds and ducked into a stall selling ribbons and lace.

She'd promised the queen she would be one of the Maypole dancers. Had Christopher promised the same thing? It was highly likely. She had no desire to spend her afternoon trapped in a mesh of ribbons with a furious Druid slayer.

"That one's a farthing, love."

Rosalind looked down at the knot of green and silver

ribbons she held in her hand and fished in her purse for a coin. "Thank you. It matches perfectly with my gown."

The older woman dressed in an old-fashioned kirtle and soft linen head covering took the ribbons from Rosalind. "Stand still, my precious, and I'll pin it onto your bodice for you."

She'd handled Christopher badly. The fact that he'd been right to question the timing of both her and Rhys's disappearance only made it worse.

"There you are, sweeting."

Rosalind smiled down at the woman. "It looks beautiful. Thank you."

"You go off and enjoy yourself now, my lady." The older woman poked Rosalind's arm. "I'm sure you've got a dozen followers just waiting to dance with you today."

Rosalind waved and set off again, only to bump into Margaret and her husband, who enthusiastically dragged her over to the Maypole and insisted she take her place in the dance. Opposite her stood Christopher, his expression savage, his blue eyes boring into hers. She quickly looked away and smiled at the man standing next to her. Perhaps if she deliberately forgot her steps, she could bind Christopher to the Maypole. She'd have liked nothing better than to leave him there trussed up like a chicken for the rest of the day.

Chapter 13

Christopher glared across at Rosalind as she chatted merrily to the man clutching the Maypole ribbon next to her. It was no surprise to see the young man's smile widen and interest deepen in his eyes. Rosalind looked beautiful. Her green-and-silver gown flattered her figure and brought to Christopher's mind images of the lush emerging season, of buds flowering, of spring matings.

Christopher frowned as his prick reacted to the thought of spring and tried to flower within his hose. He took hold of the long Maypole ribbon and clenched it in his fist. He'd dance for the queen's benefit, and try to ignore the temptation across from him. Rosalind was only angry because he'd reminded her of her duty—that was all. And he had a perfect right to remonstrate with her.

Guilt settled over him as he recalled her furious expression when he'd insulted her morals. Verily, he'd acted like a fool and then compounded his error by pretending he was the better man for putting his duty above his pleasure.

A flash of red hair in the crowd over by the king's

dais drew his attention and he realized Rhys was doing his part and keeping his eye on the royal couple. He was surprised that Rhys was willing to forget his duties in favor of a Beltaine romp. But, then again, if Christopher had Rosalind to romp with, he'd be more than willing to ignore his responsibilities.

And that made him a hypocrite. . . .

He sighed as the music started, bowed to the lady to his left, and grasped his ribbon in his right hand. The first steps of the dance were simple enough. The men promenaded in one direction and the ladies in the opposite. He barely had a chance to glimpse Rosalind before she skipped past him. When the music changed tempo, he executed a series of gliding steps that brought him back-to-back with his female companion and entwined the ribbons more tightly around the pole. He barely remembered to smile, let alone dally with each new partner as was expected. He could hardly bear the wait as Rosalind drew ever closer.

Eventually he faced her. She wouldn't look at him, her gaze firmly on her ribbon and the pattern overlying the red and white stripes of the Maypole.

"I'm sorry." That brought her head up. She sidestepped until they were shoulder to shoulder, her silken skirts catching at his hose. "I have no right to criticize your religion or your choices."

Her brown eyes flashed fire at him as they faced each other again and then repeated the same set of steps to the left. His ribbon brushed against her cheek; he wished he could let it go and simply touch her instead.

"You imply that I am a whore, and expect me to forgive you just because you smile at me?"

She danced around him and his opportunity to reply was lost as he contemplated the beaming welcome of his next partner. He set his teeth and endured the whole excruciating circle again until he was opposite Rosalind.

"I'm not smiling and I don't think you a whore, else I would already have had you."

She swayed to her left and looked back over her shoulder at him, her dark hair half covering her face. "As if I'd let you."

He shot a frustrated glance at the musicians. Why couldn't they slow down? In two more beats of the music, he would be past her again. "I don't care about the others."

She looked startled, but then it was too late and she had slipped past him again, leaving him unsure of her response and desperate to escape the demands of the dance.

And then they were back together, their maneuvers restrained by the tug of the shortened ribbons and the laughter of the other couples. He stared into her eyes. "I don't care, Rosalind. I still want you."

She stood and stared at him as the music climbed to a triumphant climax. He dropped his ribbon and pulled her into his arms. "God help me," he whispered, "I don't care what you've done. I want you."

The crowd around them was yelling in appreciation of their amorous embrace, but Rosalind was not responding.

"What is it now?" he asked.

Tears glinted in her brown eyes and she blinked hard. "I don't want you to want me despite yourself."

"What in God's name is that supposed to mean?"

"You are still judging me."

"I'm trying to tell you that I don't care. That, despite everything, you are still the only woman I want. Why does that make you weep?"

She swiped at the single tear on her cheek. "I'm not weeping."

He sighed and let her go, oblivious of the shouts and jeers of the crowd around them. A curiously dull sensation settled in the pit of his stomach and he swallowed hard. What was it about him that made everyone push him away? Did he carry evidence of his mother's sin on his very visage? He held out his hands, palms up in supplication. "What else do you want me to say?"

She shook her head and turned to walk away from him, the gauzy silver streamers of her headdress fluttering in the breeze. He wanted to go after her, to demand an answer, but he realized it would be futile. She didn't trust him, and to be fair, he wasn't sure he was worthy of her trust. Mayhap she'd sensed the lie behind his words, that if she was his, he'd never let her touch another man again.

His gaze fell on the oak barrels lined up by the food trestles. If he was destined to spend the rest of the day alone, he might as well submerge his addled thoughts in ale and prepare himself for another night hunting the Vampire.

"Sir Christopher?"

Christopher looked up from contemplating his empty cup of ale to find Rhys Williams staring down at him. Darkness now covered the site of the May Day revels, although fires roared and people gathered in tight knots to sing and drink. The air was different somehow, charged with a menace and an excitement he could almost taste.

"What can I do for you, Master Williams?"

Rhys frowned. "Get your head out of that ale, for a start. How do you expect to guard anyone when you are befuddled with drink?"

"I am not drunk." Christopher tried to conceal a belch. "I am merely merry."

"If you insist, sir." Rhys didn't look convinced at all.

"Will you be able to watch over the king and queen by yourself tonight?"

Christopher glanced around, but there was nobody else sitting at his table. He helped himself to more ale from the new jug someone had thoughtfully placed there. "I don't need anyone's assistance. I am the one who can sense the Vampire in my head."

"That's a good point, sir. I hadn't thought of that. It will make your job far easier." Rhys nodded and made as if to leave.

Christopher stared into his ale. "Are you going to her now?"

Rhys hesitated, one hand on his sword. "I'm not sure what you mean."

"To Rosalind."

Rhys stared at him for a long moment and then lowered his voice. "I'm going to celebrate Beltaine according to the customs of my religion."

"So you will be with her."

Something flickered in Rhys's eyes that mirrored all too accurately the emotions swirling in Christopher's head. "It's the first time she's celebrated Beltaine without her family around her. I have to keep her safe."

Christopher saluted him with his cup and then drank deeply. The bitter taste of the hops and added herbs made his throat burn. "Better you than anyone else, I suppose."

"I beg your pardon, sir."

"To rut with her, I mean."

He suddenly found himself on his feet as Rhys grabbed a handful of his doublet. "Do not speak of my lady like that."

Christopher laughed. "What's the matter? I flatter you, sir. I'm saying I'd rather it was you than any other man."

Rhys yanked even harder on Christopher's doublet,

his voice rough and full of anger. "And so it would be, if you hadn't turned up and ruined everything. Make no mistake, Ellis. I vowed I would not interfere in your relationship, but if you hurt her, I'll kill you and be damned to the consequences."

"I'd expect nothing less from the man she considers her dearest friend."

"Her *betrothed* when I get her safely back to Wales."

Christopher hoped his smile masked the instant denial that sprang to his lips. "Then go to your beloved."

Elias appeared suddenly behind Rhys and wrapped a hand around his throat. A dagger appeared between his fingers, and Rhys went still. "I told Rosalind to go ahead and meet you at the stone circle, Master Williams, but I'm afraid you will be delayed."

Christopher had to grab the edge of the trestle table for support. That last jug of ale must have been far more potent than the rest. "Let Rhys go."

Elias drew the tip of his dagger across Rhys's throat until a thin line of blood appeared. He inhaled deeply, as if savoring the bouquet of a fine wine. A muscle flicked in Rhys's cheek, but otherwise he showed no reaction. "Go to Rosalind, Ellis. She needs protection."

Christopher ignored Rhys and fixed his gaze on Elias. "Aren't you supposed to be helping us?"

"I am helping you." Elias smiled. "Master Williams is right. Lady Rosalind could be in danger. You must find her."

"But I don't know where she is."

Before Christopher could react, Elias's fangs sank into Rhys's neck. Rhys gave a strange sigh and slumped to the ground.

"What in God's name have you done?" Christopher went down on his knees to help Rhys, only to find Elias's dagger at his temple. "He's the only one who knows where Rosalind is! Why did you kill him?"

"He isn't dead, Sir Christopher. He'll awaken in a few hours. I give you my word on that."

Christopher got slowly to his feet. None of the masses of people carousing around the bonfires seemed aware of the drama being played out in front of them. Had Elias performed some magic to shield them from view, or was everyone simply too drunk to care? Christopher swayed as a wave of heat blossomed in his gut and spread through his limbs.

"You fool, Elias. How am I supposed to find her now?"

Elias smiled to reveal his bloodied fangs. "I can find her. I tasted her blood this afternoon." He licked his lips. "She was . . . delicious."

Christopher dove for Elias's dagger and was rewarded by another staggering wave of dizziness, which made him incapable of using his fighting skills with any accuracy. With his immense Vampire strength, Elias easily fended him off and sent him crashing to the ground. Christopher half rose, but had to remain crouched over, his hands on his knees. "Where is she?"

"I will take you there." Elias grabbed Christopher's arm, and everything blurred and speeded up. Christopher had the sensation that they were falling through the darkness. He came to himself kneeling on the scrubby grass and retching. He looked up to see Elias smiling down at him.

"How can I help her when I feel like this? Did you put something in my ale?"

Elias cocked his head to one side, his clothing immaculate, not a hair on his head out of place. "You're not stupid at all, are you? I told the Vampire Council you would be worthy of this mission and I was right." He reached down and pulled Christopher to his feet, his slight frame deceptively strong. "Do not worry. In a little while you'll feel like a new man, and you'll be more than capable of serving the Druid wench."

Elias turned Christopher around until he could see the smoke rising from yet another bonfire. "Rosalind is down there in that valley, worshipping her gods. Go and find her, and be thankful that I obey orders, or else you'd be sleeping with Master Williams and I'd be taking your place."

"What?" Christopher blinked and Elias was gone. He took a deep breath as the dizziness faded to be replaced by a sense of quivering anticipation. His heart thumped in his chest and heat shuddered through him. His harried thoughts settled on one thing. Rosalind needed him, and he had to keep her safe.

He started toward the faint flickering lights and the billowing smoke, his breathing ragged, his motion erratic. A steady drumbeat vibrated through the air, echoing the uneven rhythm of his heart, luring him onward to his fate, to his reward, to a Druid orgy.

As he began his descent into the small, bowl-shaped valley, his heavy, furred overgown caught on some branches and he shrugged out of it. He kept moving toward the flickering lights, his eyes straining in the darkness, as he searched for Rosalind.

Shadows merged into human forms, and he paused, his hand braced against an oak tree to watch. The drumming sound was louder now, and interwoven with the sound of voices. The reverberation quickened his blood and sent tremors of heat down his legs. He pulled at the tight laces of his velvet doublet and fought to free himself from its constraint.

Whatever Elias had put in the ale had made him hotter than Hades and as skittish as a stallion after scenting his mares. Christopher moved closer, his gaze fixed on a group of women who danced in a circle around the blazing fire. Their hair was unbound and they wore flowered wreaths on their heads; some wore a thin shift but others were completely naked.

Christopher swallowed as his prick hardened at the luscious sight. Without tearing his gaze away from the dancers, he unbuckled the leather belt from around his waist and allowed it to fall to the ground, taking his codpiece and dagger sheath with it. He moved even closer, aware of the men sitting in a predatory circle around the darkened edge of firelight, their gazes fixed on the dancers while they chanted and drummed.

There she was.

Christopher recognized Rosalind and found he could no longer move. Despite the shift she wore, the outlines of her body were illuminated by the flames, displaying the roundness of her breasts, her nipples, and the dark triangle between her thighs. Instinctively, his hand moved to stoke his prick and he whispered her name. He started forward, intent on reaching her and dragging her out of the dance. Just as he moved, the music changed and all the men joined the women, except one who wore the horned stag headdress of a priest.

Despite his sense that he was moving through a dream, Christopher picked up his pace and ran toward Rosalind. He inhaled the sweet smoke pouring from the fire and almost collapsed again as a fresh wave of sensations crashed over him. He caught her arm and swung her around to face him.

Her lips formed a soundless "oh" before he covered them with his own, wrapped her in his arms, and kissed her. A surge of thankfulness, fear, and pure sexual need roared through him as he backed her against the nearest solid object and ravished her mouth with his.

Her hands slid up his shoulders to pull him even closer. Through his linen shirt, her fingernails bit into his skin and he groaned with sheer pleasure. But her mouth wasn't enough; he needed to taste all of her, to own every inch of her flesh. He kissed his way down her long swanlike neck and cupped her breast, set his lips over the thin muslin, and sucked her nipple into his mouth.

She gasped and arched her back, offering herself to him, offering him everything he'd ever dreamed of. He slid his knee between her thighs until she rode him. The glorious scent of her arousal permeated his senses, adding and enhancing the otherworldly sensations created by the smoke.

He transferred his mouth to her other breast, used his fingers to keep her nipple a tight, thrusting point, and suckled hard. He groaned as her hand fisted in his hair to hold him even more firmly against her. Forgetting all about caution, he simply ground himself against her softness. He wanted her naked; he wanted his mouth on her wet quim, his tongue licking at her slick wetness as she screamed his name. . . .

He raised his head and looked into her eyes. The centers were so black that almost all the brown had disappeared. Did she even know it was him? Did it matter? He had her now, and he was never going to let her go again. With a silent plea, he took her hand, placed it over the front of his hose, and pushed himself urgently into her palm.

Her gaze dropped to his prick, and she whirled around and ran from him, laughing. For a moment he wanted to howl, but he had no time, he had to go after her, had to keep her safe, have her, swive her, *own* her . . .

As she ran, her long hair streamed out behind her. Drawn by a compulsion older than time, he followed her deeper into the center of the valley, past other couples openly copulating on the ground, past the priests, the drummers, and the dancers, his heart pounding, his cock echoing the pulsing need.

At some deep level he was aware that he was no longer himself, no longer civilized, no longer capable of denying his lust, but he couldn't stop. It was almost as if he was watching himself in a monstrous court masque or play.

He stumbled and reached out a hand to save himself, felt the shock of stone vibrate beneath his fingertips. Rosalind stopped running, and framed by the inner circle of stones, she looked back at him. She held his gaze as she stripped off her shift. Christopher took one last lingering look over his shoulder at the now distant fire and the other revelers.

He stepped through the upright stones, and almost staggered backward. It felt as if he'd ripped through an unseen curtain and entered a magical void where anything could happen. He inhaled thick, turgid air that seemed to breathe with him and emanated from the stones.

He couldn't stop.

He had to go after her.

Rosalind held her breath as Christopher paused at the edge of the inner stone circle and looked behind him. She was panting as if there was no air left within the center of the ancient sacred circle. When he entered, the stones vibrated and began to hum as if reacting to his male presence. Waves of heat pulsated through Rosalind as she stared at his long, lean form.

He walked toward her, his face ablaze with determination and lust. Strands of black hair curled around his face. His long legs ate up the ground between them, but he seemed to move so slowly that she could see every tiny motion. As he approached, he stripped off his long shirt and hose, leaving him as naked as she was. His muscles bunched and relaxed and his chest expanded as he breathed as harshly as she did. She couldn't help staring at his erect cock.

In the last remaining corner of her mind that wasn't affected by the smoke, she had expected it to be Rhys. But Belenos, the Shining One, the God of Beltaine, demanded his due, and she was unworthy to question the rightness of Christopher's presence or the God's will.

No sound from the raucous celebrations around the fire penetrated the inner stillness of the stone circle. It was as if they were alone, newborn, created by the gods to obey their dictates and explore and celebrate the very essence of life. Rosalind backed away from Christopher until she came up against the solid stone block in the dead center of the circle.

He kept coming toward her, his expression intent, his gaze fixed on her body. When he reached out a hand to cup her breast, time seemed to dissolve and become meaningless. She moaned as his thumb grazed her nipple, watched as his mouth descended to suckle her breast, as his fingers slid between her thighs to find her already wet and open for him.

She wasn't Rosalind and he wasn't Christopher. They were beyond that now, merely creatures of the gods, with no other purpose than to please each other and offer up their joining to the heavens. He leaned over her, urging her back against the warm stone, his cock a wet, hard, thrusting presence against her soft belly. She reached down between them to stroke him, gloried at the heat and stiffness, at his harsh groan when she moved her fingers over the already wet and swollen head.

His hands settled around her waist and lifted her to sit on the edge of the stone block. He pushed himself between her thighs. Her feet found the footholds carved into the side of the stone and settled there, as if this had happened before. His hips moved against hers in an urgent rhythm that echoed the earlier drums and the sound of her frantic breathing.

His fingers touched her quim, stroking and separating her swollen folds. He flicked the taut bud that made her convulse and lift herself into each deliberate caress. She sighed as he circled his fingers over her soft wetness in an endless spiral until she was moaning and mindless with the pleasure.

"Please," she whispered.

His hand was shaking as he brushed the hair out of her face and stared down at her. "Rosalind . . ."

"Please . . ."

He closed his eyes and lowered his mouth to hers. She felt the tip of his cock probe her slick entrance and went still. With a harsh groan he drew back his hips and then surged forward. Her fingernails dug into his shoulders as he thrust again, and she struggled to accommodate his thick hot length.

"So . . . tight," he murmured against her mouth. "So perfect." He began to move again, thrusting deeper with every long stroke, filling her and molding her to his desires.

She forgot everything but the feel of his body impaling hers and the slick sweat on his skin. His tongue mimicked the thrust of his cock as he groaned and plundered her mouth. Pleasure built in her quim and she began to move with him, arching her back so that he pressed hard against her needy flesh. Sensation narrowed like a sharpened blade until she had to scream into his mouth and she exploded with pleasure.

Christopher increased his pace, his cock driving harder now, his whole body trembling and shuddering with the effort of fucking her against the backdrop of living stones and the sense of an audience that fed on every sigh and thrust and quiver of their joining. He was nothing to them, just male to her female, a staff to her sheath, a source of fertile seed to fill her.

At that salacious notion, his thoughts dissolved into pure sensation. His balls tightened until his seed flooded from his prick in long draining spurts, even as she came around his shaft again. He buried his face in the crook of her shoulder, his beard rasping her tender flesh, his teeth settling against her skin and marking her as his and his alone.

He had no sense of time. It might have been seconds or hours before he managed to open his eyes and look down at her. She stared back at him, her gaze steady, her hair spread around her flushed face like a rumpled curtain of lusciousness. Her fingers drifted over her chest and traced the brand of Mithras over his heart. He eased out of her, aware of the sudden coldness on his shaft, and fought the urge to bury himself right back in her warmth.

He tried to focus on their surroundings. The ancient carvings in the stone seemed to glow in the faint light. Blackness stirred in the pit of his stomach, and even more treacherously in his mind. His knees gave way and he slid to the ground. As he did, a shaft of moonlight struck the stained rock and revealed his seed mingled with Rosalind's blood, revealed the joint sacrifice they had offered to the pagan gods on their sacred altar.

What in God's name had he done?

Christopher's vision darkened and he knew nothing more than the blessed emptiness of oblivion.

Chapter 14

Christopher opened his eyes and stared up at the painted limestone ceiling and the curved oak beam directly above his bed. He swallowed hard and shuddered at the disgusting taste in his mouth. What on earth had he drunk last night? He had no recollection of getting himself to bed at all.

He slid a hand under the covers and cupped his prick and balls, aware of both a myriad of aches and pains in his body and a sense of satiation and glorious release. What in God's teeth had he done? Unwelcome, forbidden images crashed through his mind, and he sat up, clutching the covers at his waist. He groaned as his head pounded in earnest. His torso was covered in scratches, and both his shoulders bore the marks of a woman's nails.

Rosalind . . .

Christopher swung his legs over the side of the bed and looked for his clothes. "Roper!" he croaked.

His manservant came through the door, a tankard of ale and a lump of coarse bread balanced on a plate in front of him. "No need to shout, sir. I was just coming."

"Where are my clothes?"

Roper sniffed disapprovingly as he placed the tray on the bed. "I wouldn't know, sir. I found you at the bottom of the stairs last night, naked as a babe and dead to the world."

Christopher shoved his hands through his hair. "You have no idea how I got there, I suppose."

"No, sir."

Christopher closed his eyes and tried to think. The last thing he remembered was— Oh God, Rosalind. The stone circle. He shot to his feet and had to sit down again. His legs were bruised and scratched from running through the undergrowth, and he reckoned the soles of his feet were probably filthy. He inhaled the scent of his unwashed skin, the coppery tang of blood . . .

He groaned and rubbed his face in his hands. He *had* to find Rosalind. "Get me some clothes."

Roper moved to the clothes chest situated under the small window and opened the lid. "There's no need to be rude, sir. It's not my fault that you drank too much ale last night, now, is it?"

Christopher reached for the tankard of ale and swallowed it down. At least it deadened the foul taste in his mouth. His fingers tightened on the handle. What had happened while he'd been lost to reality?

"The king and queen are in good health, Roper?"

Roper turned to stare at him, a set of black hose and a linen shirt already draped over his arm. "Of course, sir. Why should they not be?"

Christopher didn't answer. It seemed that snake Elias Warner had at least done one thing right last night. He got to his feet and washed himself in the lukewarm water Roper offered him. He ignored the scratches and cuts as best he could, each stinging reminder a scourge to his already overwrought conscience.

Roper passed him his clothing, and he quickly shrugged into his doublet and overgown.

"Do you wish me to trim your beard, sir?"

"Not this morning, Roper. I have to go out."

"The king's already gone hunting, sir, and the queen is at Mass."

"From your tone, I assume you think me deficient in my duty, but I should imagine after the May Day celebrations many of the court are still abed." Christopher shoved his sore stockinged feet into his leather boots.

"There's never been telling *you* anything, sir." Roper sighed. "I know what you're like, and I know you're up to no good."

Christopher reached for his hat and faced his manservant. "Indeed, I *have* been up to no good, and now I need to make it right."

He headed first for the queen's chapel, where he mentally added the sin of missing Mass to the enormous tally building up for his confessor's ears. He couldn't see Rosalind among the queen's women. Fear curdled his guts. He'd left her alone and unprotected in the stone circle. Anyone could've found her, touched her, hurt her . . . For God's sake, he'd done all that and more.

With a soft curse, he headed down toward the stables. If Elias had been telling the truth, Rhys would be recovered by now, and would surely know where Rosalind was. With so many out on the king's hunt, the stable yard was quiet. Only the sounds of birds chirping as they fed off the scattered grain in the courtyard and the stables being mucked out greeted him.

Christopher headed for the stall where he knew Rosalind kept her horse. A familiar auburn-headed man was grooming the chestnut mare. A wave of relief flooded through Christopher.

"Rhys." The man turned and Christopher went still. There was a bloodless look to Rhys's face that worried him. "Are you well?"

Rhys grimaced. "As well as any man can be after being bitten by a Vampire."

"Elias didn't feed from you, did he?"

"How would I know? The last thing I remember before I woke up facedown in the straw of this stall was his fangs puncturing my neck."

"Then you haven't seen Rosalind this morning?"

The faint animation faded from Rhys's face. "You *promised* to take care of her."

"I . . ."

Rhys took a hasty step forward until he was right in Christopher's face. "What happened?"

"I don't know. I woke up in my own bed."

"Where did you see her last?"

"In the stone circle."

"God's blood . . ." Rhys swore viciously as he grabbed a blanket and threw it over the horse's back. Christopher opened the stall door and barely got out of the way before Rhys galloped off. He raced to get his own mount and soon followed along behind, his gaze fixed on Rhys's distant figure, his heart pounding in his chest like a death knell.

He'd left Rosalind alone, yet again proving his unworthiness. He lifted his eyes to the bright skies and prayed to all the saints that she would be safe, offered them *anything* if she would only return to him unharmed.

Ahead of him, Rhys had tethered his horse to one of the low branches of an oak tree, and Christopher followed suit. He started down the slope toward the standing stones, aware of the heavy pall of smoke trapped within the trees of the valley and the scent of damp, scorched wood. Apart from his own harried breathing and the sound of Rhys crashing through the undergrowth ahead of him, everything was quiet.

He reached the edge of the stone circle and hesitated. There was no sense of anything magical luring him on this morning, only the dankness of rotting vegetation and tantalizing wisps of that damnable sweet-smelling smoke.

Rhys suddenly appeared to his left. "I don't see her, do you?"

Christopher shook his head. "I didn't mean to leave her, Rhys. Elias Warner put some kind of potion in my ale. I lost consciousness, and the next thing I knew I was back in my bed."

"She was unharmed when you saw her?"

"She was . . ." Christopher realized he couldn't speak. He slowly raised his eyes to meet Rhys's. "She was unharmed."

Rhys sighed. "Then perhaps she woke in her own bed as well."

"Elias Warner brought me to this place with magic. He may have returned us both to the palace."

Rhys's expression darkened. "I hope he did not. I mislike the way he looks at her."

"So do I, but isn't that better than imagining Rosalind wandering around the forest in her shift?" Christopher smashed his fist into the solid stone and enjoyed the frisson of pain that radiated through his fingers. "I won't rest easy until I see her for myself."

"And neither will I." Rhys took one last look around the deserted stone circle. "Let us go to Rosalind's."

Rhys clattered down the stairs of the building that housed the queen's ladies, his expression grim. "She's not there."

Christopher's already battered confidence dissipated even further. "Damn it. Then we'll have to seek out Warner, who is not easy to find."

Rhys strode away from the busy doorway and around the corner to a more secluded spot. "Finding him isn't a problem. He bit me last night." Rhys pushed his jerkin to one side and placed his fingers over the puncture marks that Elias had left. "He has my blood, but I also have a touch of his." He closed his eyes and concentrated hard, his brow furrowed and his mouth a firm line.

There was a popping sound, and Elias Warner appeared, his expression tranquil, his silver eyes deadly. "Why did you summon me? You know that I dislike being awakened this early in the day."

Rhys opened his eyes. "Then you shouldn't have bitten me and gifted me with your blood. Where is Rosalind?"

Elias cocked his head to one side. "How should I know?" He glanced slyly at Christopher. "Doesn't the Druid slayer know how to guard a woman?"

Christopher grabbed Elias by the throat. "You manipulated us like chess pieces last night. You must know where she is."

The Vampire blinked slowly at him. "In truth, I put her to bed. I even made sure that she was decently covered."

"She is not in her bed."

"Verily?" Elias raised his eyebrows. "I do not know where she is, then."

Christopher set his teeth. "You lie. Where is she?"

"I swear on my mother's grave—yes, she does have one; a Llewellyn killed her—I put Lady Rosalind to bed after you so unfortunately passed out. I feared for her safety."

Christopher held the Vampire's gaze for as long as he could and then loosened his hold. "Rhys? Have you got any more tricks to persuade this Vampire to tell the truth?"

"I suspect he is telling the truth," Rhys murmured. "At this point in the game, he can have no desire to prevent Rosalind from fulfilling the prophecy."

"That is true, Master Williams," Elias answered as he brushed his crumpled green doublet and straightened his ruff. "I am just as anxious to see Lady Rosalind restored to her rightful place as you are."

"Then what are we supposed to do now?"

Rhys glanced back at the palace. "We'll have to look for her. I'll start by discreetly questioning the servants. They are usually better informed than anyone else."

"And I'll check amongst my brethren," Elias said. "Sir Christopher can search amongst the courtiers."

Rhys bowed and headed back toward the stables, his expression stern, his stride purposeful. Christopher watched him leave and then turned to find Elias was studying him.

"You didn't tell him, did you?"

Christopher frowned. "Tell him what?"

"That you and Lady Rosalind sacrificed yourselves to the Beltaine gods."

"How do you know what we did or didn't do?"

Elias's smile was sweet. "I *know* human nature." He turned to leave. "And I also know something else. If you wish to find the lady, you just have to think about her."

Christopher snorted. "I'm just a human. I don't possess the ability of a Vampire or a Druid to fool with magic."

Elias paused. "What do you have to lose?"

Christopher waited until Elias sauntered away, and then he leaned up against the palace wall. Did he dare try to summon Rosalind in the same way that Rhys had summoned the Vampire? He swallowed hard and closed his eyes; pictured Rosalind's face smiling at him.

He stiffened as she seemed to look directly at him, her expression startled, a question in her fine eyes. A wave of thankfulness rushed through him. She was alive. But where exactly was she? Before he could ask, or try to focus on her surroundings, his concentration wavered and her image was gone.

He opened his eyes. At least he knew she was safe. He sighed. Now all he had to do was work out what he was going to say to her when he saw her next.

As Rosalind's image faded, a sense of coldness enveloped him and he became aware of the other presence in his head seeking his emotions. A whisper stirred his senses.

"Didst thou enjoy swiving the Vampire slayer on the very altar of her gods, my kin?"

Christopher bit down on his lip and tried to think of anything except listening to the Vampire, but it was already too late; she seemed to fill all the available space in his head.

"She spilled her blood for you. Didst that please you?"

Christopher said nothing. Mayhap she would go away if she got no response from him. He struggled to even out his breathing and deliberately dug his fingernails into his skin to remind himself of what was real, and what was not.

She laughed and the sound ripped through his mind like a knife through canvas. *"I know thou canst hear me. I know that thou gloried in thy possession of the female. Didst thou crave the power she brought you? Wilt thou use it to destroy her and her race?"*

Her mocking laughter echoed through his skull and then she was gone. Christopher raised a shaking hand and scrubbed at his face. The Vampire didn't want him connected with Rosalind; even a fool could sense that, yet she seemed almost excited by the prospect as well. He tried to think through the pain still resonating through his senses. The prophecy mentioned enemies becoming one, and the reuniting of blood. . . . Was the Vampire suggesting that his joining with Rosalind might have terrible consequences for the human race? Did she even believe he might use such power to aid her?

Christopher shuddered at the thought and resolved

to seek out Rhys. It seemed he had yet another reason to learn to keep the Vampire out of his mind. And it would give him something to do while he waited for Rosalind to return from wherever she had gotten to.

"Thank you for a lovely day, Margaret, Lord Sinclair."

Rosalind smiled as Margaret handed her a bouquet of early spring flowers. She brought them close to her face to inhale the fragrance.

"It has been our pleasure," Lord Sinclair answered for them both, his arm around Margaret's waist, his pleasant expression a balm to Rosalind's troubled thoughts. "I have long wanted to meet Margaret's oldest friend." He kissed the top of his wife's head. "And I hope you will visit us later in the year after our happy event."

Rosalind curtsied and held out her hand. "If Margaret needs me, I would be delighted, sir."

"Of course I do." Margaret half laughed back at her. "You, at least, have seen a child being born before. I have no experience in the matter at all."

Rosalind tried to keep her smile bright as her mind wandered through all the dangers of childbirth. There was no point in alarming Margaret. As her mother had always insisted, babies had to be born and women were designed by God to deliver them.

Holding her posy of flowers to her nose, Rosalind bade her friends adieu and headed back toward the queen's chambers. Her day with Margaret and Lord Sinclair had kept her away from both Rhys and Christopher, but it was only a temporary reprieve. She'd known that the moment Christopher had appeared in her thoughts, his expression grim, his blue eyes haunted.

Despite her best efforts, erotic images of their coupling danced constantly through her mind. The experience had changed her in more ways than one. Had it been like that for Christopher too? And how would she feel when she saw him again? She forced herself to think of something else.

How exactly had Christopher managed to invade her thoughts? She frowned as she approached the door. Because of their unique shared ancestry, Druids and Vampires could track those who shared blood with them whether voluntarily or not, but a Druid slayer? It seemed that Elias was right: Christopher was no ordinary slayer. She could not allow herself to forget that he could also communicate with the killer Vampire.

"Lady Rosalind."

Rosalind looked up from her flowers to find Rhys marching toward her. He jerked his head in the direction of the trees and walked away from her. Warily, she followed and gave him a bright smile, which he didn't return. He folded his arms across his chest.

"Where have you been, my lady?"

It was typical of Rhys to cut to the heart of the matter. "I spent the day with Margaret and her husband. Didn't I tell you that yesterday?"

"I can't remember." Rhys frowned as if her vain attempt to distract him had worked. He shoved a hand through his thick auburn hair. "I can't remember anything that happened before Elias Warner bit me."

"Bit you?" Rosalind grabbed his arm and peered anxiously at his throat. "He *fed* from you? Why?"

Rhys set her away from him, his expression grim. "What exactly do you remember about last night?"

Rosalind forced herself to meet his gaze. "I went to the stones. I danced, I prayed to the gods, and I woke up in my bed." She hesitated. "Did you put me there?"

"No."

"Then who did?"

"Elias Warner, or so he claims. Do you remember anyone else?"

She fought a betraying tremor in her voice. "You still haven't told me what happened to you."

Rhys sighed and massaged the side of his neck. "I don't think Elias drank from me. If he had, I'm sure I'd feel far worse today than I actually do. And I believe he was more concerned with convincing Sir Christopher to come after you than with drinking my blood."

"Why would he do that?" Rosalind whispered.

Rhys met her gaze. "Perhaps you can tell me. Did you see him?"

"Sir Christopher? I saw him at the queen's party."

A muscle flicked in Rhys's cheek. "And later?"

"What do you mean?"

"Did he find you at the sacred circle?"

Rosalind slowly let out her breath. "I think I saw him watching me while I danced, but I can't be sure." She offered an apologetic smile. "You know how potent the herbal potion can be, and the smoke from the bonfire. I was quite oblivious of everything except the ritual."

That, at least, was the truth. She'd completed the ritual, gloried in it at the time, but there was no need for Rhys to know the details until she had straightened things out with Christopher.

Rhys studied her so intently she wanted to squirm like a worm on a hook. "Why do I get the sense that you are not telling me the truth, Rosalind?"

She raised her chin. "I am telling you everything I remember clearly." Another lie. She would never forget Christopher moving over her, the strange sensation when he'd pushed inside her, the sounds of their mingled desire . . .

Rhys stepped back and bowed, his face shuttered as if she had been the one to slam the door shut. "We will speak more on this."

"I'm sure we will." Rosalind pretended to dust down her brown silk skirts. "You have never been easy to please."

"Or for you to lie to."

He didn't even smile at her attempt to lighten his spirits. Had he somehow guessed that she was no longer a maiden? Did it show in her eyes and on her face? She turned back toward the palace and kept walking, Rhys at her side.

"Sir Christopher and Elias are looking for you as well."

"Were you all worried about me?"

"Of course we were. Even Elias."

"Only because he wants me to catch his Vampire and fears that you and Sir Christopher cannot do it without me."

Rhys didn't smile. "I believe Sir Christopher and I would manage quite well. But Elias is far too interested in you, my lady. I know he wants you to kill the rogue Vampire, but it is more than that."

Rosalind shivered as she imagined the Vampire's soft white hands on her as he put her to bed. "In truth, I try not to think about him too much, but I will be careful." She reached the door of the queen's suite and turned to face Rhys. "I'm sorry for worrying you today."

He bowed. "You've been doing that your whole life and I always come back for more. Don't I?" He managed the ghost of a smile. "I'll see you later tonight at the usual place."

"Indeed." She watched him leave with a leaden ache in her heart that refused to go away. When he found out what had really happened in the stone circle, would he still want her? She doubted it. Even worse, she did not know if she wanted him to.

With a silent prayer, Rosalind picked up her skirts and ascended the stairs to her room, her steps heavy and her mood unsettled. She opened the door and saw Christopher's long, lean frame stretched out on her bed, one arm cradling his head, his booted feet crossed at the ankle.

"What are you doing in my room?" Rosalind gasped.

Christopher shot to his feet in one fluid motion. "Where in God's name have you been?"

She almost turned to flee as images of his naked body seared through her senses. He flung out a hand and closed the door behind her. She was glad to lean against it to support her shaking legs.

"I spent the morning with Margaret and her husband in London."

"Why?"

"Because they asked me to. Why not?"

"Didn't it occur to you that after last night, Rhys and I would be worried about you?"

"I assumed you and Rhys would be able to protect the king without me for a few hours." She tried to read his face. Did he even remember what had happened? Should she try to bluff her way out of it? "Rhys said that Elias bit him."

"That's true."

"Why did he do that?"

His mouth twisted. "I assume it was to stop Rhys from attending the Beltaine celebration, although I'm still not sure why."

Rosalind licked her lips. "Rhys said he was unconscious for hours."

"So I believe." He nodded. "You have seen him, then? I found him at the stables this morning and he had no idea what had happened to you. He was very concerned."

Something hot and angry stirred in her chest. "And were you not concerned as well?"

"By the saints, you know I was."

She looked up at him. "Why is that?"

"Because I deflowered you on the pagan altar. Don't you remember that, or have you conveniently chosen to forget it?"

"I remember," she whispered, unable to drop her gaze from his. "I wasn't sure if you would."

"Is that what usually happens? Some unsuspecting youth is drugged and forced to participate in a Druid fertility rite without his consent, only to wake up and remember nothing of what was done to him? Or was there more to it this time, because you and I were destined to fulfill this damned prophecy and become one?"

Her anger died, to be replaced by the taste of ashes. "I . . ." She looked down at the floor.

He took a step toward her and put his fingers under her chin. "I didn't mean that. I'm no callow youth. I knew exactly what I was doing and what I wanted." He drew an unsteady breath. "The question is, did you?"

She swallowed hard and stared at the small ruff at his throat. "Do you think I lured you to the altar deliberately?"

"I don't know." His quiet answer made her want to weep.

"I didn't know I was the Chosen. No woman does until the moment the gods make their decision. And I didn't know who would be chosen to mate with me."

He nodded. "I'll have to take your word for that. But there is something else to discuss, is there not?"

She risked another glance at his face and wished she hadn't. "What would that be?"

"The fact that you were a maiden."

"Of course I was. The Chosen always are."

"You let me believe that you and Rhys were lovers."

She jerked her chin away from his fingers. "I did not say so. You decided that by yourself, sir."

"But I would like to think that if I'd known you were a virgin, I would not have followed you to that altar."

"So you are suggesting that this is my fault, then? That you are the innocent here?"

"No! By the saints, stop twisting my words!" He slammed his hands on the door behind her head, caging her in. "I *said* I would like to think that I would've

walked away from temptation, but somehow I doubt it."
He grimaced. "I wanted you too badly. I am at fault. I
have despoiled you."

"You did nothing I did not want."

He frowned down at her. "How can you say that when
you have been deprived of your maidenhead and your
chance to make a decent marriage?"

"I was deprived of nothing. I freely offered it up in
the service of my gods."

"That is all very well, but your gods are not here to
safeguard you from the gossips on English soil."

"Who will gossip? Only you and I were there, and I'm
not planning on telling anyone else—are you?"

He stared down at her, his brow furrowed and his
eyes full of concern. "I should be down on my knees offering to marry you."

She almost smiled. "As if your family would let you
marry a Llewellyn and live."

"But—"

She covered his mouth with her fingers. "You need
not worry about me. For my kin, marrying a woman
who has been singled out by the gods is an honor, not a
curse."

He stepped back from her so suddenly she flinched.
"Rhys said that you were destined to become his wife,
no matter what happened. Is that what he meant?"

She managed a shrug. "These are our ways. You cannot understand."

A muscle flicked in Christopher's cheek. "I don't
want you to marry him."

"I don't think that is any of your business, is it?"

He picked her up and reversed their positions so that
he was standing beside the door. He placed his hands on
her shoulders. "It is my business if you carry my child.
You must swear to tell me if that is the case."

Rosalind bit down hard on her lip. "It makes no difference to our situation, does it? You still cannot marry me."

"And yet you let me make love to you."

"I did what the ritual demanded. Can't you see that?"

"No, I can't." He shook his head and opened the door, then hesitated. "And what if I hadn't got to you in time? Would you have been as willing to take any other man?"

"That isn't fair," she whispered.

"I know that, and yet I can't help thinking about it." He nodded. "Good evening, my lady."

Rosalind sank down onto the bed and listened as his booted feet clomped down the stairs. She closed her eyes and wrapped her arms around herself. It was stupid to feel hurt and vulnerable. She'd told him the truth, she was proud of being chosen by the gods. It was an honor such as she'd never dared imagine. But a part of her worried that her faith was not pure, for she doubted she would feel the same if it had been any man but Christopher. He'd been everything she had desired and more. Had the gods known that? Known that he was truly the one man whom she wanted in her heart?

Tears trickled down her face. Was it the gods' kindness or cruelty to give her this taste of ecstasy knowing she would never have it again?

Christopher knew as well as she did that there was no future for them. After all, he had said he *ought to* marry her; he hadn't actually asked her. Not that she would have said yes, but . . .

She wiped at the tears that slid down her cheeks, and vowed to put this silliness behind her. She still had a Vampire to catch.

Chapter 15

"This isn't working, Rhys." Frustrated, Christopher opened his eyes and glared at Rhys, who was whittling at a piece of wood with the blade of his dagger. "It makes no sense." They were sitting in the ruined shell of the ancient Roman bathhouse beside the stables, waiting for the light to fade to blackness.

"You are trying too hard. Just relax and try again."

Christopher gave up the effort and sat back. "Do you think she'll come?"

Rhys looked up. "Rosalind or the Vampire?"

"Both, I suppose."

"Rosalind will come."

"And I suppose I might have a warning of the Vampire's arrival in my head." Christopher shuddered at the very thought. He pictured the Vampire settled in the darkest corner of his skull like an adder waiting to strike.

"I was thinking of the *other* Vampire, Elias Warner."

Christopher tried to smile. "Of him, I have no notion. If he does turn up, I might be tempted to bloody his nose."

Rhys scowled and rubbed the side of his neck. "You may have his remains after I've finished with him."

Christopher's gaze slid over Rhys's shoulder and settled on Rosalind, who had just entered the building. She wore her boy's garb, and her dark brown hair was pulled back into a tight braid. Even though she'd made it abundantly clear that their lovemaking had merely been a matter of circumstance, he couldn't stop himself from staring at her. She looked back at him, her gaze wary and unsure.

Lust slammed through him with a force that startled him. He wanted her underneath him again, her hair unbound and curling around his skin, her luscious mouth open as she gasped his name and screamed her pleasure. In his soul, he knew his feelings had nothing to do with duty and everything to do with need.

As if unaware of the dangerous current of emotion eddying around him, Rhys patted the stone beside him. "My lady, come and sit down. Before we leave to patrol the grounds, we need to help Sir Christopher build his defenses against the Vampire."

Without speaking, Rosalind joined them and sat down, her hands clenched on her lap, her booted feet lined up together on the broken tiles.

"I was trying to explain to Sir Christopher how to build a barrier in his mind."

Rosalind nodded. "What you need to do is pretend you are building a wall made with bricks. Imagine each brick, picture it clearly, and place it onto a line inside your head."

"A line."

Rosalind glanced at him and then looked away. "Think of it as the boundary that separates the good in you from the evil of the Vampire."

Christopher closed his eyes and pictured the edge of the darkness in his thoughts. He carefully laid out a row of bricks and then another. After a short while he blinked. "But won't this wall of mine trap the Vampire within my head?"

"You have to see the wall as keeping the Vampire *out* rather than bricking her in."

"Ah . . ." Christopher concentrated again and slowly reversed his view of his brick wall. Ridiculous as it seemed, he could see it holding the darkness at bay, protecting his thoughts and inner goodness. "I have it."

"Good," Rhys said. "And you must tend to it like a zealous gardener in the spring. Keep it strong and mend any cracks, make it invincible."

"I'm not sure I can do that yet without devoting my entire attention to the effort."

Rhys chuckled. "It will become easier, Sir Christopher. Remember, Rosalind and I have had a lifetime to perfect the skill." He rose to his feet. "If you feel more prepared, perhaps we should go and seek our foe?"

Christopher stood as well and held out his hand to help Rosalind up. The moment her fingers touched his, a shock of energy shot up his arm. He dropped her hand as if she had burned him, and noticed she looked as dismayed as he did.

"What happened?" Rhys demanded.

Christopher kept his gaze fixed on Rosalind. He'd forgotten what Elias had said about his new ties with her.

"It's nothing, Rhys," Rosalind whispered, her hand clutched to her chest. "Sir Christopher accidentally pressed on the puncture marks Elias left on my wrist."

Christopher studied her. Was she lying or had he really hurt her? He dismissed that notion as he recalled the stirring sensation in his own blood, of like recognizing like, of *knowing* . . . That had been no accident.

Rhys came around to stare at Rosalind, his expression concerned. "Are you sure it was nothing more?"

Christopher sighed and braced himself for Rosalind's

ire. He was beginning to feel like one of the oddities displayed at the county fairs, a creature so unusual that everyone came to gawp at him. He guessed Rosalind still hadn't told Rhys about what had really happened in the stone circle, and he could understand why. Without Rhys, their mission to destroy the Vampire would lose a valuable resource. Not to mention Rosalind's feelings for Rhys and his for her.

"That is not the truth," he said softly.

Rosalind glared at him, but Christopher kept his attention on Rhys.

"And what is the truth?"

"Elias suggested that if I could hear the Vampire in my head, I might also be able to sense Rosalind."

Rhys went still. "He told you that?"

"Aye."

Rhys's gaze swung between him and Rosalind. "Because of the prophecy, or because you are somehow connected to Rosalind by blood?"

Christopher cleared his throat. "I'm not sure." He could give Rosalind that, a small breathing space, an opportunity for her to face her fellow Druid when she had her feelings and her explanations sorted out. "But I can sense Rosalind now."

"Can you sense him?" Rhys asked.

Rosalind nodded and kept her gaze on the cracked mosaic floor.

"This mission becomes more and more fantastic every moment," Rhys sighed. "Sir Christopher, you are not what I imagined at all."

"I'm not particularly happy about these developments myself," Christopher muttered as Rhys headed for the exit, Rosalind at his heels. His life had never been easy, but at least he'd known whom to hate and whom to protect. Now those old certainties were fragmenting before his eyes.

He lengthened his stride and caught up with Rosalind and Rhys. The palace grounds seemed quieter tonight. He imagined many folk were sleeping off the excesses of their May Day celebrations rather than carousing anew. He stopped as something shifted and whispered through his mind. "The Vampire is close."

Rhys took out his dagger. "Can you be a little more specific?"

"Not really. It's hard to protect my mind and allow the Vampire in at the same time."

Rhys ignored his sarcasm and motioned to Rosalind to stand behind him. Christopher tried to concentrate. "She is"—he pointed ahead of them—"somewhere over there."

"The queen's apartments," Rosalind answered. "Let's go."

She sprinted off into the darkness, the two men following along behind, daggers drawn, and swords ready at their sides. "I can smell her too," Rosalind said over her shoulder. "She must be close."

"Let's enter here." Christopher overtook Rosalind and headed for the secluded servants' door he remembered in the back of the building. After a quick look inside, he ushered Rhys and Rosalind through the door and paused to listen. There were no sounds of violence, but that didn't mean the queen was safe.

Rosalind started moving off down the hallway, but Christopher grabbed her arm. "She's not here."

She glanced up at him, the frustration on her face evident even in the faint candlelight. "Where, then?"

"I'm getting a sense of her moving below us."

Rosalind turned and headed back toward a small door set in the underside of the staircase. "There are secret passageways that connect this wing of the palace to the king's."

"Ah," Rhys murmured. "And how would you know that, my lady?"

Rosalind ignored him and opened the door to reveal a narrow passage that sloped downward and then spiraled away to the left. Christopher took a lighted candle from one of the sconces on the wall and handed it to Rhys, then took another for himself. Rosalind led the way through the tunnel, stopping at every bend to listen. Christopher tried to remember both to hide behind the newly constructed defenses in his mind and yet keep track of the Vampire. It proved so taxing he kept bumping up against Rhys.

Eventually, Rhys grabbed him by the shoulder and reversed their positions, leaving Christopher in the middle with himself at the rear. Rosalind beckoned them onward again, her slight figure crouched low, and her gaze fixed on the outline of the exit door. Christopher inhaled the unpleasant stench of the river and something far worse. He reached out to warn Rosalind, but it was too late; she had already opened the door.

A shrieking sound filled his senses as something fell upon Rosalind and he struggled to get out of the passageway to aid her. Even as he ran toward her, she kicked out at her attacker and he saw the glint of fangs as the creature's head snapped back. Before he could move, a blur of motion to his left brought his dagger hand up, and he instinctively slashed at the approaching Vampire.

Rhys joined the fight, and for a while Christopher heard nothing but the hiss of Vampire breath, his grunts of effort and pain, and Rhys's steady cursing in Welsh. In one appalled corner of his mind, Christopher watched himself parry the Vampire's blow. He hadn't been trained to fight Vampires—they were his allies. But as the Vampire launched another attack, Christopher realized he had no choice but to keep fighting or he might lose his life. He used his sword to hack at his assailant's legs and then brought him down to the ground.

"Rhys!" he yelled.

Christopher just managed to roll out of the way before Rhys's heavy sword came down and severed the Vampire's head at the neck. He remained on his back as Rosalind came into view, fighting another Vampire, her expression feral, her dagger hand already stained with blood. He looked up at Rhys. "Should we help her?"

Rhys shrugged as he finished off his opponent with a lethal sword lunge. "She won't thank you for interfering."

Christopher watched with a combination of admiration and terror as Rosalind twirled like a dancer in front of the confounded Vampire and finally stabbed him through the heart. The Vampire fell to his knees and Rhys administered the final blow. The thump of the Vampire's head hitting the tiled floor sounded very loud.

Warily, Christopher looked around. Despite the fact that they were in the king's chambers, there was no sign of any panic—of any humans, in fact. Had the Vampires thrown a magic circle around themselves?

"Where is the female Vampire?" Rhys asked as he wiped down his sword.

Christopher concentrated. "Not here anymore. Perhaps she just wanted to test our readiness to fight to protect the king."

"Then I hope she appreciated our effort." Rhys swiped a hand across his forehead. "I thought Elias said the other Vampires wouldn't attack us."

"He did," Christopher answered, sitting up with a grunt. "I wonder what he'll have to say about this."

Rhys sighed. "Alas, I cannot command his presence. The blood effect only lasts for a short while."

"A pity." Christopher stood up and regarded Rosalind, who was also cleaning her weapons. "Are you all right, my lady?"

She looked up from her work. "Of course I am."

"Then why am I sensing your pain?"

She glowered at him as Rhys stalked over to her. "Why did you have to say that? Rhys loves to fuss over me."

Christopher bit his tongue from revealing just how much he would cosset her if she would only allow him to. He moved closer, his attention fixed on her right hand, which she held awkwardly against her chest. Rhys touched her elbow, and something primitive and possessive stirred in Christopher's chest. He didn't want Rhys near her ever again.

"Rhys, shouldn't you take care of disposing of the bodies before someone discovers us?"

Rhys reluctantly stepped back. "I suppose I should." He frowned at Rosalind. "Will you let Sir Christopher take care of you while I am gone?"

Rosalind stood up, her face flushed and her balance unsteady. Both men reached for her, but she stepped back, her head held high. "I do not need taking care of. I'm perfectly capable of tending my own hurts."

Rhys met Christopher's gaze. "I'll leave her in your capable hands, Sir Christopher. Perhaps while I'm gone you could clean up in here and check on the king."

"Of course." Christopher nodded, his attention still on Rosalind, who had sat down again as if someone had chopped at her knees. "I'll do my best."

He made sure that the king was indeed oblivious of the commotion, and then set about restoring the darkened stairwell to rights. He even ventured into the dank-smelling laundry shack at the rear of the palace to get some cleaning cloths to wipe up the blood. As he worked to restore order, he could feel both the ebb and flow of Rosalind's pain and the Vampire's ghoulish satisfaction. She enjoyed games and she obviously enjoyed bloodshed even more.

When he'd finished cleaning, he went back to kneel at Rosalind's feet and closed his fingers around her wrist. "Let me see."

For a moment, he thought she would resist him, but she relaxed her arm and brought it down to her lap. He turned her hand over to examine her palm and the dagger slash that marred her skin. It was still bleeding sluggishly, and he frowned as he examined it.

"It's a shallow cut. I don't think you've done any permanent damage."

"I know." She tried to ease her hand out of his grasp.

"It still needs cleaning, my lady. Hold still." He tipped clean water from a jug he'd secured in the washroom onto a soft cloth, then dabbed at her hand. He was as gentle as he could be, because he could feel her every twinge in his head. It was most peculiar to feel her thoughts, to share her pain, to feel how desperately she was trying to keep him out of her mind.

Rosalind looked down at the top of Christopher's head and watched his long, elegant fingers touch her skin. She tried not to shiver. She craved his touch—wanted to throw herself on his chest and feel his arms close around her. It was a most unpleasant sensation for a woman who prided herself on her independence.

"I can do this for myself."

"I know." He looked up at her and she couldn't help staring into his intense blue eyes. "You don't need me at all. You've made that quite clear."

She had to swallow hard. "You would feel the same if you'd had to fight for your right to be considered a competent slayer."

His mouth kicked up at the corner. "I know everything there is to know about fighting for one's place. My family distrusts me for reasons other than my sex." He checked her hand again and ripped off a long strip of the cloth. "I'll bind this for now. I'm sure you'll make a far better job of it yourself when you retire to bed."

She waited as he deftly bound her hand and tied the bandage in place. He dropped a kiss on her palm and then released it. "And I wasn't just talking about your competence as a slayer, which is all too evident."

Rosalind cradled her throbbing hand against her chest and looked anywhere but at Christopher. They were surrounded by the undead, the scent of blood was choking her, and underneath it all she could sense his steady unswerving presence in her head.

"Why are you making this so difficult?" she whispered.

"Making what difficult?"

"The time we spend together. Can't you just let me be?"

He rose slowly to his feet and dropped the blood-stained cloth into the jug. His expression was icy. "I can only apologize again for my unwanted attentions, my lady. Unlike you, I cannot seem to stop caring what happens to you."

She bit down hard on her lip until it hurt. "I don't want you to care."

He bowed. "So you said. Unfortunately I'm having a difficult time convincing myself to let you go."

"I am not yours to keep or let go."

He raised an eyebrow. "I've had you, though, haven't I?"

She felt her cheeks heat and also stood up. "We agreed that we were not responsible for what happened. Why must you bring it up again?"

He scowled at her. "I agreed that our union was arranged by your gods and, for some unknown reason, the Vampire Council, who both believe we are central to this cursed prophecy. I also agreed that such a union would never be acceptable to either of our families." He took a step toward her. "I did *not* agree that I wouldn't be affected by it. You're in my head now, damn it."

She could only stare up into his face. What did he want her to say? To confess her own sense of confusion and continuing desire? What good would that do either of them?

"Christopher . . ." She hesitated as she heard Rhys's familiar voice behind her. Christopher stepped away and presented her with his back as he cleaned his sword. She turned to face Rhys and his Druid companions, who began the unpleasant task of removing the bodies to the sacred stone circle, where they would stake them through the heart with silver. It was best to be thorough. A badly killed Vampire could rise again and wreak havoc on those unfortunate enough to encounter him.

The men were efficient, and Rhys and Christopher continued to clean up the hallway until not a trace of Vampire blood or their recent struggle remained. Rosalind didn't try to help, knowing that both of the men would stop her. And she didn't relish another fight. The physical encounter with the Vampires had worn her out. The emotional one with Christopher had been even harder.

She tried not to look at Christopher as he moved with efficient grace around the cramped space, but it was impossible not to admire him. He was tall and elegant but as strong and well muscled as Rhys, and moved with the grace of a cat.

Rhys held out his hand to her and she took it gratefully.

"I'll escort you to bed, my lady."

Sir Christopher bowed to them both. "And I'll keep watch and ensure that the king remains in good health."

Rosalind was torn between annoyance at his abrupt departure and relief that he wouldn't be following her back to her bed. She wasn't sure if she would be strong enough to keep him out.

She and Rhys walked in silence back to the other wing of the palace, past the posted guards and the occasional hurrying courtier, past the deserted and trampled garden where the Maypole was being dismantled.

"Rosalind . . ."

At the door to the queen's apartments, Rosalind turned to Rhys and her faint smile died. "What is it?"

He regarded her for a long moment. "My men just told me they saw you at the Beltaine festival last night."

"So?"

His smile was bittersweet. "They thought you were beautiful and that you made a fitting sacrifice to the gods."

She held his gaze. "Thank you."

"Is that all you have to say?"

"I'm not ashamed of being the Chosen."

"I'm sure you're not. It is an honor." He shifted his stance so that his shoulder leaned against the doorjamb, blocking her way. "The question is, why did you not share that honor with me?"

Rosalind considered him carefully. "You were not there."

"That is one answer, yes."

"And there is another?"

He reached out and brushed his fingertips over her cheek. "Did you fear to tell me because you thought I would no longer want you?"

"That was part of the reason."

His expression softened. "It is an honor to mate with one of the gods' chosen. You know that."

"Then you would still marry me?"

"Of course." He paused. "Rosalind, is there something else you need to tell me?"

She summoned all her courage. "I always thought

that if I was Chosen, it would be with you, Rhys, but it wasn't. I'm so sorry."

"I was delayed by that snake, Elias Warner." He swallowed hard. "So, who was it, the male? Anyone I know?"

Rosalind looked down.

Rhys slowly straightened as stricken comprehension dawned on his face. "The blood link with Sir Christopher. He was *allowed* into the sacred circle?"

"Yes."

"And he took your maidenhead?"

"He had no choice—you know that. The gods are all-powerful."

"The Druid slayer took advantage of you." Rhys slammed one gloved fist into the other and started to pace. "He thinks to bind you to him. I will make certain he never comes near you again."

"Rhys, I didn't stop him. I am equally to blame."

"You are an innocent compared to him."

Rosalind grabbed his arm and made him face her. He deserved the truth—even if she knew it would just make things worse. "No, I am not. I do not regret what happened. Do you understand me?"

He blinked slowly and took a step backward, his hands curling into fists at his sides. "It seems you have made your choice. Good night, my lady."

Rosalind swallowed back a desire to cry. "Rhys—"

He held up his hand. "I need to think on this. I'll be at the stables at dawn tomorrow."

She could do nothing but watch him walk away from her. She had no ability to change either what had happened or the effect it would have on them all. But, for a moment, she wished with all her heart that she hadn't had to hurt her best friend in the world.

Chapter 16

For the first time in a long while, Rosalind found herself reluctant to get dressed and meet her fellow Vampire hunters. Seeing Christopher was difficult enough, but now she was at odds with Rhys. She feared that despite what he believed, he would never come to terms with what had happened to her within the stone circle.

Perhaps she could delay meeting with them for at least a while. She did have a duty to the queen. As she left her room, Rosalind smoothed down her embroidered blue kirtle and settled the lace at her bodice. Her cross of amber and gold, her favorite, nestled between her breasts. It had been her mother's. A wise woman, courageous even in death. The least Rosalind could do to honor her memory was pretend she was capable of the same.

Queen Katherine sat surrounded by a circle of her ladies, all of their heads bent industriously as they sewed a long altar cloth for the chapel. The queen looked up as Rosalind curtsied to her.

"Ah, Rosalind. Have you come to join us?"

"I'd be honored, Your Majesty." Rosalind drew up a stool and found a space between two of the queen's waiting women. She focused her attention on the gold border of the altar cloth and fashioned her stitches to fit the chain that had already been outlined.

When Rosalind looked up, the queen's hands had fallen idle, and she was studying a painted miniature that hung at her waist. It was an image of the Virgin Mary with the Christ child held on her lap. Was the queen thinking about her own child, Mary, whom the king had forbidden her to see?

The king's cruelty no longer surprised Rosalind, but it still hurt to see the queen separated from her child and unable to please her husband. For a fierce moment, Rosalind wished her loyalty did not lie with the king, but with his estranged wife instead. The queen deserved to be free of her husband.

Soon Rosalind's neck was aching from staring so critically at her work and she fought a yawn. She'd much rather be wielding a dagger than a needle. The queen glanced at her.

"Did you not sleep well, my dear?"

Rosalind felt herself blush as some of the other women tittered and looked up at her as well. For an awful moment, she wondered if everyone knew what she had done on Beltaine night. "I apologize, Your Majesty. I had a restless night." Suddenly she beheld in her mind's eye an image of Christopher searching for her. She struggled not to look startled.

The queen's smile was sympathetic. "When I cannot sleep, I take up my rosary and pray to Our Lady. I find it helps me enormously."

"I shall try that, Your Majesty," Rosalind murmured, ever more distracted as the tantalizing scent of orange blossom now reached her nose.

"Perhaps Lady Rosalind might care to promenade in

the gardens with me, Your Majesty, and blow away those cobwebs?"

Rosalind didn't need to turn around to know that Christopher had found her. The queen smiled at him and then at Rosalind.

"I think that is an excellent idea, Sir Christopher. Please take your time."

Christopher stepped forward and bowed. He had the audacity to wink at the queen, who chuckled. "Do not fear, Your Majesty. I shall treat Lady Rosalind as a precious jewel who needs to be sheltered and protected from every element, foul or fair."

Even as she rose to her feet and curtsied to the queen, Rosalind scanned the faces around her, trying to determine which one of the dozen or so ladies smelled like dried orange blossom. Christopher took her arm and led her gently, but inexorably, toward the door.

The moment they left the queen's sight, she shook off his hand. "Why did you have to arrive at exactly that moment?"

He glanced down at her, his black hair whipping across his face in the breeze. The weather had turned as uncertain as her mood. "Because you are supposed to be meeting with me, Rhys, and Elias. We were concerned when you didn't arrive."

"I was attending the queen as is my duty, and if you had left me alone for another moment, I might have worked out which of the women seated around that altar cloth was the Vampire."

"You sensed the Vampire?" He frowned. "One of the reasons I came to find you so quickly was that I felt a threat to you. I wonder if it was her."

Rosalind stared at the ground and stamped her cold feet. "We'll never know now, will we?"

Christopher started walking again, reclaimed her hand, and tucked it into the crook of his elbow. "But don't you think it is interesting? There might be a way to use the link between us to find the Vampire."

"Well, we certainly failed to do so this time," Rosalind muttered.

"That's because we weren't aware of the possibilities. Now that we are, perhaps we can share our sense of the Vampire's presence with each other."

"I suppose that could work."

Christopher opened the door into the chapel and glanced down at her as she passed under his arm. "Did you not sleep well, my lady? You seem a little out of sorts."

She found herself glaring up at him. "I wonder why."

His eyebrows rose. "You are not happy?"

"Why would I be? You are being far too pleasant to me this morning."

His smile disappeared and he regarded her levelly. "You told me plainly you wished our relations to return to how they were before. I am simply trying to do as you bid me."

She continued to glower at him, aware that she was being unreasonable, but unwilling to admit it. "I *wish* you would leave me alone."

"And that is not possible until we catch this Vampire." He bowed and closed the chapel door with such force that all the candles flickered. "So perhaps you might turn your considerable skills to aiding the capture of the Vampire rather than sulking."

"I am not sulking!"

Christopher didn't answer her, his attention on Rhys and an obviously disgruntled Elias Warner, who stood near the door to the bell tower at the very rear of the chapel. Elias gave an elegant shudder and huddled deeper into his fur-lined cloak as Rosalind approached.

"Lady Rosalind, I'm so glad you have finally joined

us. I'm not at my most comfortable in this accursed place, as your companions well know."

She could understand Elias's reluctance. Most Vampires avoided sanctified Christian spaces. Only a very few could tolerate being inside a chapel, and Elias was obviously uneasy. She had to admire Christopher's cunning, though. Meeting Elias at the chapel would hopefully undermine his normally impenetrable defenses.

"We wanted to ask you a few questions, Elias," Christopher said. "It won't take long."

"I should hope not," Elias answered. The alabaster cast of his skin made him look as pale as one of the statues adorning the chapel. Rosalind wondered when he had last fed.

"Last night we were attacked by four Vampires in the king's apartments," Christopher said. "You told us that no Vampire would interfere with our mission."

Elias blinked slowly. "You were attacked? That is not possible."

"Are we to believe you did not know?" Rhys challenged him.

"I was not in this realm last night. I was with the Vampire Council discussing your lack of progress." His flat golden gaze searched their faces. "Now, as you are all present and still breathing, I assume you defeated these Vampires."

"We did, but that isn't the point. You told us no one would hinder our cause."

Elias tilted his head thoughtfully. "Obviously this rogue Vampire is stronger than I imagined. She took advantage of my disappearance and used her powers to bend some weaker beings to her will."

"How could she do that?" Rosalind asked.

"The Vampires who attacked you were probably ones she had made. They are more susceptible to their creator's power."

Christopher frowned. "This is not very welcome news. How can we focus on killing her if we have to worry about being attacked on all sides?"

Elias straightened his fur cloak. "I will speak to the Council about this matter and seek their guidance."

"And in the meantime?" Rosalind said. "We are at risk. I cannot truly believe that one Vampire is more powerful than all of the rest of you."

Elias threw her an angry smile. "Believe it. Focus on slaughtering the Vampire. You have all the necessary tools now."

Rhys cleared his throat and Rosalind was forced to look at him for the first time. He looked exhausted, his mouth a hard line, his gaze dangerous, as if he had made some hard decisions and was determined to see them through. "Are you talking about the link between Lady Rosalind and Sir Christopher?"

Elias gave an exaggerated sigh. "I'm talking about all the links between us. We are all involved in this mess."

Rhys persisted. "That is not exactly helpful, Elias. In what way are you and I involved?"

"We are involved, Master Williams. I can promise you that. We are part of the whole." He glanced at Rosalind. "She is the center. She has bound us all to her cause, can't you see that?"

Rhys grimaced. "I suppose she has. She has certainly 'become one' with her enemy."

Rosalind flinched at his harsh tone. Christopher stepped closer and took her hand. She was suddenly grateful for both his touch and his solid presence.

"What else can we do to ensure the Vampire's death?" Christopher asked.

"Work together. Stop bickering amongst yourselves." Elias shoved past Christopher, almost knocking him into the wall. "Now I must bid you all good day!"

As he strode out of the chapel, Rosalind stared after

him, almost wishing she could follow along behind. Anything would be better than having to face the two men beside her.

Rhys leaned up against the door, his arms folded over his chest. "He's right, you know. We do need to work together." He glared at Christopher. "We must put our individual feelings aside until we have defeated our foe."

"I'm not sure I believe you." Christopher let go of Rosalind's hand and strode toward Rhys. "From the look on your face, and the disparaging way you just spoke of my lady, you are not at peace at all."

Rhys met Christopher's gaze, his hazel eyes full of fire. "If I had my way, Druid killer, I would challenge you to a swordfight for what you did to *my* lady."

"Challenge me, then."

"Christopher . . . Rhys!" Rosalind remonstrated, but she was unable to get between the two men. "Stop this!"

"You only say that," Rhys said, sneering, "because you know I cannot oblige you. We both have our orders."

"Still, I'll fight you, if your honor demands it." Christopher paused. "And if the lady wishes it."

Rhys's fighting stance seemed to crumble and he put his dagger away. "How can I kill you, when it would destroy her?"

"Please!" Rosalind cried. "We are supposed to be trying to work together! Can we not put this behind us?"

Christopher looked over at her. "It's all right, Rosalind. Rhys and I know our duty. Neither of us wants to cause you pain."

"He's correct," Rhys said. "I'll keep my thoughts to myself until we've caught this Vampire." His cold gaze returned to Christopher. "But there will be a reckoning between us."

Christopher bowed. "I'm sure there will, but until then, Lady Rosalind needs both of us, don't you think?"

His mild tone made Rosalind feel ashamed. "I'm sorry I've been difficult. I will do my best to concentrate on the matter in hand."

"Thank you," Christopher said simply. "That is all I ask. And you, Rhys?"

"I have already offered to do my part."

"Then we are all in agreement," Christopher stated. "Shall we meet back here at midnight?"

Rosalind and Rhys nodded, and Rhys turned toward the door. It was only after he had left that Rosalind realized he hadn't looked her in the eye once. That hurt more than she could possibly have imagined.

Christopher held out his hand. "I should escort you back to the queen. She will be wondering what has become of you."

She laid her hand on his black velvet sleeve, felt the roughness of silver thread beneath her fingers, and traced the spirals. It was now obvious that the path she had chosen meant that Rhys would no longer be quite so willing to shield her from all harm. She couldn't ask him to, not after what had happened with Christopher. She glanced up at her companion's dark features. Christopher wanted to defend her as well, but she had to stand alone.

A gust of wind shook through her and she shivered. If Elias was right, they were all at the mercy of the prophecy and its foretelling of death. All she could do was hope to God that they saved the king, and remained alive themselves.

Rosalind checked that her silver-tipped dagger was in its sheath and that her sword was tightly strapped to her side. She felt more anxious than usual, as if time was running out for them to catch and destroy the Vampire they sought.

She glanced up at Rhys, who was studying the terrain, his narrowed hazel gaze intent on the comings and goings outside the king's apartments. Christopher was also quiet, blending into the shadows in his usual black garb. A sudden resolve shook through her. They had to succeed soon. She couldn't stand it.

"Sir Christopher?"

"Aye?" He did not look at her, his blue gaze seemingly intent on something in the distance.

"Can you sense the Vampire yet?"

"I am trying." He closed his eyes and a shudder ran through him. "She is stirring, looking for blood, seeking to create mayhem."

"Can you share her thoughts with me?"

"I don't know." He frowned into the darkness. "I'll try."

Rosalind opened her senses, and felt the shock of the Vampire's black thoughts trying to seep into her mind. Determinedly, she contained the evil and turned back to Christopher. "I'll send you my sense of her as well. Perhaps together we can find her."

He nodded, and she felt their minds blend with a shocking compatibility that she had never expected to experience. It was as if they were two parts of one reunited whole. Was this how it had been before the Vampires and Druids separated all those centuries ago? Had each side taken something magical and vital from the other? Her fear of the Vampire resurfaced and she struggled to maintain the connection. Only *Vampires* mind-mated, not Druids. What was she doing? She could not understand how they were able to communicate in this way, and she wasn't sure she liked it at all.

They spoke together. "She's near the queen's chapel."

Rhys was already moving as they spoke, and Rosalind headed after him, dagger at the ready. The chapel was unlocked, but the vestibule was empty. Christopher pointed to the flagstones.

"She's underneath us again. How can that be?"

"This palace was built on top of several other old buildings. There are many secret passageways that connect the different wings." Rhys took out a key and opened the smaller arched door that led down to the crypt. "It's unlikely that she has a resting place in the Christian crypt, but she might in one of the other tunnels."

Rhys locked the door behind him and then knelt on the floor and upended a huge flagstone to reveal another set of spiral stairs.

"If the Vampire is indeed one of the queen's ladies, she must have to attend to the queen on a regular basis. Would she still have a coffin to sleep in, or would she be missed?" Christopher asked.

"That's a good question." Rhys lit the small lantern concealed on a ledge beneath the stone. "I suspect she is old enough that she doesn't need to sleep every day."

"But even the most powerful Vampires need the restorative powers of the earth and the darkness at some point," Rosalind said.

Christopher glanced at her. "Which makes them easier for you to kill, yes?"

Rosalind met his gaze. "We are not murdering them in cold blood. They are already dead, Sir Christopher. They have no souls."

He turned abruptly away from her and refocused his attention on Rhys. Rosalind bit her lip. Christopher was still protective of the Vampires, and she hadn't yet managed to convince him otherwise. In truth, she was unlikely to convince him of anything ever again. The thought of not seeing him made her spirits plummet and he looked back at her.

"Are you all right, my lady?"

His sensitivity to her merest thought was annoying, but at least it saved her from having to reply. She grabbed the tinderbox and shoved it into the leather pouch hanging at her waist. The passageways were subject to mysterious drafts and she had no intention of ending up stranded in the dark.

"Are we all ready?" Rhys asked. "Perhaps you should lead the way, Sir Christopher, seeing as you have the best connection with the Vampire." He placed himself firmly behind Sir Christopher, leaving Rosalind to bring up the rear.

The tunnels were complex and winding. Rosalind had memorized the route to the chamber she and Rhys trained in, but after that she was at Christopher's mercy. He seemed to know exactly where they were headed, his steps unerring. She allowed her mind to follow along with his, felt an ominous cloud of bloodlust and evil stir and take shape in his thoughts.

She found herself licking her lips, mimicking the Vampire, and immediately shuddered. Was Christopher doing the same, were his thoughts turning to feeding and inflicting pain? And did those dark thoughts excite him? They stirred something deep inside her, which she struggled to fight off. Behind the Vampire's compulsion, she could sense Christopher's confusion and his determination weakening. His defenses weren't strong. What if they couldn't prevent him from being taken over by that pulsing need to kill? Imagining what he could do if he turned on them in this confined space, Rosalind concentrated even harder on sending him her defenses.

Christopher suddenly stopped and looked to his left. A small chamber was haphazardly stacked with cheap wooden coffins, some of them open, overturned, or destroyed. Rhys pointed, his eyebrows raised, but Christopher shook his head. Even Rosalind knew that the Vampire they sought would never rest in such a paltry box. They continued onward more slowly, the beat of the

Vampire's excitement like a drum in Rosalind's head. She kept the link with Christopher, felt him struggle to bear the weight of such malevolence.

Rosalind caught the scent of blackcurrants and looked up to catch the slither of movement just before the black-clad Vampire came down on top of her. She had no time to warn the others, and barely a second to leap to the side to avoid being crushed. It was a woman, but young, the ends of her long black hair whipping across Rosalind's face and momentarily blinding her.

With a flick of her wrist, Rosalind managed to break the Vampire's intended hold and elbowed her in the face, felt the sharp edge of fangs scrape against her skin. The Vampire squealed as Rosalind brought her dagger up between them and stabbed her in the chest. She slid to the floor, her nails scraping down Rosalind's hose, ripping the fabric as she fell.

Rosalind looked to her right, and saw that Christopher was just about to dispatch his opponent with a competent thrust of his sword. Rhys was farther down the passageway, struggling with two of the creatures. She could see other Vampires emerging from the chamber they had passed, obviously alerted by the threat.

She ran back to aid Rhys, Christopher at her heels, and together they helped him dispose of his attackers. Like enraged bees guarding their plundered hive, other Vampires continued to spill from the chamber. There was no way back to their original entry point, so the three of them ran farther into the maze of passageways.

Rosalind tried to mark the places they turned, but it was hard to concentrate with the Vampires right behind them. Her ragged breathing bounced off the walls and then Rhys's salvaged lamp went out. For a stark moment she drew in breath to scream. Someone grabbed her arm, and pushed her forward through a yawning black opening, then drew her to one side. They sank down to the floor, their backs to the wall. Rosalind struggled to breathe normally in the thick, all-encompassing darkness.

"I had to stop," she heard Christopher whisper. "I can't keep the Vampire out of my mind when I'm trying to fight and run. I don't want her to know where we are."

"I'll help you." Rosalind took some deep breaths and concentrated on sending her energy into Christopher. She helped him rebuild his defenses, brick by painful brick. Eventually, she felt him relax.

"I think she's gone to ground again. Thank you."

She was painfully conscious of his warmth along her left side, the sigh of his harsh breath on her earlobe. "Where is Rhys?"

He stiffened. "I thought he came in here ahead of us."

"Rhys?" Rosalind whispered. "Are you here?"

There was no reply, and Rosalind swallowed hard. "Do you think he went further into the tunnels?"

Christopher cursed. "He was ahead of us, so he must have."

Rosalind half struggled to her feet. "We should go after him."

"He's probably found a way out by now. If we go chasing after him, we risk rousing the Vampires again. Our best plan is to wait here until it gets lighter and retrace our steps to the chapel."

Rosalind subsided onto the hard floor. "But Rhys—"

"Is an extremely talented Vampire slayer. He'll be fine."

"I suppose you're right. But I know he would come looking for me if I was lost."

"Of course he would. He's a gentleman."

"Are you saying that a woman wouldn't bother?" She

tried to scramble to her feet, elbowing him in the ribs in the process. "I should go after him."

"Rosalind." He yanked her back down. "You are staying with me, and that is the end of it. I've already left you in danger once; I'm not going to do it again."

She eased away from him, and immediately regretted the loss of his warmth and the security of his touch. "I was quite safe at Beltaine."

"You were not." There was an edge to his soft reply that echoed off the stone walls of the chamber.

"I woke up in my own bed; what could be safer than that?"

"Courtesy of Elias Warner. God knows what that man might have done to you while you slept."

"Elias has always been . . . pleasant to me."

"Of course he has, he wants you."

"He wants me to fulfill the prophecy, and I'm still not sure if I understand exactly what that entails."

Christopher sighed and his leather jerkin creaked as he settled himself back against the wall. "I don't think Elias wants us to understand anything. He enjoys watching us stumble around in the dark."

"Then he will enjoy hearing about this." Rosalind wished Christopher hadn't mentioned the darkness. She listened intently, but there were no sounds of movement coming down the tunnels. "I think we caught our Vampire by surprise. I don't think she was ready for us to find her so quickly. That's why she sent the other Vampires against us."

"You could be right. Perhaps we should think up a way to combine our abilities, trap her somewhere, and finish her off."

"That would be nice. Then we could leave the court." She sighed, the sound loud in the small chamber.

"You want to go home?"

She turned to view his faint profile. "Don't you?"

"You have an annoying habit of avoiding my questions by asking your own." He cleared his throat. "I don't really have a home. I was sent away to school or I lived as a guest with one or another relative."

"Your parents didn't leave you any property?"

"There is a house in Aragon." He paused for a long moment before continuing. "But it holds too many unhappy memories."

"Is that where your mother died?"

"You could say that."

"What do you mean?"

He stood up and walked toward the opening of the chamber. "Do you think we should start to make our way back to the chapel or should we wait a little longer?"

Rosalind got up too and followed him. She put her hand on his arm and felt his muscles flex as if readying for battle. "I thought you said we should wait. If you don't want to answer my question, you just have to say so."

He turned to face her. "I'll answer you. I'd rather tell you myself than wait for Elias to blurt it out." He removed her hand from his arm. "While my mother was giving birth to me, she was taken by a Vampire, and turned. No one knew how this would affect her child. As you might imagine, I was the subject of much speculation and distrust."

Rosalind brought her hand to her mouth. "While she was giving birth? That is tragic."

"She did not think it so. She had arranged it with her Vampire lover. It was a deliberate attempt to deprive my father of his son as well as his wife. Unfortunately, my father arrived and tried to save me. They killed him and disappeared, leaving his body sprawled over mine. I was handed over to his reluctant family to rear."

Rosalind reached out and stroked his cheek. "How terrible. And you feared you would become a Vampire?"

"No one knew what would happen. There have been instances of Vampires turning babies at birth and, indeed, giving birth to Vampires, but they are rare. Despite my mother's hopes of taking me with her, neither family really wanted a half-breed. They are notoriously unstable and unpredictable. The Vampires would probably have killed me on sight, so I suppose I was lucky."

"You don't smell like a Vampire." The words came out before she realized it.

She sensed rather than saw his smile. "Thank you, I think."

"You must have spent your whole childhood terrified that you were going to change."

He swallowed so hard that she felt the tremor run through his jaw. "Childhood was not a particularly pleasant time for me."

Rosalind gave in to temptation, leaned into him, and rested her forehead on his chin. "When I was born—a female with the mark of Awen—many suggested that I was an abomination and that my father should sacrifice me to the gods."

His hand brushed over her hair. "We are a fine pair of changelings, aren't we?"

She raised her face until she could just about see him. "As a Druid I knew I would always have to hide a part of myself. And then I spent my childhood being looked at as an oddity among my own people. But at least my parents claimed me and insisted I was a gift from the gods, so I did not have to fear for my life."

She used her fingers to trace the stark line of his cheekbone, the harsher texture of his tight beard, and finally the softness of his lower lip. Inside, her emotions spilled and boiled, desperate to get through to him, to acknowledge the loneliness at the center of him, to offer him her own.

"Rosalind," he whispered fiercely. "Don't you dare feel sorry for me."

She stilled her fingers. "I'm not. I'd simply like to get hold of a few of your family and bang their heads together for treating you so appallingly. You were only a child, and it was no fault of yours that your mother betrayed your father. What were you supposed to do?"

Christopher almost smiled at her indignant tone. He could sense her tangled thoughts, her fierce desire for him fighting her lingering doubts about his heritage. She had more courage than anyone he had ever met and, incredibly, she was on his side. His throat was tight and he was hanging on to his composure by his fingernails. Wasn't it ironic that his worst enemy understood him far better than any member of his own family? He'd fought so hard to be accepted by his father's family, to prove himself worthy of being initiated into the cult of Mithras, only to find himself trapped in a cause he no longer believed in.

Rosalind sighed and he realized that her body was aligned with his from toe to shoulder, the hilt of her sword digging into his thigh and her head fitting neatly into the crook of his neck. He wanted to put his arms around her and keep her safe, hold her against his heart. He wanted to kiss her more than he wanted to breathe. . . .

With all the care he could muster, he gently set her away from him. "We should make our way back to a point in the tunnels we recognize. Did you say you had a place down here where you trained with Rhys?"

"Yes." She sounded a little dazed and he knew why. The link between them left them both reeling with the need to be close, to be together. Christopher set his teeth. Which was why they had to move on, or he would take her down to the floor and swive her with all the ferocity of a starving man.

He motioned at the entrance. "Come, then. We can proceed as slowly as we like. With your sense of smell and my ability to detect the rogue Vampire, we should be quite safe."

Rosalind didn't reply, but at least she followed him without protest, her dagger at the ready. He'd never had a fighting companion before, and he found her presence remarkably comforting. With Rosalind at his side, he felt more optimistic of success than he ever had in his life.

Chapter 17

Rosalind paused as Christopher peered into yet another of the endless caverns that lined the tunnels they traversed. She could only wonder what the original purpose of the catacombs had been. They had seen no sign of Rhys or any of the Vampires. She had no idea how long they had been down in the depths of the earth, but she had a sharp longing to breathe fresh air and see the sky again.

His fingers closed around her upper arm and his mouth brushed her ear. "We are near the chamber with the Vampire coffins. At least the bodies have gone. Can you sense anything?"

She shook her head, and his teeth grazed her skin. "I feel nothing." Nothing about the Vampires at least, and nothing she was prepared to confess to him at this moment. "And you?"

"No. Let's move past and hope they don't see us."

They crept forward again, but there was no movement in the room stacked with coffins. Either the Vampires had left in pursuit of Rhys or had returned to their rest. Rosalind let out her breath as Christopher quickened his pace and headed toward another place where two tunnels intersected each other. She used her fingers to feel the stones at all four corners, and discovered one of the marks she'd made with her dagger.

"It's this way."

"You marked our path?"

"I tried to. It became difficult because we were moving so fast." She felt his approval wash over her and shrugged. "I'm used to searching for Vampires underground."

"Of course you are." He turned away and walked on, his shoulders set. She gazed after him. She understood him better now, both his defense of the Vampires and his struggle to fulfill his mission. But it didn't change who she was, and what she did. Would he ever come to terms with that?

She caught up with Christopher and inhaled the scent of leather warmed by exertion and his own particular spicy scent. She directed him through three more junctions until they came to a part of the tunnels she recognized.

"This is the passage that leads back to our training room and the chapel."

"Let's get out of here, then." He sounded as grim as she felt. After what seemed like forever, they arrived at the bottom of the spiral staircase.

Rosalind frowned. "There's no light up there."

Christopher started up the tight stairwell, and his voice echoed down to her. "Someone has replaced the stone."

"It's all right. There is a ring set in the underside to push up on."

She heard his harsh breathing and a faint curse. "It's not moving."

"What do you mean?" Rosalind scrambled up the stairs and wedged herself into the narrow space beside him. She lent her weight to the attempt to push up the stone, but it wasn't budging. "Someone has put something over the top."

Christopher slumped down beside her. "Aye."

They stared at each other in the darkness. Above them they heard the church bell boom four times, indicating that the night was almost over. Rosalind swallowed. She was so close to getting outside. Her fingernails bit into her palms as she fought her fear. She could not go back down there again. She *couldn't*.

"Are you well, Rosalind?" Christopher asked, the mere sound of his voice doing more to calm her than she could have imagined.

"I want to get out. I *need* to get out."

He squeezed her hand and lifted it to his mouth, brushed his lips over her bandaged knuckles. "We will get out. I give you my word. I have no liking for being shut up in small spaces either."

"Or the dark. I am not much fond of it." She tried to laugh as she said it, but knew she couldn't fool him.

"I'm not surprised considering what you hunt in it. You must have witnessed many gruesome sights that haunt your dreams."

"Yes." She heard nothing but a certain matter-of-factness in his tone. Being a slayer himself, he seemed to understand her fears, and would not belittle them. Simply knowing that helped calm her anxiety and made her feel less of a coward. "We have to hope that Rhys is free and will come back and rescue us. Until then we should go back to the training room. There are candles and weapons stored there."

"Agreed." Christopher shifted to one side to allow her to descend before him. "Let's assume that Rhys will come. If he doesn't, we'll have to try to get out the other way."

"Past whatever the rogue Vampire was trying to

defend," Rosalind whispered. "Probably her resting place."

Christopher kissed her cheek. "If we stumble upon it and the Vampire is there, we'll deal with her together. But let's hope for better things."

He kept hold of her hand and she retraced her steps to the chamber Rhys had prepared for their training. There was nothing to cover the doorway, but at least they would have additional weapons and some light. She felt her way to the back of the room and retrieved a candle from the stash tucked into an alcove in the wall. Her hands shook as she took the tinderbox from her leather pouch. It seemed to take forever to produce a spark strong enough to ignite the candlewick.

Christopher knelt down beside her and she angled the candle toward the iron-bound chest. "There are more weapons in here, but Rhys has the key."

"I'll force it open if I have to, but let's pray we don't need to be that heavily armed."

She focused on his face, and saw the lines of strain revealed by the tiny flickering light. She imagined she must look the same. The energy produced from the fight had dissipated, leaving her shaken and cold. She melted some wax onto the corner of the chest and affixed the candle to it.

"I don't suppose you stored any food down here?"

"We have ale." She pointed at another alcove. "It's over there."

Christopher located the pottery jug and carefully unstoppered the seal. He offered it to Rosalind, and she took a small swallow before handing it back. He drank too, the scent of hops now mingled with the deadening smell of decay and damp.

Rosalind shivered and Christopher put the jug down. "Are you cold, my lady?"

She tried to smile at him. "No colder than you are, I warrant."

He nodded at the wall. "We should sit together and share our heat, mayhap."

"You don't sound very happy about that."

"And you know why." He sat with his back to the wall and opened his arms. "But there's no point in freezing to death."

She regarded him for a long moment, but he looked more resigned than aroused, and the temptation to share the heat radiating from his body was too much to resist. She crawled over to him and arranged herself on his crossed legs, her back to his chest. He brought his arms around her and sighed.

"It's all right. You can lean back."

Rosalind gradually relaxed her spine, until she fitted seamlessly against the hard curves of his chest and leather jerkin. The candlelight flickered as drafts whistled and moaned along the tunnels. Rosalind shivered even harder. She hated inactivity, and had driven her mother near mad as a child with her constant desire to move.

Christopher tightened his arms around her. "Try to relax. I suspect it will be a while before Rhys works out what has happened to us."

"If he is alive," Rosalind blurted out.

Christopher's lips brushed the top of her head. "Of course he is alive. He is an extraordinary fighter, and I have no doubt that he escaped."

"He is excellent. He taught me."

"So I understand." His voice was low and comforting, and she closed her eyes to hear him more clearly. For the first time in a long while, she felt almost safe in the dark.

"May I ask you something?" Christopher murmured.

"Of course."

"Did you tell Rhys what happened at the stones?"

"Yes."

"How did he take it?"

"As you might imagine. He was not pleased."

"I'd like to say that I'm sorry I took you from him, but I'm not."

"I am not a possession." She looked back over her shoulder at him. "He doesn't *own* me any more than you do."

"That's not what I meant." He shifted beneath her and she became aware of the hard length of his cock pressed against her buttocks. "I just want you to know I don't regret making love with you. But I can understand how Rhys might feel, because if it was the other way round, I would feel the same."

"Even though you were drugged and lured into the circle and forced to couple with me?"

He picked her up and reversed her position so that she faced him. "Are you still angry I said that? I told you it wasn't true."

She couldn't help touching his cheek. "But you *were* coerced, and you must wonder if what you felt for me had any foundation in reality."

He raised his eyebrows. After the hours of darkness, it was a relief simply to see his face. "Is that how it seems to you, then? That what we shared was not real, because it was Beltaine?"

"I'm not sure," Rosalind whispered. "It was my first experience. I have nothing else to compare it to."

He regarded her for a long moment. "Rosalind, what exactly are you saying?"

She held his gaze. "What if no one comes? What if tonight is the last night of our lives? Wouldn't you like to know whether there really is something between us other than potion-induced lust?"

She knew she was behaving in a most unladylike way,

but then she had always been an original, not content to wait to be asked, and never content to sit and be admired for her womanly virtues.

He grimaced. "Be careful what you ask for, my lady. If I take you, it changes nothing. We are still on opposite sides."

She scowled at him. "I thought you wanted me."

He slid his hand into her hair and brought her face so close to his that their noses touched. "God's teeth, you know I want you." He used his other hand to press her fully against his groin and groaned. "I'm already hard and ready for you."

His mouth came down on hers and she welcomed him inside, met his tongue with her own, and enjoyed the duel. He kissed her until she shared every breath with him, and could no longer tear her mouth away from his. His hips rolled against hers, driving heat and desire to her quim, making her wet and needy.

He wrenched his mouth away and held her by the shoulders. "I want you, Rosalind. Don't ever doubt that, but if I have you again, I don't know if I'll be able to walk away from you."

For the first time in her life, she didn't want to think about that, didn't want to contemplate a future without him.

"Could we not pretend we are just Rosalind and Christopher?" she whispered. "That here, in the darkness, we can just be ourselves?"

"Rosalind . . ."

She sensed he was going to refuse her again and she couldn't bear it. She shook off his grasp, knelt between his thighs, and dropped her hand to the front of his hose. She tugged at the points that connected his codpiece to his breeches. He grabbed for her wrist, and for a moment, she thought he meant to stop her. Then he cursed and helped her rip at the eyelets and shoved his linen away to reveal his erect cock. He gasped when she wrapped her hand around him.

She studied his swollen flesh, dipped her finger to sample the wetness that escaped from the very tip. His hips angled toward her and he whispered her name. She tightened her grip and felt the hardness beneath the soft skin. His hand covered hers, and he showed her how to slide her fingers up and down his shaft.

While she watched him writhe under her hand, his own hands roamed over her body, inciting a roar of sensations that begged to be satisfied and released. His long fingers slid beneath her jerkin and hose, down over her buttocks, and touched her already wet core. He began to rub her there, his fingers echoing the rhythm of hers, her wetness mirroring his, his gasps of pleasure echoing her own.

He shoved down her hose and pulled off her boots so that she was bared to him below the waist. He reversed his hand so that he worked her from the front. His fingers circled and aroused the tight bud at the center of her need, until she was mindless with want.

"Please . . ." She moaned as he slid a finger inside her and moved it back and forth, taking her to a whole new level of urgency. Her hand froze on his cock as she used all her concentration to absorb the sensations he aroused in her. He kissed her and she took each slow thrust of his tongue and gloried in it.

She made herself pull away and meet his gaze. "I want *you*, Christopher Ellis, for yourself, and for myself."

He leaned his head back against the wall, his blue eyes narrowed, and settled his hands around her waist. "And I want you, Rosalind Llewellyn, without the aid of any love potion."

He lifted her over him, and helped her guide the thick crown of his cock inside her. She gasped as he slowly filled her and she sank down onto his full length.

"Do I please you, my lady?"

He was still watching her, his teeth settling into his bottom lip as if the feel of her pained him.

"Your sword is indeed mighty, my lord."

"And your sheath fits it to perfection." His gaze fell to where they were joined. "Perhaps you should ride me and test my stamina and steel." He took her hands and anchored them on his shoulders. "Go ahead, my lady. I promise I won't fail you."

Rosalind rose onto her knees and then sank back down again, felt him shudder as she slid over his hardened flesh. He caught her hips in his hands and helped her find the rhythm she needed, his fingers biting into her skin as she rode him and used him for her pleasure. She forgot everything but the taste of his mouth, the ache of need, and the building, frantic urge to bind him to her, to make him lose control and give her what she demanded.

He whispered into her mouth, "Give me your thoughts."

At first, she struggled to open herself in yet another way to him, but he was there, waiting for her, his mind as chaotic as hers, his desires just as potent. She saw herself as he saw her, their mouths fused, tongues entwined, her body molded to his and cradling his aching, thrusting prick. His desperate need blended with hers, until she could no longer tell where his thoughts ended and hers began. She let him feed her rising passion and her frantic need for culmination. He reached between them and plucked at her throbbing bud and pleasure overwhelmed and consumed her like a raging fire.

Despite the conflagration that burned equally brightly in his mind, he managed to lift her off him before he came, his seed hot and wet on her belly as he shook and groaned under her. She slumped over his chest, as weak as a newborn, and just as defenseless. If the Vampire appeared now, she would be unable to shield herself.

Christopher's right hand slid off her hip and came to rest on the floor. She noticed his dagger lay an inch from his fingers, wondered if he was any more capable of defending them than she would've been. She didn't want to move and face the dawn, didn't want to have to walk away from him again. She swallowed hard.

He stroked her cheek. "What's wrong? Did I hurt you?"

She struggled to sit upright. It felt as if she were tearing herself in half when she pulled out of his arms. "You were right, Christopher. This was a mistake."

Christopher felt her words like a blow. But that was no matter; he was a master dissembler, had been all his life. "I apologize, my lady. I'd hoped it would be somewhat longer before you realized that." With unsteady hands, he attempted to tidy his clothes, cursed at the ripped points, and hoped his hose would stay up until he could escape this hellhole and put on a new pair.

She scrambled off his lap, her cheek reddened either from embarrassment or from the caress of his beard. Wisps of her hair had escaped her braid to curl around her heart-shaped face. He wished he'd undone her braid and allowed her glorious hair to cloak them.

"That wasn't what I meant."

She fumbled to put on her hose and boots, then finally stopped fussing and focused her gaze on his. "I *meant* it will be even harder to forget you now."

Her softly spoken words eased past his defenses and completely unmanned him. What could he say? Even if he agreed with her, it made no difference. They were both far too strong-willed to give up their chosen paths, and betraying their ancient names was out of the question.

"I should have resisted you."

She half smiled at him then. "I shouldn't have insisted."

"I'm older than you are. I'm supposed to know better." He shoved a hand through his disordered hair. "I also know how powerful the bond of sex can be. Why do you think my mother left my father for a Vampire? Once they formed their blood bond, she cared nothing for my father."

"Why don't you hate the Vampires?"

He made a helpless gesture. "Because as a child, I often thought I would have been better off if my mother had taken me with her. Perhaps I imagined that by joining the struggle I could protect them all, and that maybe my mother would hear of it and be proud of me. . . ." He paused. "It seems that whatever they are, or whatever I am, I simply cannot bear for my mother and her kind to be hunted."

Rosalind let out her breath. "I think I would feel the same. Even though you aren't a Vampire, you are tied to them despite yourself."

He forced himself to keep looking at her. "Yet I've formed a Vampire-like bond with you."

She frowned. "Does that frighten you?"

"Yes, and it should frighten you."

Her smile was hesitant. "I am not worried that you'll murder me, if that is what you are thinking."

"I am not concerned that I'll want to hurt you. It's that I don't know how I'll react to seeing anyone else touch you. And that includes Rhys."

"You won't hurt him."

Her quiet confidence was both shocking and humbling, and somehow only served to increase his anger and frustration. She thought she was so knowledgeable, this Vampire hunter, but she could not understand as he did the power of the Vampire bond, the way it could compel someone to hurt and destroy. "How do you know that, when I'm not sure of it myself?"

"Because I know you." She leaned forward and touched his forehead. "Here."

He closed his eyes at her gentle caress and wanted to drag her back into his arms. He knew it would be a mistake and yet he still wanted it desperately.

"We should go back and try the chapel exit again."

She sighed as if he had disappointed her, and moved away. He watched her pick up the candle and light a new one. She gave him one last long look over her shoulder before she stalked toward the exit. What did she expect him to do? Rearrange the entire order of the universe simply to accommodate their desires? And even then she wouldn't thank him for it, would hate him for changing her.

And so he would hurt her.

He had no choice.

Chapter 18

Rosalind walked ahead of Christopher along the tunnel leading back to the chapel. Her muscles felt sore, aching as she stretched her legs. She had tried to make him acknowledge the link between them, but she'd only managed to stir his fears and remind him of all the reasons why they were *not* meant to be together.

Reasons that were true, and thus very hard to ignore in the cold light of morning. Rosalind sighed and her breath frosted in front of her nose. After they killed the Vampire, they would be leaving court. She would have other battles to fight and so would he.

A thought occurred to her and she turned her head. "Christopher? Is your mother still living?"

"As far as I know. If you consider a Vampire to be alive."

He sounded guarded again, his tone faintly self-mocking as though he refused to acknowledge the pain her question must cause him. "Why do you ask?"

"Because you said that the rogue Vampire spoke with a Spanish accent."

He stopped. "I think I'd know if it was my *mother.*"

"You've never met her. How would you know?"

He started walking again and almost knocked her into the wall when he pushed past her. "It isn't my mother. This Vampire sounded very old—*ancient*."

Rosalind could not disagree, for she had had the same impression. "What about your other relatives in Aragon?"

"What about them?"

She followed after him, pitching her voice as quietly as she could. "Mayhap, because of your unusual birth, you have the ability to communicate with *all* the Vampires who share your mother's blood." He'd reached the bottom of the stairwell and was staring upward as if she didn't exist. "Christopher, is it possible that your mother turned other members of your family?"

"Of course it's possible, but I've never heard of it."

Rosalind frowned at his abrupt tone. "Or perhaps it is even more complicated than that. The Vampire who turned your mother—his blood may have entered you as well. Was he from Aragon?"

"I have no idea."

"Well, don't you think you should find out? If we can trace your Vampire bloodlines, we might find the name of the female who threatens our king and queen."

Abruptly, Christopher stopped and dragged her back into the shadows. There was a grating sound from above. A moment later, a familiar bird whistle echoed down the stairwell. Rosalind clutched at Christopher's arm.

"It's Rhys!"

She stepped forward and ran up the stairs, found herself being lifted out of the hole and hugged tightly in Rhys's arms.

"Thank God you are safe," Rhys murmured. "I lost you in the tunnels and I couldn't get back because of the Vampires."

She allowed him to hold her, enjoying his soft, familiar Welsh accent and hard strength. He smelled like home. She fought back a wave of emotion and opened her eyes to see Christopher watching her over Rhys's shoulder. There was no warmth in his gaze, and more than a hint of possession. Had she been wrong to assume he wouldn't harm Rhys? Was it possible that his Vampire blood could defy and supersede his humanity? That he'd inherited enough Vampire instincts to protect his bond with her at any cost?

She disengaged herself from Rhys's arms and checked him for injuries. Apart from a bruise on his cheekbone, he looked unscathed. She stepped back as he turned to Christopher and held out his hand.

"Thank you for keeping her safe, sir."

Christopher took his hand and shook it. "I hardly did that. The lady is more than capable of looking after herself. You have trained her well."

Rhys smiled. "That is the truth." He glanced back at the heavy carved oak stool that had been placed over the entrance to the secret stairwell. His expression hardened. "Let's get this back to its proper place, and then we can discuss who got through a locked door and put it there."

Rosalind touched his sleeve. "I am too weary to talk now. May I meet up with you later?"

Rhys frowned. "Are you not well?"

She summoned a reassuring smile. "I just need to rest."

Christopher nodded at her and then at Rhys. "I can tell you everything you need to know, Rhys. Let Rosalind take her rest. If you don't mind sharing it twice, you can tell her your own tale when she returns."

Rhys stared hard at Rosalind and then sighed. "All right, my lady. You do look rather tired. I'll see you later."

Rosalind walked away from them before Rhys could

question her any more closely. When she opened the outer door of the chapel, she was surprised to see that it wasn't even fully light yet. The merest hint of the dawn hovered over the hills to the east. There were very few folks about, and she was glad to get back to her bed without causing comment or suspicion.

She locked her door, took off her boy's clothing, and washed quickly before falling into bed. She would sleep until the light through her window woke her, and then she would seek out Elias Warner. If anyone knew about Christopher's Vampire kin, it would be Elias.

With a groan, Rosalind flipped onto her front and buried her face in the bedding. If she couldn't have Christopher, and she already knew in her heart that it was impossible, she had to get away from him. The worst way to heal a wound was to constantly poke and prod at it.

A clean break was always the best. Rhys had told her that. He'd also said that mortal wounds hurt less than superficial ones, which might account for her current state of numbness. Rosalind wiped a tear from her cheek. She had to kill the Vampire so she could go home. So this would all be over.

She curled up into a ball and imagined Christopher smiling at her as their bodies moved together in perfect harmony. He wouldn't appreciate her going behind his back and consulting with Elias, but there was nothing else she could do. She needed to end this—not only for her sake, but for his.

Elias was so easy to find that Rosalind suspected he had been waiting for her. He sat in the window seat in the queen's music room, quietly tuning a harp while one of the queen's ladies read from Sir Thomas More's *Utopia*. He looked up at her from under his long eyelashes as she curtsied to the queen and then came and sat beside him.

"Lady Rosalind, what a pleasure. You look exquisite this morning."

"Thank you, Master Warner." She settled her brown satin skirts around her and smiled at him, keeping her voice to a whisper. "Did you speak to the Council?"

"I did. They said they will investigate the matter immediately."

"You might also tell them that we were attacked again last night."

He did not seem surprised. "Indeed."

"And you allowed it to happen?"

"By the time I returned from my meeting, everything was over and done with. There was nothing for me to do but dispose of the bodies."

"You could have let us out of the tunnel."

Elias's eyebrows rose. "You were trapped? How awful."

Rosalind fixed him with her most quelling stare. "You don't remember sealing the flagstones with that heavy stool?"

"Why do you assume it was me?"

"Because most of your kind cannot tolerate being inside a church."

His slight smile disappeared. "I didn't trap you down there. If I had, you wouldn't have survived."

For some reason, she didn't doubt him. She fought the sudden chill his words caused in her stomach.

"And, in truth," Elias continued, "you deserved to be trapped. You had no reason to go blundering into that chamber. You terrified those Vampires."

"We were going after the rogue Vampire, not seeking other victims. They attacked us."

"Why would they do that, Vampire slayer?"

She held his cold gaze. "Because the one we seek

stirred them up. I suspect she has her resting place down in the tunnels somewhere, and was caught unprepared when Christopher and I found her so close to her lair."

"You found her together?" He nodded and played the last lilting notes of his song. "How interesting."

"Isn't that what you hoped for? That Sir Christopher and I would join together to defeat the monster?"

He smiled at her. "I hoped so, yes, but I wasn't exactly sure what would happen between you." He held out his hand. "May I escort you outside?"

Rosalind glanced back at Queen Katherine, but she was now listening to a reading from a book of sermons, her rosary beads in her hands, her expression remote. It occurred to Rosalind that since she'd been back at court, the king hadn't once visited his wife even to share her bed. It was hardly surprising that the queen sought comfort in her religion and her few attendants.

She nodded and Elias laid the harp aside. At the door they bowed to the oblivious queen. Rosalind placed her hand on his slashed and beribboned blue sleeve and he escorted her into one of the courtyards.

"Sir Christopher has surprised me. I believed he would have some unusual abilities, but even I wasn't sure exactly how they would manifest themselves."

"You make him sound like an interesting experiment rather than a human being."

Elias gave a soft laugh. "Well, he is rather unusual." He glanced sideways at her as if daring her to ask why. She kept her gaze uninterested.

"Indeed. As I understand it, he springs from two ancient and well-respected cultures."

Elias stopped walking and smiled at her. "He told you, then? About his birth."

"What he told me is between us." Rosalind stared down Elias. "However, I would like to know if his mother turned any other members of his family."

"She did not."

"Then what about the family of her lover? Christopher might be connected by blood to that family too. Do you know if any of those females might be at court?"

Elias considered for a moment and then nodded. "That is an excellent thought. I will look into it immediately."

Christopher walked with Rhys to the stables and tried to concentrate on what the other man was saying. It was difficult when he was so exhausted from their night in the tunnels—and from struggling with his conscience over Rosalind.

"Was Rosalind all right? She does not . . . enjoy the darkness," Rhys said as they passed the ruins of the Roman bathhouse.

Christopher forced himself to focus. "She was a little scared of the dark. She didn't tell me why, but I found it quite surprising for such a bloodthirsty slayer."

"She fell into an open grave one night. The Vampire she was chasing dragged her down under the mud and tried to suffocate her." Rhys's smile was wry. "She thinks I don't know where her fear came from, so don't tell her."

Christopher sighed. "I'll not tell her anything but what's necessary to finish off this Vampire."

"And then you will leave her alone." It wasn't a question.

"I will." Christopher could not keep the pain out of his voice. "Rhys, the last time I suggested you were the only man I could bear to see with Rosalind, you tried to throttle me. But I need to know. Will you take care of her when I'm gone?"

"I told you that I would."

"Even knowing what happened between us?"

Pain flashed in Rhys's hazel eyes. "That doesn't

change anything. What occurred in the stone circle was willed by the gods. I can no more change their course or their actions than I can change the path of the sun or the moon."

Christopher let out his breath. "I am glad to hear it. I truly am. I can't change what happened either, nor would I want to. But I cannot marry her." He sucked in an unsteady breath. "If there are consequences——"

"I'll take care of Rosalind," Rhys said. "I give you my word."

Christopher gripped Rhys's shoulder. "Thank you. She is . . . an extraordinary woman."

"Aye." Rhys started walking again. "She is very dedicated to our cause and one of the finest slayers I have ever trained with."

"And a feisty, outspoken baggage," Christopher added, his throat tight with a mixture of relief and the beginnings of grief. He had to let her go, and at least with Rhys she stood a chance of being happy. "I pity any man who takes her on."

"Then pity me, Sir Christopher, because persuading her to marry me will be a Herculean task." Rhys grimaced as they arrived at the queen's quarters. "I think I'll go back and try to sleep for a while. My shoulder is aching like the devil"—he gingerly touched the bruise on his cheek—"and my head is still ringing from the impact of that Vampire's skull as he dropped down on me."

"Then go and take your rest, and I'll see you later."

Christopher headed off toward the gentlemen's sleeping quarters, his conscience, if not at rest, at least a little easier. The sooner they caught the Vampire, the sooner he could be gone from Rosalind's life. And, as hard as that would be, the longer he waited, the worse it would get. He had no illusions now as to the bond that had formed between them. Letting her go would be like tearing his soul in two.

At least she would have Rhys. . . . Tension knotted in Christopher's gut at the very thought of Rhys bedding his woman. What would he have when she was gone? A Druid-hating family who treated him with suspicion, and a Vampire family who had abandoned him to his fate. Perhaps they were right and he simply didn't deserve to be loved. He was tired of trying to please everyone, of trying to be accepted. With a sigh, he shoved his ridiculously maudlin feelings to one side and concentrated on finding his way to bed. If they were to get rid of the Vampire and free them all from this hell, he needed his wits about him.

Rosalind was the first to arrive at the ruined bathhouse behind the stables. She sat down on a pile of bricks and contemplated her booted feet. She'd spent enough time crying over what she could never have. If her grandfather could see her now, red-eyed and despondent, he would surely be disappointed in her. It was time to move on, face her demons, and dispose of them.

"My lady."

She looked up as Rhys and Christopher arrived together and managed to nod at them. The bruise on Rhys's face had darkened and covered most of his left cheekbone, but he didn't seem to be in pain. She avoided Christopher's gaze. If he looked as wretched as she felt, it would undermine her resolve to appear unaffected, and if he looked as if nothing was wrong . . . that would probably be worse.

Rhys sat next to her and patted her knee. "So, tell us, have you a new idea for capturing this Vampire?"

Rosalind cleared her throat. "If Christopher and I can combine our thoughts, we might be able to summon the Vampire to us."

"And then what?" Christopher asked.

"While we distract her, Rhys can kill her."

"It sounds too easy—and far too dangerous," Rhys said. "How do we know what effect summoning a Vampire of that power and age will have on you both? What if she is able to overpower your thoughts and take over your minds?"

Rosalind glanced up at him. "It is a risk we will have to take. We cannot allow this Vampire to get so close to the king again."

"I agree," Christopher answered.

Rhys pursed his lips and whistled. "Mayhap we can contain her powers by summoning her to the stone circle. Surely Druid magic will be in the ascendant there?"

"That might work." Christopher nodded and looked directly at Rosalind. "Are you willing to risk it?"

She allowed herself to gaze at him, devoured his beautiful face, aware that if they succeeded, she would never be able to look so freely upon him again. He met her gaze head on, his blue eyes full of resignation and longing. He might hide it better, but she knew he was in as much pain as she was. And somehow, that was comforting.

Rosalind stood up. "Then let it be tonight."

Chapter 19

It was cold within the stone circle, the space unwelcoming without the Beltaine fires and the presence of the gods. Rosalind shivered as she stepped over broken stones, fragments of animal bones, and oak tree roots that had forced their way through the perfection of the space. It was hard to imagine how the temple might have looked before the Romans came and destroyed everything in the name of Christianity.

"Wait."

Rhys held up his hand as a slight noise rustled one of the rowan bushes to Rosalind's left. She turned to face the threat and found Elias Warner at the pointed end of her dagger. He stuck out his tongue and touched the tip to the point of her blade.

"I am more than willing to share my blood with you, my lady," Elias murmured. "You only have to ask."

Rosalind flicked her wrist and brought her dagger down to her side. "What are you doing here?"

He shrugged. His green and silver jerkin matched almost perfectly with the ivy-clad stones. "The Vampire Council thought you might need me." He shuddered extravagantly. "Although, as usual, your choice of venue leaves much to be desired."

"We wish to catch the Vampire, that is all."

"And you think you can trap her here? I wish you good luck."

"But you are here to help us, aren't you?" Rosalind smiled sweetly at Elias. "I'm sure you can think of several ways to block or control her power."

"I'll do my best. I am as eager to see her gone as you are."

Rosalind headed toward the center of the circle, to the slab of rock fashioned into an altar. She placed her hand on the stone. It stirred beneath her touch as if it remembered her recent blood sacrifice. Christopher appeared beside her, dressed in his habitual black, his expression as solemn and steady as she assumed hers was.

"Should we hold hands?" he asked.

She didn't want merely to touch his hand, here, where their bodies and minds had joined together; she wanted all of him. Emotion surged through her and she forced it down. There would be time to weep after they had caught the Vampire. "Yes, that sounds like an excellent idea."

Christopher positioned himself opposite her, their hands linked together on top of the stone altar. Elias and Rhys took up stations at either end of the stone so that they formed the shape of a cross.

Elias chuckled and began to recite. "The kiss of the rose is death to kin. And three will stand alone."

"Elias," Rhys growled. "This isn't a joke. If you don't want to be here, then leave. Rosalind needs to concentrate."

Elias's smile died. "Master Williams, I don't wish to be here at all. I suspect we shall regret this. But, like you, it seems I have no choice."

Christopher squeezed Rosalind's hand. "Shall we try, then?"

She met his calm gaze across the altar stone and nodded. "Yes."

She closed her eyes and slowly allowed her mind to open and merge into Christopher's, felt him do the same. Their thoughts flowed together as harmoniously as a river, light to dark, love to hate, despair through hope. What one of them lacked, the other supplied as if they effortlessly completed each other. When Rhys spoke, the sound was hollow, as if they were underwater.

"Command her with your blood, Sir Christopher," he urged. "Call her to you. Help him, Rosalind."

Rosalind took Christopher's command and amplified it, sent it hurtling out into the night sky like a challenge. Around her, the stone circle seemed to echo the demand until she wanted to cover her ears. She felt the Vampire stir and then her startled response. A roaring sound filled her ears and she was aware of Christopher's fingers slipping through hers. She tried to hold on to him, but he was gone, leaving her in the center of a swirling, screaming black vortex—and face-to-face with the Vampire.

It took all her courage and strength to look at the woman directly. She wasn't particularly tall, and her long white hair was shrouded in a hooded black cloak that cast her features into shadow. Her body glimmered and shifted like a candle flame, as if she wasn't quite whole, as if touching her would be impossible. For the first time, Rosalind doubted that a mortal weapon would have the ability to kill her. With a start she realized they were standing atop the altar, and she had no idea where the men were; she was cut off, inside the Vampire's magic.

"So you thought to capture me, child?"

Rosalind fought the prickles of fear that ran along her skin as the Vampire spoke. The foreign sound was like dead leaves rustling on the pathways or fingernails scratching on glass.

"Did you think that by summoning me, you would be in control?" The Vampire laughed, her mouth a black hole surrounded by the thinnest red lips and the longest fangs Rosalind had ever seen.

Rosalind struggled to find her voice, not yet sure if the Vampire was truly there, or simply invading her thoughts. "I do not seek to control you, only call you to account for your actions. You have killed innocent humans and been found guilty by your own race. They have condemned you to death, not I."

Rosalind tried to look around, but she could see nothing beyond the black whirlwind and the Vampire.

"Yet you are to be my executioner."

"I serve my people."

"Who hate mine."

"With good reason." Rosalind tried to inch her hand toward her dagger. If she could reach it, perhaps she could finish this once and for all. Then she screamed as the dagger was ripped out of its sheath and flung into the chaotic twisting darkness.

The Vampire laughed. "I can see your murderous thoughts, Druid. Do you really think I'd allow you to finish me off with your little silver blade?"

Desperately, Rosalind tried to reconstruct her shattered defenses. Sharing herself with Christopher had weakened them considerably. Could she reconnect with him? She needed his strength.

"Where is Christopher?" She didn't mean to blurt out his name, but she couldn't help herself.

"My kin?"

"Yes. Is he all right?"

"Do you think I care for him?" The Vampire's face twisted. "He is an abomination, neither Vampire nor human. He was simply a means to an end."

"What do you mean?"

"He gave me what I wanted, which was access to you."

"And what do you want with me?"

The Vampire laughed. "You are a brave little thing, aren't you? That's why I have chosen you to do my work."

Rosalind forced herself to hold the Vampire's burning gaze. "I will not do anything willingly for you. I would rather die."

"You do not need to die, Druid. If I wish I could simply turn you into a Vampire and order you to kill the king yourself."

"No Vampire dares turn a Druid. Legend has it that combining the blood of both races again would create a being more powerful and dangerous than any of us. You would not risk such a thing." Rosalind prayed the Vampire wasn't insane enough to try just that.

"Foolish girl, do not bait me. You do not know what I am capable of." The Vampire pointed into the darkness. "What of these three men who willingly gathered around the altar for you tonight? Do they mean nothing to you?"

It was hard not to let her voice shake. "If it is me you want, you don't need them. Let them go."

The Vampire leaned so close that the scent of decayed orange blossom almost made Rosalind gag. "But I do need them. They are my hostages. What happens to them next is entirely up to you." She snapped her fingers and the mist dispersed to reveal the three men, each bound to one of the standing stones with the trailing ivy. Moonlight illuminated their faces, but Rosalind could see no sign of awareness. It was as if they were awake, but in a trance.

"What have you done to them?" Rosalind whispered.

"Nothing yet. They are merely deep in dreamland. Would you like to know what they dream of?"

The Vampire grabbed Rosalind's shoulder and spun her around to face Elias. Sharp fingernails dug into Rosalind's flesh and she winced. At least the pain proved that the Vampire was present in some form.

"This fool who has betrayed me to work with you—what do you think he fears most?"

Rosalind gasped as the Vampire forced her mind into Elias's and made her experience the cold panic of his dreams.

"What do you see, slayer? What does he fear?"

"He fears you, even more than he fears the Council; fears he will fail to stop you. There is something else, something he hides so deeply that even he is afraid to acknowledge it." Rosalind gasped. The Vampire had some kind of grip on her mind; she was unable to resist the compulsion to speak. She tried to fight it, and found only an ironclad power that entrapped her thoughts, turned them back on her, and laughed at her struggles.

"And what else?"

Rosalind moaned as she was propelled deeper into Elias's mind, saw images of herself, felt tainted and consumed by Elias's lust. He wanted her body and her blood, wanted her enslaved to him forever. Like a swimmer desperately seeking air, she forced herself upward. She tried to grab hold of the Vampire's robes as she recoiled. "No!"

"Elias desires you. He's fascinated by your beauty and your ability to kill. But he would not die for you. He is far too selfish for that."

With a snap of her fingers, the Vampire extracted them both from Elias's mind. He sagged against his bonds as if weakened by their invasion.

Rosalind tore her gaze from Elias and tried not to

look at Rhys, used all her remaining strength to painstakingly rebuild her defenses for the ordeal she suspected was to come.

"And then we have the Welshman."

"Please don't." Rosalind licked her lips. "Rhys has
done nothing to warrant your anger."

"Except try to kill me and my followers!"

Rhys strained against his bonds as Rosalind and the
Vampire invaded his mind. Rosalind tried to hold back,
but the Vampire was relentless, forcing her through
his memories of her. She felt his love, his longing, his
utter devastation and growing anger at her joining with
Christopher.

"Stop it!" Rosalind found her voice and shoved her
hands over her ears to shut out his anguish. "I don't
want this!"

"Why should you be spared? You have betrayed his
love," the Vampire whispered. "You have destroyed him
with your unnatural lust for a Druid slayer."

"I know!" Rosalind found herself glaring into the
Vampire's cold burning red eyes. "I know what I've
done to him."

"And you don't regret it, do you? Because you'd
prefer to spread your legs for my kin, a man who kills
your people and mine, a man who cannot be trusted by
anyone."

And then Rosalind was screaming as the Vampire
threw her into the chaos of Christopher's thoughts; his
fear for her bundled up with his fear of himself, that he'd
become a Vampire, that he'd be forced to kill for her
love.

Rosalind fell to her knees as tears streamed down her
face. She was surrounded by pain, by yearning, by the
needs of all three men, and she was trapped in the center, a conduit for all of their emotions.

A conduit . . . Beneath her fingertips, the stone undulated and started to warm. Her gods were stirring; she wasn't entirely alone.

Vampires were descended from the Druids; surely like called to like? But how could that help her? The men were tied to the upright stones. Could they feel it too? The ebb and flow of energy? She wasn't yet sure, but at least it gave her hope.

"See what you have done, Vampire slayer? You have taken three good men and destroyed them. Now what do you intend to do about it?"

"Make it stop!" Rosalind cried. "Take me out of their minds."

The Vampire grabbed Rosalind's braid and forced her to stand upright. "I can make it stop. I can kill them all for you. Is that what you want?"

"No!" Rosalind tried not to scream her denial. "You have caused this, not I!"

"How very selfish of you, my dear."

Rosalind sagged as she was suddenly freed from the others' minds, but the Vampire continued speaking.

"But it only makes me more certain that you are indeed the person the prophecy speaks of. The one who will help me rid the world of this king."

In the very recesses of her mind, Rosalind felt something stir, some sense of Christopher searching for her beneath the fear. Even as she sought to protect him from the Vampire, she tried to send him strength, strength that she didn't even have, strength that she needed to protect herself.

The heat building up in the stone intensified, and she wondered if the Vampire was aware of it.

"Why do you hate the king?"

The Vampire raised her chin. "You should know why. You attend the queen and appear to care for her."

"I do care for the queen. I've known her since I was a child."

"And I've known her since she was born. I've protected her and her family from vermin like you for generations. I don't need to wait for permission from the likes of Elias Warner and the Vampire Council to kill my enemies!"

Rosalind licked her lips as Christopher tentatively touched her mind. "But why now?"

"Because the king is determined to set the queen aside—to betray his true wife with that upstart whore, with that . . ." The Vampire shook her head, her attention focused completely on Rosalind. "I decided it was time to use the prophecy for my own ends. Because of what will come next. Because of you."

"But I had no part in the creation of the prophecy," Rosalind said desperately. The Vampire kept speaking as if she hadn't heard her.

"It was time for the prophecy to come to fruition. I arranged for a few corpses to turn up close to the king and queen to garner the interest of the Druids and the Vampire Council. I needed a reason for them to think the king was in danger and send for those they thought best to fulfill the terms of the prophecy."

"You wanted the prophecy to come true?"

"Of course, Vampire slayer. I needed you and my kin to come together and serve me."

"Serve you?"

"Indeed." The Vampire smiled and Rosalind fought a grimace. "And you have amused me greatly."

Rosalind sensed Christopher trying to escape his bonds. The Vampire's gaze flicked to the circle of stones and Rosalind willed him to be still.

"The king needs to die."

Rosalind shuddered at the Vampire's flat tone.

"I once thought to turn him and use him as my vessel. But he has a stubborn mind and a devout faith. And despite his wickedness, the queen still loves him. I would have to dispose of her to gain true power, and that I would never do."

Rosalind tried to think through what the Vampire was telling her. There was something she was missing, something obvious, but trying to keep the Vampire occupied while protecting Christopher was tearing her mind apart. "So you wish to murder the king and rule in his stead?"

The Vampire fixed Rosalind with her empty stare. "If he insists on annulling his marriage to the queen, it is the only solution. And through your unnatural bond with my kin, you will help me achieve my aim. Your family is the only one granted instant access to the king. No one will question you when you come to kill him at my command." She smiled, displaying her fangs. "And when he's dead, you will be put to death as well, and the Vampire Council will thank me for ridding them of the last of the cursed Llewellyn family."

Rosalind backed up a step and realized she was close to the edge of the altar. "I've already told you I will not do it."

"Then you don't care about the fate of these men?" The Vampire gestured at Elias, Rhys, and Christopher. "If you do not aid me, I will kill them all." She laughed and clapped her hands together.

"I think you are insane." Rosalind flinched as the Vampire's fangs snapped a whisker away from her throat. It was hard to breathe, let alone frame words. "Let them go and I'll consider what you want me to do."

"You think me a fool?"

"Leave them alone!" Rosalind gathered the power the stones were channeling through her and threw herself at the Vampire. Energy and exultation shot through her and she grabbed for the Vampire's throat. But before she could reach her, she felt herself falling. She had a sense of time blurring, of the stone circle distorting until it swallowed her up and she lay in the darkness under-ground. The only sound was that of her frantic breath-ing. There was no sign of any of the men or the Vampire, and her dagger had miraculously been restored to her hand.

"You may choose one, Vampire slayer." The voice of the Vampire echoed inside her head. "Choose one to save—the others are mine to kill."

Cautiously, Rosalind sat up and looked around. Had the stone circle freed her from the Vampire or not? It seemed unlikely. She was surrounded by tunnel en-trances made of a shining black rock that gleamed like burnished steel. Although there was no natural light, Rosalind could see perfectly well. She took a deep, steadying breath. She only knew she had to find the oth-ers and free them from the Vampire's clutches.

She closed her eyes and thought about Elias, found her feet moving in the direction of one of the tunnels before she even questioned the impulse. Her boots sounded loud in the confines of the circular space and she slowed to a walk. At the end of the tunnel, Elias was leaning against the wall, arms folded over his chest, his fixed silver gaze seemingly unaware of her presence.

Rosalind studied him for a long moment. She tried to think like the Vampire. Surely Elias was valuable? He was the Vampire's link to the Council and she was unlikely to dispose of him. Elias also meant the least to Rosalind, so she calculated that the Vampire would not enjoy killing him.

"I'm sorry, Elias," Rosalind whispered, even though she didn't think he could hear her. "I can't save you."

She turned back and left him standing there, her heart thumping hard in her chest. That had been the easiest of the choices she had to make; now she had to decide what to do next. She returned to the center of the maze and took a moment to compose herself. Her panicked thoughts swirled around in her head, making it almost impossible to breathe, let alone think.

Whom should she leave, and whom should she save? The Vampire obviously thought she would be unable to make a choice, and it was possible that she was right. Rosalind sought for calm. Rhys was her dearest friend and her future. Christopher was . . .

Rosalind closed her eyes as a sob tore from her throat and she pictured the man she had to find.

Chapter 20

Christopher regained consciousness and tried to open his eyes. He knew something was terribly wrong. Try as he might, he couldn't seem to move his limbs. It felt like one of his old nightmares, when he lay paralyzed in bed as his mother returned for him, fangs extended, intent on turning him.

He licked his lips and tasted blood, felt a familiar but growing excitement run through his senses. He inhaled slowly and his heart rate increased. Where was he? He only knew he was no longer at the stone circle, but underground. He tried to focus, aware only of his heart pumping away, of his senses sharpening as his fangs elongated. . . .

Terror gripped him. He threw his head back and it banged on solid rock. He didn't have fangs; he wasn't one of them! With elaborate slowness he uncurled his tongue and licked along the line of his teeth, shuddered when he met his extended incisors. This was not real. It couldn't be. Dear God, the Vampire must have . . .

He opened his eyes. Where was the Vampire and where was Rosalind? He couldn't sense her in his mind at all. Panic rose in his chest and threatened to suffocate him. He tried to remain calm as his vision turned red. He must focus on the image of Rosalind, loving him, sharing herself with him . . .

Fear stirred and he choked it down. Was Rosalind still alive? He tried again to get a sense of her, almost whimpered with relief when he felt her again. She wasn't dead. Thank God for that, at least. He tried to move away from the rock, but something held him fast.

What would happen when the Vampire released him? Christopher groaned silently. He would take blood from the first human he saw. He swallowed hard, aware that the thought excited him beyond measure. What if that human was Rosalind or Rhys? Was that the Vampire's plan, that he should drain them dry in his frenzied lust for blood?

He groaned and slammed his head back against the wall again, enjoyed the pain that shot through him. He was still unable to tell if he was trapped in his own mind or was in the real world. He sensed movement in the tunnel and tried to focus. Was the Vampire coming back or was it something even worse? Did he even want to be rescued now? He inhaled the scent of human blood and his whole body trembled. He fixed his gaze on the approaching figure, his thoughts in utter and complete turmoil, and began to pray.

Rosalind approached Christopher as cautiously as she had approached Elias. His eyes were open, but she could not tell if he was aware of her presence.

"Christopher?"

"Go away, Rosalind." He licked his lips and turned his face away from her.

Her heart twisted at the desolation in his voice. He sounded as if he was in pain. Did he know? Did he already hate her? She gathered herself to explain.

"Christopher, I need you to listen to me." He didn't

answer, just licked his lips and swallowed convulsively, his whole body shaking.

Rosalind took a step closer and he recoiled. "Don't touch me," he hissed. "I am no longer safe, and I will hurt you if she lets me free."

"You'll not hurt me."

He groaned. "Can't you see what she has done to me? What she's made me?"

She gently put her hand to his cheek. "I see only you, Christopher."

He stiffened and slowly met her gaze. "And what do you see?"

"You, trapped by the Vampire's magic. What else is there?"

"I don't believe you," he said, struggling against whatever was pinning him to the wall. "I know what I feel!"

"I promise you," Rosalind said. She stroked his cheek, then his shoulder, trying to calm him. "She made you dream of what you fear the most. It is not real. You are not a Vampire."

"But I feel it inside, trying to rip its way out of me!"

She took his jaw in her hands, forcing him to look her in the eyes. "You are not a Vampire."

He let out a groan. "Then tell me where we are, and what is happening."

Rosalind took a deep breath. "The Vampire wants me to kill the king."

"But she knows you will refuse."

"Yes, but she's threatening to kill you all if I do not do her bidding. I tried to use the power of the stone circle against her, but I think I failed and she brought us all here." Her voice faltered. "I'm not even sure if this is real. It feels like a nightmarish game."

"A game?" He tried to focus on her, his eyes narrowing at her obvious unease. "We are part of a game?"

Rosalind wrapped her arms around herself. "She wants me to save one of you. I fear I am still trapped in her wiles, and all I can do is play out the game and hope that . . ." Her voice faltered and she could only stare at him.

"What?"

"That I will choose wisely." She choked back a small sob as Christopher's eyes widened and he looked over her shoulder. Rhys was stumbling down the tunnel, his expression haunted. "I have chosen Rhys."

The hope in Christopher's eyes turned to dust and his face became a mask. "Of course you have. Now leave me be."

"It's not what you think." Rosalind began to speak faster, her voice rising as Christopher seemed to waver and dissolve in front of her eyes. She realized it was her own tears distorting his image. "Let me explain. . . ."

But Christopher was no longer looking at her, and Rhys was making her turn away from her lover, making her abandon him in the maze.

Rhys's grip loosened, and Rosalind cried out as she was thrown upward toward a tunnel of light. She emerged into the stone circle again, crying and shaking. The Vampire was nowhere to be seen. Rosalind fell to the ground and beat her fists on the dirt.

"I chose, damn you. Now do your worst!" she screamed into the emptiness before collapsing onto the stone altar again. Soft laughter filled her ears and she looked up once more into the Vampire's shadowed features.

"You have surprised me, Vampire slayer. I thought you would choose my kin. I thought you would sacrifice everything for love."

Rosalind couldn't speak as she struggled to understand the sudden change in her surroundings. Had she been anywhere, except her mind and her own worst nightmares? She was back on the altar with the Vampire. The three men were still tied to the upright stones. Even as her mind wrestled with the trick played on her, her body refused to accept it; it continued to shudder with grief at what her choice might mean.

The Vampire scowled down at Rosalind. "The Druid circle has drained my powers tonight, but you will kill the king for me, Vampire slayer."

The Vampire disappeared so quickly that Rosalind gasped. She fought to catch her breath before slowly sinking to her knees. She wanted to retch. She wanted to crawl into bed and never get out again.

"God, what in Hades happened?" Rhys whispered as he opened his eyes. "Are we still alive?"

Rosalind searched his face for any memory of exactly what had transpired. "The Vampire outwitted us."

Rhys cursed and rubbed his face. "I don't remember anything except being slammed against this rock."

"She trapped you in your worst nightmares, and made me share them with you."

Rhys shuddered and muttered a prayer in Welsh. "Are you all right, *cariad*?"

"I'll recover soon enough." Rosalind tried not to let her voice shake as she got down from the altar. Elias was stirring too, his eyes unfocused, his mouth an uncertain line. Logic said that if Elias was unharmed, Christopher would be too, but Rosalind couldn't look; she was too afraid.

She walked over to Elias and waited until he focused his gaze on her. "Are you all right, Elias?"

"No thanks to you." He glared at her and pretended to brush the dust from his clothing. "I told you this was a mistake. She could've killed us all."

Rosalind sighed and put her dagger away. It seemed he had no idea that she'd abandoned him to the Vampire either, or she was sure he would've mentioned it. "You're right. I misjudged both her power and her purpose."

He turned away from her and disappeared without another word. Rosalind didn't blame him. She'd let them all down this night, had shown how weak she really was, and how overinflated her opinion of her own powers was.

Elias was gone, Rhys was patrolling the stone circle, looking for his weapon, but Christopher still stood against the upright stone. She forced herself to cross the space between them, aware that he was watching her. There was no welcome in his face, no hint of the love and concern she'd unconsciously expected.

"Are you all right, Christopher?"

He continued to stare at her. "Why do you ask?"

Rosalind made a helpless gesture that encompassed the whole stone circle. "Because I put you all in danger."

He leaned his head back against the stone as if he was exhausted and briefly closed his eyes. "Aye, you did."

Fear clenched in her chest. She couldn't sense him in her head anymore, but it wasn't due to the Vampire's tricks; he was deliberately blocking her. "Are you angry with me?"

"You do not think I have the right?"

She bit her lip. "It depends on what you remember."

"Obviously more than Elias and Rhys." A muscle twitched in his jaw. "We have a special bond between us, do you not remember?"

"You saw what happened?"

"Aye." He pushed himself away from the stone and towered over her, his blue eyes dark, his expression remote. "You chose Rhys's life over mine."

Rosalind grabbed his sleeve. "I had no choice. If you will just let me explain—"

He removed her hand from his arm. "There's nothing to explain. You chose well. Rhys will always be with you, won't he? You chose your future."

He tried to step around her, but she blocked his path. "No, that's not how it was. I—"

Christopher pressed three of his fingers over her lips. "I understand. You made your choice, and by God, now you have to live with it. Let me be." He shoved past her and stalked out of the circle.

Rhys appeared at Rosalind's elbow, his dagger and Christopher's in his hand. He stared after Christopher's departing figure. "What did you say to the Druid slayer to make him storm out of here as if the hounds of hell were after him?"

Rosalind shook her head. She couldn't tell Rhys what she'd done; she'd only hurt him too if she tried to explain her desperate logic. Rhys slung a comforting arm across her shoulders, and walked with her toward where they had left the horses.

"Don't worry, *cariad*. We'll catch the Vampire next time."

His comforting words almost made Rosalind cry, but she was beyond tears. Christopher's rejection hurt so profoundly she felt as if she were bleeding inside. And Rhys couldn't help with that. She had only her own fear and inadequacy to blame.

Rosalind scrubbed at her tired eyes. She knew how vulnerable Christopher was, how his family had convinced him he was never good enough. And what had she done? Shown him that he wasn't good enough for her either. What a fool she was! She was a failure both as a lover and as a Vampire slayer. How in the name of all the saints was she going to make it right with him? She already missed his presence in her mind.

She stared out into the midnight blue sky and caught the soft, welcoming whinny of her horse on the night breeze. She had to talk to Christopher. She had to prevail upon his sense of duty to continue their fight against the Vampire. For if he was forced to be with her, eventually, surely, if God was indeed merciful and just, she would get the chance to explain what she had done.

ChapteR 21

"Sir Christopher . . ." Through the locked bedchamber door, Christopher heard Rhys sigh. "You cannot avoid me forever. I have your dagger. Don't you want it back?"

Christopher contemplated the small window and his ability to fit through it. He was not in the mood to speak to Rhys. He'd slept badly, dreaming over and over of becoming a Vampire, and had woken up sweating and cursing . . . and missing Rosalind so much, it hurt to breathe.

At least it wasn't she standing outside his door. He wasn't sure if he ever wanted to see her again.

She had abandoned him, left him there at the mercy of the Vampire, and expected him to understand. Oh, he understood. He just didn't have the stomach to listen to her excuses. The truth was simple: he was not enough for her, would never be enough for her. . . .

"Sir Christopher?" Rhys rattled the door again.

With an irritated grunt, Christopher sat up and went to the door to let Rhys in. The Welshman looked his usual calm, competent self. In the stream of sunshine pouring through the window, his auburn hair shone like a fox pelt. He held out the dagger to Christopher.

"I had the smithy put a new edge on it. The silver was tarnished by the Vampire's powers."

"Thank you." Christopher restored the dagger to its usual place and sat back on his bed. He looked up at Rhys, who had made no move to leave. "Is there something else I can do for you?"

Rhys leaned back against the closed door. "Perhaps you can explain why Rosalind is moping around like a wench who has lost her reason to live."

Christopher shrugged. "Because she put us all in danger with her latest plan to capture the Vampire? That would seem the most obvious reason."

"We all agreed to her plan. I seem to remember that you were particularly keen."

"Because I want this whole damned mission to end," Christopher replied. "Don't you?"

"In some ways, yes, because I don't like being at court, but in other ways? I find myself at a loss for how to deal with my lady."

Christopher forced a smile. "I'm sure you'll master her one day."

"But I don't want to master her." Rhys scowled at Christopher. "It would be as thoughtless and cruel as crushing the dreams of a child."

"Better that dreams are crushed early, Rhys. You can't have her thinking she can twist you around her thumb." And what in God's name was he doing giving advice to Rhys about Rosalind? He had no idea who or what she was anymore, or what she wanted.

Rhys half smiled. "The truth is—she knows I'm as weak as water where she is concerned."

"And what does that have to do with me?" Christopher stood up and pretended to look for his jerkin. "I have hardly managed to endear myself to her recently."

"Oh, but you have."

Christopher met the other man's gaze. "Not anymore. She has made her choice, and you have already promised me you will take care of her."

Rhys frowned and advanced toward him. "What choice did she make?"

Inwardly, Christopher groaned as he pulled on his leather jerkin. "She wants you."

"When did she tell you that?"

Christopher glared at Rhys. "Why does it matter?" He focused his attention on buttoning his doublet. "And why are you still here?"

Rhys grabbed him by his shirt and shoved him against the wall, his forearm braced against Christopher's throat. "I do not appreciate your levity or your disrespect for my lady."

"And I do not appreciate being mauled. Get your hands off me."

"Considering what you have done to her, Ellis, I should be pounding you into a pulp."

"I did nothing she did not want." Christopher groaned as Rhys shoved him hard against the wall. "Ask her yourself."

"I know what happened. I also know that she has been foolish enough to fall in love with you, so why in God's name would she tell you that she wanted me?"

"I swear she chose you over me, now release me."

"Ah." Rhys stepped back as if Christopher suddenly made sense. "That's women's logic for you. She can't have you, so she'll take me instead."

"That is not my problem anymore—it is yours. I'm quite happy to leave her in your capable hands." Christopher cursed as he twisted one of the silver buttons so hard it came off and bounced along the oak floorboards.

Rhys bent to pick up the button. "You're lying, but

I'm not a fool. If you won't fight for her, I'll take her and keep her safe." He paused for a moment as if expecting Christopher to refute his claims and then continued. "How are we to complete our mission if you and Rosalind will not speak to each other?"

Christopher fixed him with his most intimidating stare. "You don't need me anymore. The Vampire used me to get at Rosalind through our bond. Rosalind can communicate with the Vampire perfectly well without me."

Rhys looked puzzled. "Rosalind didn't tell me anything of this."

"It transpired when we were in the Vampire's thrall." Christopher stalked across the room, held the door open, and looked pointedly at Rhys.

"Is this why you refuse to talk to Rosalind, then? You feel slighted, excluded, scorned?"

"I will feel anything you like if you will just get out of my bedchamber."

Rhys held his gaze. "I never thought you a coward, Sir Christopher."

"I'm not a coward. I've just become unnecessary. Ask Rosalind. She'll agree with me."

Rhys smiled and Christopher fought a sudden desire to drag Rhys back into the room and shove his fist right into the man's face. "Why do you think I am here, Druid slayer? Rosalind told me to come."

"You said she wasn't speaking to me."

Rhys shrugged. "That doesn't mean she isn't speaking to me. She wants to catch this Vampire, and she is willing to do whatever it takes to achieve her aim. You share a unique bond with her that could save us all. Are you as stalwart a fighter as she?"

Christopher sucked in a harried breath. "Damn you both. I want this Vampire dead."

Rhys handed him back the silver button from his

jerkin. "Then we will see you tonight in the king's bed-chamber."

"What?"

"You wish to catch the Vampire, don't you?" Rhys bowed and headed out of the door. "I will see you later, my friend."

Rosalind paced nervously around the king's private audience chamber, her attention fixed on the door. The walls of the king's inner sanctum were covered with colorful tapestries depicting the fall of Eden, which deadened the sound of her footsteps and kept the room far warmer than most of the palace.

"Sir Christopher will come. I promise you."

She halted and glared at Rhys, who lounged at his ease in the window seat. "Why should he?"

"Because he wants to finish this as much as you do."

Rosalind huffed out a breath. "I suppose he can't wait to see the back of me."

"He has cause."

"What do you mean?"

Rhys shrugged. "He said you chose me."

"I . . ." Rosalind stared at Rhys and shook her head. "What is the point? The man is as stubborn as a donkey."

"Rather like you, then."

Rosalind narrowed her eyes at him. "I would've thought you'd be more pleased to be 'chosen.'"

"My, you're conceited, aren't you?" Rhys's smile grew serious.

"So you don't want me either?" Rosalind flung up her hands. "Good! Because I am tired of dealing with men. I really don't need any of you!"

"That's the spirit, my lady. Keep that up and we'll all be wishing you to the devil very shortly."

Rosalind scowled at Rhys, but he pointed at the door. "I think I hear the Druid slayer."

She swung around to face the door and tried to compose her features. Christopher came in without knocking. He wore his habitual black garb and a smile that was as false as paste jewelry. He bowed with exquisite precision.

"Good evening, my lady. Master Williams."

Rosalind nodded at him. "Good evening. It is good of you to join us."

"It's always a pleasure, my lady. How could you doubt it?"

His smile was flirtatious, his mind completely closed to her. She was reminded of when they first met and she'd thought him a frivolous fool with no substance. She knew better now, but it didn't mean she could regain his trust. She doubted he'd willingly lay himself open to hurt more than once.

She took a deep breath. "I need your help."

He raised a supercilious eyebrow. "Are you sure?"

"I wish to convince the Vampire that I will do her bidding and kill the king."

"And how do you intend to do that?" Christopher strolled across to a chair by the fire and sat down. One long leg crossed over the other.

"It shouldn't be too difficult." She managed a smile. "She knows what I did to you. She believes I sacrificed you for Rhys. All you have to do is summon her in your mind and tell her that I am willing to kill the king if she will help me get you back. You can even laugh about my chances of success. I'm sure you'll enjoy that."

Christopher went still. "You want me to tell the Vampire you are going to murder the king."

She opened her eyes wide at him. "Yes. It's quite simple."

"You expect me to convince her I hate you so much

that I would deliberately betray you? And that you care enough about me to even consider such an exchange?"

Rosalind struggled not to flinch at his harsh assessment. "That is hardly the point, is it? You just have to convince her I am willing to slaughter the king."

"And what happens when she realizes that you have no intention of murdering the king at all, and turns her power on you?"

Rosalind met his skeptical gaze. "By then it will be too late. I'll already have killed her."

Christopher stood up and paced the floorboards, his expression thunderous. "This is ridiculous. How are you even going to be sure that the Vampire is physically present?"

Rhys cleared his throat and Christopher swung around to glare at him. "Because after we alert the king to our plans and clear the guards, we'll make it easy for the Vampire to follow Rosalind in."

"Why can't we simply surround the queen's quarters and kill her there, then?" Christopher asked. "This seems far too dangerous and too complicated."

Rosalind forced out the words. "Because the Vampire likes games. If she thinks I have capitulated to her will, she will want to gloat in person. And she will enjoy the challenge of getting into the king's quarters to watch the king suffer and die by my hand."

Christopher exhaled. "I don't like it."

"You don't have to like it, Sir Christopher. You merely have to play your part," Rosalind snapped. "Are you willing to do this, or not?"

He faced her, his blue eyes intense. "I'll do it, but only because I wish to fulfill my pledge and see this Vampire dead."

Rosalind held his gaze. "Now you know how I felt the other night." She swallowed hard. "I'll wait here until I hear from Elias. Then Rhys will come to you and ask you to summon the Vampire. Meanwhile, I'll make sure the king knows I will be sneaking into his bedchamber, apparently with the intent to execute him."

"What if the Vampire decides to kill the king herself?"

Rhys laughed. "It won't be the king in that bed. It'll be me."

Rosalind smiled at Rhys. "That will certainly make things a little less dangerous. While you wait in the bed, Sir Christopher and Elias can track the Vampire's progress and make sure she arrives to see me perform the terrible deed."

Rhys bowed at them both and headed for the door. "I'll go and find Elias and report back."

Rosalind found herself alone with Christopher and turned away to the fire on the pretext of warming her hands.

"Do you want me to stay with you until Rhys gets back?"

"That isn't necessary, sir." She didn't dare look at him, couldn't bear to see the coldness in his gaze. "You probably have far better things to do."

She gasped as he gripped her arm and spun her around to face him. "Rosalind, I'm aware that you aren't telling me the whole truth, but at the moment, I'm damned if I can separate the facts from the lies."

She stared at his black velvet doublet and neat silver-edged ruff. "I'm not going to beg. Either help us or don't." She raised her eyes to his face. If he stood any chance of convincing the Vampire that he was truly done with her, she needed him to remain angry. "Mayhap I should try to contact the Vampire by myself, after all."

"Don't play with me. I said I would do it and I will." A muscle flicked in his jaw. "I've made my peace with my confessor. I should be the one to kill the Vampire. After all, unlike you, I have no one who cares what happens to me. No family to mourn me, no lover waiting patiently in the background to claim me."

Rosalind desperately wanted to reach out and comfort him, but it would not do. She struggled to sound unaffected. "Your part is to communicate with the Vampire. I cannot trust you to do more. The blood ties you share might make you unwilling or unable to actually kill her."

He jerked away from her as if she'd slapped him. "No one is as capable of killing as you, Vampire slayer." He schooled his expression and bowed. "Until tonight, my lady."

She didn't bother to reply and he left the chamber. Rosalind found a chair and abruptly sat down, her head cradled in her hands. Deceiving Christopher was one of the hardest things she had ever had to do. She had no idea if she was going to survive the night, and she had wanted more than anything to tell Christopher she loved him.

Christopher made his way to the queen's receiving room and settled himself in the corner of the music room with his lute on his knee. It was getting late and the chamber was already bathed in candlelight. The queen looked tired and distracted, her attention drifting between her ladies' conversation and her rosary beads. Christopher studied the circle of women who surrounded the queen. If the Vampire was truly one of them, she should receive his message all too clearly.

Strumming the lute in a minor key, he closed his eyes and began to dismantle some of the wall he'd built so painstakingly in his mind. He allowed cracks to open up, bricks to be displaced, until the darkness encroached on the light and on his deepest feelings. Of course, to complete the trap, he had to allow Rosalind back into his mind as well, and that was far harder than dealing with the Vampire's desires. Ever since he'd shut Rosalind out, he'd felt incomplete—as if she had made off with the better half of his soul.

Like a fisherman tickling a trout, he played out his lure, tantalized the Vampire with thoughts of Rosalind's plan to kill the king, her determination to do it now, to finish it now, to force Christopher back to her. He showed the Vampire a final image of Rosalind inside the king's private apartments, creeping toward the royal bedchamber.

As the Vampire's excitement grew, he struggled not to react to the waves of triumph and bloodlust that saturated her thoughts and forced all common sense out of his head. When he found himself licking his lips and picturing the bloodied corpse of the king, he forced his eyes open and laid the lute down. He didn't wait to see if the Vampire followed him but hurried from the room without asking the queen's permission. From the frenzy of vicious enjoyment and anticipation in his mind, he knew the Vampire would take the bait. Rosalind was correct about the Vampire's overwhelming arrogance. Now all he could do was try to prevent a catastrophe. He wished he had the strength of will to destroy the Vampire before she ever reached the king's privy chamber, but he feared Rosalind was right. He wouldn't be able to kill her while she still inhabited his mind and influenced his thoughts.

In the hallway outside the queen's rooms, Christopher pressed himself back against the wall as a black-cloaked figure flew past him. He tensed as a hand grabbed his shoulder, and spun around to face Elias, whose silver eyes gleamed with anticipation.

"Sir Christopher." Elias nodded in the direction the woman had taken. "That was Lady Celia Del Alonso; apparently she is related to your mother's Vampire mate. She has been with Queen Katherine since the queen was born."

"Is there no way to dispose of her now, before she even reaches the king?"

"She's stronger than I, and you are her blood kin, so I doubt it." Elias grimaced. "I suggest we follow the original plan. I know a back way to the king's apartments. We can get there before the Vampire."

Christopher nodded and followed Elias into the shadows and through a series of corridors and passageways that brought them to a solid stone wall. Elias pointed to a crack of light in the center. "There's a peephole here and below it the mechanism to open the secret door."

"Where are you going?" Christopher hissed.

"I'm going to cut off her exit from the rear." Elias's fanged smile was deadly. "She will not escape us again." He bowed to Christopher and left him the burning torch. "Good luck."

"And to you."

Christopher strained to see through the peephole. He could just make out a large form in the bed topped with a hint of auburn hair. Rhys—at least he hoped it was. Beyond that was the door to the elaborate golden chamber. There was no sign of Rosalind. He assumed she would be waiting on word of the Vampire's arrival to proceed.

He sent her a quick warning and hoped she understood it. The Vampire should be close now. He daren't seek her in his mind; his defenses were too weak. With a blink, he cleared his vision and saw the door open. His hand closed on the metal ring that operated the secret panel. Rosalind appeared, her expression determined, her dagger held high in her hand.

She advanced toward the bed, and Christopher held his breath. She wore her boy's clothes, her hair tied back from her face in a single braid. Was Rosalind aware that the Vampire had appeared in the doorway behind her? A wave of dark compulsion flooded through him, and he saw Rosalind falter. Would she be overcome with the desire to kill? Did the Vampire have that much control over her?

He felt Rosalind reach out for him, and tried to stop them both from drowning in the Vampire's savage urge to kill. Rosalind moved closer to the bed, her expression desperate, her dagger hand shaking. He wanted to join her, wanted to hold her hand and help her plunge her blade into the quivering flesh of the king. . . .

Without further thought for his own safety or concealment, he threw his remaining strength into Rosalind's mind and tried to block the Vampire's command. He felt the Vampire's outrage at his presence as she howled in his head.

"Let the Vampire slayer do her work! Let her kill the unfaithful one! Help her!"

"I cannot!" Christopher shouted.

As he fell into the room, Rosalind screamed and her dagger hand stabbed downward toward the recumbent figure on the bed. The Vampire shrieked in triumph as the figure in the bed bellowed in apparent pain. She edged closer into the room, her maniacal laughter echoing off the paneled walls. Christopher managed to get to his feet and struggled to release his sword from its sheath. He charged around the huge canopied bed, just as Rosalind swiveled and plunged her dagger into the Vampire's breast.

Rhys erupted from the bedclothes too and tried to pull Rosalind free of the Vampire's flailing hands. Christopher froze as the Vampire looked at him, her face wild, her mouth open as she screamed in his mind.

"Help me, my child! Thou art my blood-kin; I command your obedience. Kill the man who seeks to bed your woman."

And, God help him, for a moment Christopher's gaze swung toward Rhys, his rival for Rosalind's affections, a man who stood in Christopher's way, and was now so vulnerable to the slash of his blade. . . .

While he was distracted, the Vampire's fingers closed around Rosalind's throat and she drew her upward until her feet dangled in the air. Christopher cringed as the Vampire's screams echoed inside his head.

"You fools! If you kill me, he wins—don't you understand? He will be victorious and you will face an enemy ten thousand times as strong as I am!"

The Vampire extended her huge fangs and bent toward Rosalind. It was as if something snapped inside Christopher's head and everything suddenly became clear. No Vampire could allow another to kill his bonded mate. With a yell, Christopher grasped his sword two-handed and swung sideways at the Vampire, slicing through the column of her neck.

She fell forward on top of Rosalind, and Rhys struggled both to disentangle himself from the bedclothes and separate Rosalind from the Vampire. Christopher braced his foot on the bed frame and pulled out his sword, then hacked down once more to completely sever the Vampire's head from her body.

The stench of blood and orange blossom filled his nostrils and he gasped for breath. Something inside him screamed as if he'd cut himself open, whether it was the Vampire, or Rosalind, he could no longer tell. He couldn't see anything of Rosalind, only hear Rhys cursing as he tried to release the Vampire's death grip on Rosalind's throat even as the Vampire's body continued to twitch and convulse and spurt black blood.

Christopher fought back an urge to retch and allowed his sword to drop to the floor. Heedless of the carnage, he climbed onto the bed.

"Is she all right?" he asked as Rhys finally managed

to roll the headless Vampire to one side to reveal Rosalind's blood-soaked frame. "Did she bite her?"

"I cannot tell! There is too much blood." Rhys was struggling to detach the Vampire's fingers from around Rosalind's neck. "If I can't get them off, I'll need your dagger to cut them."

Christopher swallowed hard as he viewed the lacerations on Rosalind's throat and the paleness of her complexion. He shoved his hand beneath her doublet and tried to ascertain if she was breathing. Without looking away from Rosalind, he called out, "Elias, are you there?"

"Yes, Sir Christopher?"

"Help us, damn you!"

Elias strolled over to the bed and inhaled slowly, as if sampling the finest Flemish wine. He studied the positions of the Vampire and Rosalind and then closed his eyes and spoke in a language Christopher only vaguely recognized. "Gellong yn rhydd."

The dead Vampire's fingers fell away from Rosalind's throat and, with a snort of disgust, Rhys rolled the Vampire's body onto the floor. Elias poked the corpse with the toe of his boot.

"I expect you'd like me to take care of Lady Celia's body."

Rhys looked up. "I'd rather do it myself."

"You suspect I might attempt to revive her?" Elias chuckled. "How could I do that when her head is separated from her body? Besides, I have no wish for her to live again. She is far better off dead."

Rhys looked at Christopher. "Do you want to go with him and make sure that he disposes of the body properly?"

"No."

Elias cleared his throat. "Perhaps some of your companions would aid me, Master Williams?"

"Aye," Rhys said. "Three of my men are stationed in the courtyard beside the door. They should be easy to find, as the king has commanded everyone else to leave this area. Go and bring them here."

Elias sauntered off as if he wasn't wading through a bloodbath. Christopher met Rhys's gaze. "She still isn't awake."

"I know that." Rhys gently explored Rosalind's throat. "I can't feel any bite marks. I believe she has swooned."

"I never swoon." Rosalind opened her eyes and squinted up at them. "I stink of Vampire blood. Did we kill her?"

"We did." Christopher's heart thudded with relief and he found himself smiling down at her, his bloodied, battered, and unbowed Vampire hunter.

Rosalind's faint smile wavered and died. "She almost bespelled me again. If it hadn't have been for Rhys's quick wits and your mental support, I would have failed." She closed her eyes and turned her face into Rhys's lap. "Perhaps I'm not quite as accomplished as I would like to believe."

Christopher wanted to pull her into his arms and tell her she would never have to fight another Vampire again, that she could stay with him and be safe forever. But he couldn't dishonor her in that way. Her work was her life. And she'd already made her choice.

He stood as, behind him, he sensed movement. It was Elias returning with the other Druids. He paused to wipe his sword blade on the already ruined sheets and then stepped back. He managed to catch Rhys's eye. "I must get cleaned up. Mayhap I'll see you tomorrow."

"Thank you, Sir Christopher. You have proved to be a good man and a worthy ally. I would be proud to have you at my side in battle."

"I extend you the same compliment." Christopher was going to say more, but Rhys was stroking Rosalind's hair away from her anguished face, and he couldn't bear to watch. He bowed and turned for the door. There was no longer any reason for him to be in this room, let alone at court. All he had left was to leave as gracefully as he could.

"Christopher!"

He froze when he heard her voice, and for a terrible moment he couldn't walk away. But to stay would bring him nothing but heartache, and he was done with love for a lifetime. He forced himself to put one foot in front of the other, and somehow kept going until he reached his room.

Roper gave him hell about his ruined clothing and no credit for finally killing the Vampire. His feelings were too deadened to defend himself and, eventually, even Roper gave up. At last he lay alone in bed, unable to sleep.

Suddenly warmth flooded his senses. She was seeking him in his mind. He swallowed hard and opened his eyes as his beleaguered body stirred to life and wanted . . .

Rosalind allowed one of the female Druids who served the queen to strip her out of her blood-soaked clothes and help her into a warm bath. Even her hair required washing and she had no energy left to tend to it herself. The maid had to aid her, her voice soothing, her hands gentle as she rubbed soap into Rosalind's tender scalp.

The Vampire had been defeated and Rosalind should be feeling joyful. Instead all she felt was empty. She'd almost succumbed to the Vampire's compulsion to kill the king, and without the help of the others she would have failed again. Perhaps the naysayers were right and she would never be strong enough to defeat the most dangerous of the Vampires by herself, her female mind too weak to defend itself.

She waited as the maid rinsed her hair and helped her out of the bath before dismissing the woman with grateful thanks. Her room was cold and her bed looked more inviting than ever. She shivered as she braided her hair and put on her warmest night rail. If she wanted, she could go home now, her task completed, her honor apparently satisfied—until the next time she showed how weak she really was. . . .

Rosalind climbed into bed and pulled the covers up to her chin. Her thoughts strayed to Christopher's abrupt departure and unconsciously she sought him in her mind. His dark thoughts flowed with hers, reliving the Vampire's last terrible moments, their joint anguish as they fought her dark compulsion. His feelings of unworthiness, coupled with those of her betrayal, swamped her senses, and she reached out to comfort him. By the lady, she wished he was with her now, his strong muscular body wrapped around hers, his arms holding her close . . .

His mind slammed shut, pitching her out and downward into the desperate hell of her own emotions. She closed her eyes tight and concentrated on sleeping. She deserved to be shut out. Hadn't she betrayed them all?

Chapter 22

"Yes, Your Majesty, you are safe now."

"You are sure of this, Lady Rosalind?"

"Indeed, sire." Despite her throbbing headache, Rosalind managed to smile at the king, who stood beside her staring at his ruined bedchamber. It was early morning and the room looked even worse than it had the night before. Blood splattered the carved paneling and the bedsheets were scorched and soaked in the Vampire's blackened blood.

"Of course, we will make sure that all traces of the Vampire are removed from this room before you sleep in it again."

The king glowered at her. "In your struggle, you have ruined a fine set of bed hangings sewn with real gold thread that were a gift from the King of France."

Rosalind's smile disappeared. She hoped the king didn't expect her to pay for them. She had a suspicion that it might take her several lifetimes.

"But that's all right, my dear. I never liked them anyway." The king's laughter boomed out and rebounded against the walls, making Rosalind wince. He beckoned her back into his adjoining private audience chamber and settled himself in an enormous gilded chair. "Now tell me how a slip of a girl like yourself managed to kill this Vampire."

"I did not do it alone, sire. Master Rhys Williams and Sir Christopher Ellis helped as well."

"Ah, yes, I remember your recent request to allow Sir Christopher greater access to my person. Master Williams is a Welshman, I assume."

"He is indeed, sire, and a loyal associate of the Llewellyn family."

The king sat back in his chair and eyed her. "Which one of you delivered the killing blow?"

Inwardly, Rosalind sighed. Were all men obsessed with combat and the bloody annals of war? "I stabbed the Vampire in the heart, while Sir Christopher sliced off her head."

"It was necessary to completely behead the Vampire?"

"Yes, sire, to prevent her from coming back."

The king shuddered and crossed himself. His fingers lingered on the crucifix around his neck. "And what was Master Williams doing while you placed yourself in such mortal peril?"

"He was lying in the bed pretending to be you, sire. He has red hair."

King Henry laughed again and slapped his thigh. "I almost wish I'd seen it. A fair maiden like you, stabbing one of these ungodly creatures through the heart."

Rosalind shivered as she struggled not to relive the awful moment when the Vampire had tried to squeeze the life out of her. "As I said, you should be safe now, Your Majesty."

The king nodded. "I am right glad to hear it. I wish to meet with Master Williams and Sir Christopher to express my thanks to them in person."

Rosalind curtsied. "I'll arrange that with your chamberlain, sire."

The king waved his hand in dismissal. "We'll have to think of some reward for you as well, eh, my lady?"

"There's no need, sire. I was just honoring my family's vow of service to yours."

On that note, Rosalind backed out of the royal presence and walked slowly along to the queen's quarters. It was a brightly sunlit morning with the promise of warmth to come.

"Good morning, Lady Rosalind."

Rosalind looked up to see Elias Warner approaching her, his expression bland. Metallic threads in his silver doublet caught the light and the reflection made her blink.

"Good morning, Master Warner. I have just had an audience with the king. He was most pleased to hear of the successful completion of our mission. As you requested, I didn't mention your part in our little adventure."

Elias bowed and then continued to pace alongside her, placing her hand on his arm. "Thank you. I am quite happy to remain in obscurity. My part was rather small, in any case."

"Do you think so?" Rosalind regarded him carefully. "I believe it was you who suggested to Sir Christopher that we had an unusual bond that might be helpful."

"You flatter me, my lady. My role was simply to facilitate matters when necessary, rather than direct them."

"What a wonderfully diplomatic answer, and how utterly untrue. You have done nothing but manipulate us from the beginning."

Elias raised his eyebrows. "Are you feeling unwell, my lady? You sound a little overwrought."

Rosalind tried to organize her thoughts. There was something she needed to ask Elias. She couldn't think how to frame the question without inciting his wrath, but in truth she was almost too tired to care. "I'm concerned about something the Vampire said."

Elias patted her fingers and then brought them to his mouth to kiss. "The Vampire is gone. Perhaps you should stop worrying about that crazed old woman."

Rosalind carefully eased her fingers free. "She was obsessed, I grant you that, but she was also convinced that you were hiding something from us."

"Why would I do that? I act solely on the orders of the Vampire Council."

"Their dislike of this particular Vampire seemed very personal to me."

"You think so?" Elias managed a tight smile. "I have no idea why."

They stopped by the door to the queen's apartments and Rosalind hesitated. She decided it was best to speak to Christopher before she proceeded to air her suspicions. "You are probably right, Master Warner. I am a little overtired."

His smile was tender and she was reminded of the images she'd seen in his mind: his fascination with her, his desire to have her in his thrall. "That isn't surprising considering your recent victory, Vampire slayer." He bowed low and kissed her hand. "I assume you'll be leaving court now." Elias sounded a little disappointed.

"I haven't heard from my grandfather yet, but I am sure he will want me home."

"I will miss you, my lady."

Rosalind summoned a smile. "I'm sure you'll find plenty of other ladies to amuse you, sir."

"I'm sure I will, but they won't be you." Elias smiled beguilingly, but she refused to comment on his provocative remark so he carried on speaking. "And Sir Christopher?"

Rosalind shrugged. "I have no idea what he will be doing."

Elias paused. "You have not seen him?"

"There is no need for me to see him. The Vampire is dead."

"Ah. I should imagine that this is difficult for you both."

Rosalind stared intently at Elias. Was that a hint of sympathy in his voice? Surely not.

He continued. "I suspect Sir Christopher has enough Vampire blood in him to bond for eternity."

At that, Elias bowed and turned away, leaving Rosalind standing alone. As usual, he'd stirred up her thoughts and made her imagine things that could not be allowed to happen. Rosalind checked that Elias had indeed disappeared and turned back toward the stables. She needed to talk to Rhys.

Christopher rested his crossed arms on the door of the stall and spotted Rhys crouched in the straw, his horse's foot stuck between his knees as he picked at a loose nail in the shoe. Christopher waited until Rhys released the horse's foot before announcing his presence. He doubted Rhys would appreciate being kicked in his manly parts if the horse took fright.

Rhys stood up and wiped his hands on his leather jerkin. "What can I do for you, Sir Christopher?"

Christopher followed Rhys to the pump in the stable yard and waited while he washed his hands. "Something's been bothering me."

Rhys half smiled. "Let me guess. You've finally realized that you have been behaving like a complete fool by ignoring Lady Rosalind and you want to make your peace with her before you leave."

Christopher frowned. "No. That's not it."

"Are you sure? Because you have been a fool." Rhys paused. "She loves you, despite who you are and what you mean to her family. That is a gift I would never turn away."

Christopher set his jaw. "Be that as it may, there is something else I need to speak to Rosalind about. Something the Vampire said."

Rhys looked away from him, past his shoulder. "Then you are in luck. Lady Rosalind is here. You can ask her yourself." He bowed and took himself off, leaving Christopher staring at the water pump, painfully aware of Rosalind's sweet scent behind him, the sudden catch of her breath, the imagined warmth of her skin . . .

"Oh . . ."

She sounded disappointed. He turned around and she frowned. "I wanted to ask Rhys about something. . . ."

He fixed on a smile. "Can I help you?"

She regarded him steadily with her beautiful brown eyes. "I thought you didn't want to have anything more to do with me."

"Needs must, my lady." He inclined his head the barest inch. "I believe we have some unfinished business."

Her face softened and she clasped her hands together like a supplicant. "I'm so glad you've decided to give me a chance to explain. When I was in the Vampire's thrall, she made me choose one of you to save, and naturally I thought of you—"

"Naturally." He snorted. "And then naturally you chose Rhys."

"Because I had to."

"As you keep saying." He ran a hand over his face. "This isn't what I wanted to discuss, and you are not saying anything you haven't already said before. Please excuse me."

"Don't walk away from me." She grabbed hold of his velvet sleeve and he stopped moving.

"Let go of my arm."

"Or what?"

He palmed his dagger and brought it to lie against her flushed cheek. "Or I won't be responsible for my actions."

She stared up at him. "As if you would hurt me."

"As if you'd let me." He took a deep, steadying breath. "I do not want to listen to you, Rosalind."

"Why not?"

"Because you have already made yourself very clear."

Anger glittered in her eyes. "Do me the courtesy of hearing me out, and then I will let you go without a single murmur."

He put his dagger away and she released her grip on his sleeve. With an elaborate bow he gestured at the ruined bathhouse and she sailed past him, her brown silken skirts rustling in the straw. She took up a position in the center of the space and he strolled toward her, hands clasped behind his back to stop them from shaking.

"Well?"

She glared at him and lifted her chin. "As I was saying, the Vampire was going to kill all of you unless I chose one to save. I quickly realized I didn't need to save Elias, for the Vampire had implied that she thought he might be of use to her when she ruled the kingdom. That left you and Rhys." She sighed and looked away from him. "I thought I would go mad having to make such a choice."

"Yet you managed it." He was proud of the lightness of his tone, glad that his hard-won defenses still worked against her.

She shot him a death-glare. "Because I remembered something important. Blood ties are vital to the Vampire kind. Protecting their bloodlines is an instinct, like a human woman protecting her young. I knew that she would never willingly kill one of her blood. I knew she would never kill you." She let out her breath. "So I chose

Rhys. He was the only one of us who was of no use to the Vampire, and had no claim on her."

Christopher let Rosalind's words sink slowly into his mind, felt them heal parts of his soul he hadn't even realized were hurting. He'd felt that terrible reluctance to kill his own blood, had only conquered it when the fate of his bond mate was in the balance. The once impenetrable walls of his defenses crumbled even more and he struggled to speak.

"It was fortunate for you that your wild gamble paid off, then, wasn't it?"

"My wild gamble?"

He raised an eyebrow. "What else would you call it?"

"A reasoned decision in the face of appalling odds." She scowled at him. "That, no doubt, is what you would call it if a man had to make such a choice!"

"I don't think I would have been able to make such a choice," he said wonderingly. "I don't know that I'm strong enough."

"It doesn't make any difference, though, does it?" She sighed and her head drooped forward like a wilting flower. "You've already decided I don't deserve to be forgiven."

"It's hardly as simple as that."

She held his gaze. "Yes, it is, Christopher."

"As I said, perhaps I don't have your courage." In truth, he could hardly believe her ability to stand in front of him and share her feelings so easily. She humbled him, made him want to leap the abyss for her instead of standing back in the shadows afraid to draw attention to himself.

Her brown eyes snapped fire. "Then perhaps you should find some."

He took a deep breath. It was time to jump or fall to his death. "And tell you that I love you, and that I wish to God I could be worthy of you?" He smiled. "That is all true, my lady, and it doesn't change anything at all."

She blinked hard and he realized she was close to tears. "How can you say it doesn't change anything?"

He took her trembling hand, brought it to his lips and kissed the palm. "You're right. My love for you has changed everything for me and it will always endure. In my soul I am yours, my lady. You have made me whole again. I will never forget you, and I'll never find your equal."

For a moment he let her inside his thoughts. She experienced the truth of his words, of his love for her, and of his complete conviction that she was better off without him.

"Do not think like that! You are one of the most worthy men I have ever met." She cupped his jaw. "I have never doubted your courage or your ability to survive the most difficult of birthrights."

He was saying good-bye to her, withdrawing his mind from hers even as he stood in front of her. Physically present, and yet not with her at all.

She reached out to embrace him. "Christopher—"

A shout from behind him made him pull away and turn. Rhys stood waiting, his expression resigned.

"The king wishes to see us in his private chambers."

"All of us?" Rosalind asked. "But I have already seen the king."

Rhys gave her a searching glance as he took her elbow. "All of us, my lady, and we'd better hurry."

"His Majesty the king will see you now."

The king's servant flung open the doors of the audience chamber and bowed low. Rosalind took a step inside and then stopped at the sight of all the people gathered around the seated king. Christopher's warm hand flattened against her back and urged her forward.

The king nodded genially at them. "Lady Rosalind, Master Williams, Sir Christopher. Thank you for attending to me."

As if they'd had a choice. Rosalind curtsied low and rose to see the anxious, tearstained face of Queen Katherine. What had the king told her about the death of one of her favorite ladies-in-waiting? Rosalind tore her gaze from the obviously distraught queen and stiffened at the amused glint in Elias Warner's eyes.

King Henry smiled. "I wish to extend my thanks to you for preserving my kingship."

All three of them murmured something about it being an honor to serve the king, who then gestured at Rhys.

"Master Williams, we shall pay you a royal pension for the rest of your natural life."

Rhys dropped down onto one knee. "Thank you, sire."

King Henry nodded and then turned his gaze to Christopher. "And you, Sir Christopher, will become a baron. Our secretary and the Guild of Arms shall consult with you about the disposal of your new lands and your responsibilities."

Rosalind glanced at Christopher as she felt tears threaten. At last he would have somewhere to call home, something that belonged to him alone.

Christopher knelt too. "Thank you, Your Majesty. I am . . . overwhelmed by such generosity."

Rosalind was still smiling when the king's benevolent gaze fell on her. "And as for you, Lady Rosalind, we have an even greater prize." He winked at her and nudged the queen, who tried to smile. "What could be sweeter than to help the cause of true love?"

Rosalind swallowed hard. "I don't understand, sire."

The king nodded. "The queen tells us that one of the reasons your grandfather sent you to court was to find a husband. Is that true?"

"It was certainly on his mind, sire, but—"

The king continued to speak over her pathetic squeaking. "And she has revealed a sad story of love lost between you and Sir Christopher."

Rosalind's throat went dry.

"It seemed to us, that in addition to ennobling Sir Christopher and endowing him with land, the least we could do was double your present dowry and present you to him as the perfect bride."

"But—"

The king waved his hand. "Do not thank us, Lady Rosalind. We've already sent a letter to your grandfather and one to Sir Christopher's uncle apprising them of my decision." He smiled. "You will be very happy together."

He rose to his feet and ushered his private chaplain in front of Rosalind and Christopher. "Let's have the betrothal ceremony now while we are present."

Christopher got to his feet and cleared his throat. "Your Majesty is most generous. But, sire, I'm not sure—"

The king's good humor abruptly deserted him and he scowled. "Are either of you already betrothed?"

"No, sire, but our families will not approve of this match. In truth they—"

King Henry cut him off. "Then this union will bring them together." The king's thin lips narrowed. "I'm tired of feuding families. You will obey."

Rosalind cast an anguished look at Rhys, but he shook his head. They could not afford to offend the king to his face. Her grandfather would have their heads, if the king did not.

King Henry gestured at Rosalind. "Take his hand, my lady, and all will be well."

It would not, but Rosalind did as the king said and heard the chaplain speak the sacred words of betrothal over them. Even as she stood obediently in front of the king, her mind scrabbled like a trapped rat to work out a way to escape this disastrous ambush. But she could think of nothing, and Christopher stood just as silently by her side.

Within a heartbeat they were betrothed by the king's command and neither of them could do a thing to stop it.

Chapter 23

"What in God's name are we going to do?" Rosalind said beseechingly to Rhys. The king had stayed for only a moment to kiss Rosalind heartily and slap Christopher on the shoulder before departing with the queen and Elias in tow. "What was the queen thinking, telling the king we were in love?" Her voice had risen to an unladylike screech.

"Stay here, my lady," Rhys said, headed for the door. "I'll catch up with the king."

She was left staring at Christopher, who appeared as astonished as she was. "How did this happen?"

Christopher shrugged. "The king's will is indeed allpowerful."

"You don't sound very angry."

A smile quivered at the corner of Christopher's mouth. "Well, it is rather amusing, isn't it?"

"In what way?"

"We've spent our entire time together denying our attraction because our families are sworn enemies, and the king decrees we should be married."

She stormed up to him, her hands on her hips. "And that is amusing?"

His smile died. "Perhaps not to you, but for one glorious moment I felt as if my every desire had been granted."

Her eyes softened and she sighed as he drew her into his arms. "It felt that way to me too."

He kissed her forehead just below her pearl-edged hood. "It's certain our families will object to the king's edict, but I'm not sure how they are going to break it without offending him. Mayhap we will find ourselves married indeed."

She shoved at his chest. "You are the most provoking and contrary of men."

"How so?"

"Because before the king declared we should marry, you seemed content to walk away from me."

"I certainly wasn't content, my lady. I was simply trying to do the right thing." His smile was inviting as he took her hands in his. "But as we are now betrothed, it is only right that we enjoy the liberties that exalted position offers."

He slid a finger under her chin to raise her face to his and kissed her mouth, kissed her again until she opened her lips and let him inside. When he finally pulled away, she was gasping.

"They'll never let us marry."

He met her gaze, his own unflinching. "I know, but for this one night, let us forget that."

She scowled at him. "You have behaved abominably. Why should I forgive you anything?"

"You shouldn't." He smiled into her eyes. "Yet in my heart, I am convinced that you will make the effort to understand my fears and forgive them." For a moment he rested his forehead against hers. "As you said yourself—you know me."

She sniffed. "You are conceited. And overconfident."

"Aye." He kissed her nose. "You were right to choose Rhys. You are a brave, shrewd warrior, whereas I behaved like a complete fool."

She gazed up at him. "I like it when you apologize, especially when you agree that you have been foolish."

"I thought you might."

Rhys reentered the room. "I talked to the king and . . ." He grinned at Rosalind, who snatched her hands out of Christopher's grasp. "Are you playing fast and loose with my affections again, my lady?"

"No, she is simply enjoying her brief betrothal to me," Christopher answered for her. "We both know that it cannot stand."

Rhys nodded. "The king has agreed that the wedding can be delayed until both families have a chance to receive the news. That, at least, gives us a few weeks. It will take some clever plotting and some substantial gifts to get the king to release you from the betrothal. Both of your families are skilled at such negotiations, but it will take time." He bowed to Rosalind. "The king also told me that he expects you both at his table this evening at dinner. I suggest you act suitably overjoyed."

Rosalind narrowed her eyes at him. "You seem remarkably cheerful for a man whose intended wife has just become betrothed to another man."

Rhys studied them both, his expression serious. "Make no mistake, my lady, I want you, and I am willing to wager that in the end I will have you."

"You are far more patient than I, sir," Christopher said. "I do not know if I could wait for the lady one more day."

Rosalind cleared her throat. "And I am not a bone to be fought over. I will decide where my heart lies and to whom I will eventually plight my troth."

Rhys bowed. "We will leave on the morrow. Bring her to me in the stables at first light."

"Aye," Christopher agreed. "I'll keep her safe till then."

Rhys extended his hand and they shook. "And I will do the same thereafter," he said.

Rosalind ran to Rhys and wrapped her arms around him. "Thank you," she whispered. "I do not deserve such kindness."

He kissed her cheek and held her away from him. "That is true. Perhaps I will find another wench who will torment me more than you, and marry her instead."

She smiled at him. "Mayhap you should."

Rhys bowed once more and left her with Christopher, who reclaimed her hand. "I had better pack my belongings." He grimaced. "I expect my uncle will be seeking an explanation of my latest misconduct."

"At least now you have your own land and home to escape to, my lord."

"I'd forgotten that." He smiled. "Now go and pack, and I'll come and call for you before the banquet. Wear your best gown and let's pretend we really are celebrating our betrothal."

The banquet passed in a swirl of toasts and congratulations. Christopher stayed by her side, a constant reassuring presence, his hand in hers, their fingers entwined, the promise of further joys in his every look and word.

Together they walked up the stairs to her room and Christopher locked the door behind him. He came across the small space to her and dropped to his knees. Apart from the moonlight, only a single candle illuminated the chamber. In its flickering light, Rosalind stroked the blue-black of his hair with her fingertips.

"Let me worship you tonight, my lady. Let me show you how I would love you if we were to remain together for all our natural lives."

He took his time removing her cumbersome clothing, so much time that Rosalind grew impatient. But he would not be hurried, his intention to enjoy every inch of her skin with his mouth and his hands evident in each slow caress and gentle touch. She moaned as he kissed her knee, untied her garter, and rolled down her stocking. She wanted his hands higher, wanted him pressing her down into the soft feather mattress, and wanted to drown there with him in a sea of sensation.

"Rosalind."

She managed to open her eyes to watch him shed his long shirt and bare his muscular chest, reached out to touch the hard planes of his furred stomach. He caught her hands and laid her more fully back on the bed and came down over her. His bare legs rubbed against hers and she shifted restlessly against him.

She lay as quietly as she could while he took down her hair and spread it on the pillow around her. His delight in the task was evident both in his total absorption and the look of awe on his face.

"You are beautiful, my lady."

"So are you."

"Flatterer." He chuckled and kissed a path down the side of her throat until she was arching up beneath him. The rasp of his tight beard against her breast and the hot wetness of his tongue as it closed around her nipple made her clutch at his hair. He murmured his approval against her flesh and continued suckling, drawing her other nipple to a hard, aching point between his finger and thumb.

By the lady, she wanted to open her legs to him, to feel him there, hot and hard and ready to penetrate her already wet and swollen quim. His hand drifted down over her hip and curved inward toward the juncture of her thighs.

"Please, Christopher . . ."

He made soothing noises against her breasts as his long fingers discovered the lush secrets of her hidden flesh, and he slowly rubbed her bud. She rose against his hand, no longer capable of lying so quiescently. His mouth moved lower until he was kissing her belly, and then lower still to tangle with his own fingers to probe and suck at her most intimate and sensitive flesh.

"Don't stop," Rosalind managed to gasp as she threaded her fingers back through his crow black hair and held on tight. "I need . . ."

But he knew what she needed, coaxed her pleasure from her with his mouth and his fingers, and then did it again and again until she was screaming his name. He grabbed her flailing hand and wrapped it around his prick. She gasped as his thick, wet length surged between her fingers and she gripped him even harder.

"Don't make me spill yet, love." He groaned. "I want to be in you."

He reversed his position and was suddenly looming over her, his legs between hers and his face inches from her own. "I love you, Rosalind. Let me show you how much." He angled his hips and his prick slid over her wet, waiting quim. "Let me inside you."

She reached down between their bodies to grasp his shaft and guided him where she needed him to be. He whispered her name like a benediction as he slowly pushed inside and filled her completely. "Give me your mind, as well, love. Let's make this the perfect union of body and soul."

"I love you, Christopher."

His smile was beautiful to her. "I know."

Willingly, she opened herself to him though her torrent of lust, love, and grief was so powerful she feared it would overwhelm him. But she found the same in him, and worried no more. He took her mind as he took her body, completely, carefully, and with a reverence that undid her so she wanted to hold nothing back from him. In his arms, she could be soft and feminine, and yet she knew he would never use those things against her, that he loved her purely and simply for herself.

He started to move faster, his long, even strokes becoming shorter as he gathered her to him and pumped hard. She wrapped her arms and legs around him and took every shuddering breath and jolt, clung to him like waterweed and felt his pleasure shoot through him as if it were her own.

She held him tight when he collapsed against her breasts, and let him lie there. This night was for celebrating their love. She would gladly bear his weight if it meant she had more memories of him to help her through the long, lonely, anguished times she was sure would come.

Sometime during the night, Rosalind found herself tracing the raised outline of a brand on Christopher's chest with her fingertips. His hand closed over hers and she realized he was awake.

"Does this offend you?"

Her fingers stilled. "Is it an old wound?"

"It's the mark of those who worship Mithras. A brand shaped like a bull's horns."

"Ah." She didn't take her hand away. "Rhys told me you were a member of that cult."

"I'm ashamed to say that he is right. When I was a lad, I begged my uncle to allow me to join." He let out his breath. "He refused at first, because my blood wasn't considered pure enough, but I kept insisting I was worthy, and when I was sixteen he allowed me to be initiated. I've regretted it ever since."

"You must have known that the cult's sole purpose was to kill Druids," Rosalind said carefully.

"I did." His fingers tightened over hers as if in a silent apology for the hurt he knew he was inflicting. "But I wanted so terribly to belong to something and to finally gain my uncle's approval that I convinced myself that the cult's vows were mainly ceremonial. In truth, I didn't even realize that there were many Druids still living."

He kissed the top of her head. "When I was faced with the prospect of killing in cold blood, I realized I couldn't do it. If a Druid was attacking an innocent Vampire, of course I was quite capable of doing my duty, but I refused to hunt Druids simply to slaughter them."

He drew her even closer. "My uncle proclaimed me a coward, and banned me from the Mithraic rites, but I don't think he was terribly surprised. He knew he still controlled me, for I was bound by the vows I'd taken with no possibility of escape. That was good enough for him."

Beneath her cheek, his muscles had tensed as if he thought she might repudiate him. Cautiously, Rosalind accessed his mind and found nothing but a strong desire to confess all to her and accept the consequences. She could only offer him honesty in return. It was too late to shy away from what either of them was capable of.

"I too would feel obliged to defend any of my people if they were being attacked by an enemy," she whispered. "I understand what you have done."

He kissed the top of her head and then rolled her onto her back again. "Thank you." He kissed her mouth, whispered the words between kisses, his hands moving over her. "Thank you for understanding. I swear, I have never hunted—" She kissed him back and stopped his words, even though they echoed in his thoughts as he deepened the kiss and set about seducing her with his body and his mind.

By the morning they'd coupled so often she was sore, but she didn't care and she knew he felt the same. There was an urgency to their joining that spoke of long separation, of new love stifled, suffocated, and lost . . . He helped her dress in her traveling clothes and she aided him too, their faces as solemn as if they dressed for a funeral.

It was raining, a light misting that made the pathways treacherous and turned the trees into dripping gray ghosts. They walked through the muted darkness to the stables and paused, as if by mutual consent, in the ruined bathhouse. At the last, Christopher held her face between his hands, his warm breath clouding her vision. "Rhys will take care of you."

"I am quite capable of caring for myself."

"I know that, but . . ." He took a deep breath, then hurried on. "If you think to marry him after all, I will understand."

"That is very agreeable of you, but I'm not sure he wants to marry me anymore, and that is probably a good thing." She tried to pull away from him, but he held fast.

"You know how I feel, damn it. I'd be happy to tear any man limb from limb for daring to smile at you, let alone touch you. But we have to be practical."

"Why must we?" Desperation laced her words. For the first time in her life, her needs as a woman surpassed her need to be a Vampire slayer.

A muscle twitched in his cheek. "Because I can't be with you, and Rhys can. He is a good man."

"I know that." She echoed his words. "But he isn't you."

Anguish flared in his blue eyes. "What do you want me to do, Rosalind? Take you away from your family and keep you for myself? That would be cruel and you know it. You'd grow to hate me more than you love me. And where on this earth could we live where I could keep you safe from my Vampire family?"

"That's not important—"

"And what about your people?" he roared at her.

"Do you think they would still accept you if you were married to me?"

She bit down on her lip to stop it from trembling. "My family loves me."

"You would be cast out, and you know it." All expression disappeared from his face. "Rosalind, I've lived without a family, lived with the scraps of other people's affection and their mistrust. I would rather kill myself than subject you to the same."

"Because you love me."

"Aye."

She pressed her hand over her heart. "But it hurts, Christopher. I don't know if I can bear to leave you like this."

He briefly closed his eyes. "Don't do this. One of us has to be strong. Please."

Tears stung her eyes and she dropped him an awkward curtsy. "Then I suppose I should leave."

He reached her before she could take a step and kissed her hard, his mouth hot and savage against her cold, numbed lips. "Go to Rhys, my love."

She stumbled away, her gloved hand pressed to her mouth, and found her way to where Rhys stood already waiting with their baggage-laden ponies. She didn't look back even though she knew Christopher was still there. She couldn't or she would start begging, and damn him, he was right. It seemed she couldn't have everything.

A shadow moved through the dawn light, and she recognized Elias Warner swathed in a black cloak. His smile screamed *victory* and Rosalind was reminded of what she wanted to tell Christopher: her fear that the Vampire's warning about "his victory" referred to someone other than the king. Someone very dangerous.

With a gasp, Rosalind turned in the saddle to shout back at Christopher, but Rhys was urging their mounts into a trot and the stables were rapidly disappearing in the haze of rain. She had to warn Christopher, she had to tell him things were not as they seemed. . . .

Christopher stood still and forced himself to keep breathing. He heard the horses whinny and Rhys shout for them to move along. He was doing what was best for Rosalind.

And it was ripping his soul apart.

He started running toward the stable, slipping and sliding in the rain-drenched earth. He couldn't let her go. Why shouldn't he be happy for once? What did he owe his uncle and the Vampires anyway? The cult of Mithras was a sham. He needed Rosalind more than anything and he would fight the whole world to keep her.

He gasped as a hand shot out and grabbed his upper arm, making him fall into the mud. By the time he regained his footing, there was no sign of Rosalind or Rhys in the stable yard or on the faint horizon.

He struggled to his feet. "What in God's name are you doing here, Elias?"

"I see your betrothed is leaving you, Sir Christopher, or should I say, my lord?"

The gloating satisfaction in Elias's voice made Christopher stiffen. "Why does that bring you such pleasure?"

"The Vampire Council will be pleased to see the back of a Llewellyn Vampire slayer. She fulfilled her part in the prophecy admirably, but, as you have found out, she is still a danger to us all." He cast a sideways look at Christopher. "Unlike you, we have not all been seduced by her charms."

"Really? You seemed rather enamored of her yourself."

Elias's smile remained undimmed. "Ah well, I did not bond with her as you did. It seems you have just enough Vampire in you to please the lady and not enough to cause any upset to the balance between Druid and Vampire. A perfect choice to fulfill the prophecy and destroy your Vampire kin."

"And you were not willing to take the risk of losing your immortality just for a prophecy that might fail."

Elias nodded. "There is that, but for Rosalind Llewellyn? I admit I did consider it." He smiled. "How droll that the king would insist on a betrothal right there in front of him. It will be interesting to watch the noble Llewellyn and Ellis families trying to extricate themselves from this calamity."

Christopher frowned as Rosalind screamed something in his head and his own doubts returned in force. *"Ask Elias what the Vampire meant when she said there was something more powerful coming after her. Ask him why they decided she needed to die."*

"Tell me, Elias, why was it so important for the Vampire Council to rid themselves of this Vampire? I would have thought they would enjoy watching her gain control of the king, or even disposing of him."

Elias's smile died. "That is a vicious slander. We seek to live in peace with the human world."

Christopher stepped closer. "Why did you want her dead?"

"She was half mad! The Vampire Council cannot allow someone like that loose in the human world. It is harmful for all of our kind."

"Because she was hindering your plans?"

Elias turned his face away. "I have no idea what you mean, my lord."

Christopher grabbed him by the throat. "I think you do. What is coming next? Tell me, or I will slit your throat and leave you here to bleed for the wolves."

Even though Elias could easily have broken Christopher's hold, he didn't even bother to struggle. "Someone better. A woman who will do her duty to the Vampire Council."

"What?" Christopher cursed silently and shifted his grip on Elias, only to have him disappear with a mocking laugh.

Christopher stared at Elias's boot marks in the mud as they were gradually obliterated by the rain. There was another coming. One who had the support of the Council and new designs on the king.

He studied the faint horizon and slowly grinned. It seemed the prophecy had not been fulfilled. Whether she realized it or not, Rosalind Llewellyn, Vampire hunter extraordinaire, uppity baggage and his intended wife, would be returning to court—and to him—after all.

ABOUT THE AUTHOR

Kate Pearce was born into a large family of girls in England, and spent much of her childhood living very happily in a dreamworld. Despite being told that she really needed to "get with the program," she graduated from the University College of Wales with an honors degree in history. A move to the U.S. finally allowed her to fulfill her dreams and sit down and write that novel. Along with being a voracious reader, Kate loves trail riding with her family in the regional parks of Northern California. Kate is a member of RWA and is published by Signet Eclipse, Kensington Aphrodisia, Ellora's Cave, Cleis Press, and Virgin Black Lace/Cheek.

Rosalind Llewellyn slid off her horse and immediately grabbed hold of the bridle. After she'd spent a long day in the saddle, her legs seemed unwilling to deal with the hardness of the ground and bowed like the branches of a willow tree. She glanced around the familiar stable yard of Richmond Palace and heaved a sigh. It was late evening, and everything was quiet. Despite her long absence, nothing had changed. Even the same horses' heads were framed in the half-open stalls and the same voices called out to one another.

She glanced across at her companion, who was busy removing their belongings from the packs and simultaneously inquiring as to where he should stable the horses. Rhys looked the same as well—if she discounted a certain grim set to his features when he glanced at her.

"You seem a little out of sorts, my lady."

"Of course I am. My cousin Jasper is perfectly capable of guarding the king. I'm not sure why I had to return to court at all."

Rhys grinned at her as he led the first of the horses into one of the vacant stalls. "Coward."

The smell of fresh grain and horse dung drifted back to Rosalind. She waited for him to return, her hands planted on her hips. "What exactly is that supposed to mean?"

He took her horse's bridle in his gloved hand. "You know."

"Have you forgotten that I almost died last time I was here?"

"Oh, I remember." His smile faded. "I was right there beside you. You probably don't remember that part, being as you were too busy making cow eyes at Christopher Ellis."

"I was busy trying to kill the Vampire!"

He bowed. "As were we all. It didn't stop you becoming involved with that soul-sucking Druid slayer, though, did it?"

He stomped off again and Rosalind could only stare helplessly at his broad back. It was true that she'd become intimately involved with Christopher, but Rhys knew perfectly well why that had happened. Between her Druid gods and the king, she had been caught very neatly in a sensual trap that she had still not managed to escape.

Rhys returned, and Rosalind touched his leather-clad arm. "If you want to return to Wales, I would quite understand."

He looked down at her, his hazel eyes full of wry amusement, his lilting voice lowered to a soft murmur. "Are you trying to get rid of me?"

Rosalind sighed. "I'm trying to avoid hurting you."

"Because you plan on taking up with Lord Christopher Ellis?"

Rosalind raised her chin. "I *am* still betrothed to him." She frowned. "I am somewhat obliged to seek him out."

"Obliged, eh?" Rhys flicked her nose. "*Cariad*, you can call it what you like, but I know that you want him and that you don't want me. I'll try not to let it interfere with my job of protecting you."

"I don't know what I want anymore," Rosalind

groused and moved out of the way of an incoming horse and rider arrayed in the king's livery. "I have not heard from him these many months."

Rhys helped her over the stable wall, his hands firm on her waist. "He could hardly come prancing into your grandfather's stronghold, now, could he? He would've been killed on sight."

"That's true, I suppose, but it would have been nice if he'd made the attempt!"

"Sometimes I'm glad I'm no longer one of your suitors. You have a somewhat bloodthirsty streak." Rhys handed her the lightest bag, which contained her jewelry, coins and favorite silver dagger. "The position of your lover seems fraught with danger."

"I can't help that." Rosalind took the well-worn path that wound up from the stables to the main wing of the palace. She couldn't help but glance at the ruined Roman bathhouse, where she'd met with Christopher and the others on her last visit to court. Was he even here? She had no sense of him yet. In the last year, she'd perfected her barriers against him in anticipation of having to see him again, especially if he turned up on the opposite side of a fight.

She straightened her shoulders and focused on the welcoming lights streaming out of the palace. She would talk to Jasper tomorrow and see what calamity had arisen that had made him insist she return to court. When she'd left a year earlier both she and Christopher *had* suspected another Vampire plot was in the offing.

Rhys paused by the doorway into the maids of honor's quarters and deposited her bags on the ground. "Your grandfather wrote to Queen Katherine to ask for permission for you to return to court, but from what the stable boy just told me, I'm not certain if she is still in residence here."

"Then where is she?"

"I'm not sure." He grimaced. "Apparently, the king does not wish to gaze upon her visage. She reminds him of his lack of an heir."

"That is so unfair."

"I agree. The queen is steadfast in her love for the king, but life can be cruel sometimes."

Unwilling to delve into the thorny subject of love with Rhys yet again, Rosalind rose on tiptoe to pat his cheek. "I'm sure I can prevail on someone to give me a bed. Thank you for coming back with me."

His smile this time was definitely rueful. "I didn't have much of a choice, did I? Your grandfather was most insistent that I accompany you." He paused. "And who is to say but that Lord Christopher Ellis might come to regret your betrothal and send you back into my arms."

"Rhys!"

He winked at her and disappeared into the darkness, heading for the stable yard. Rosalind stared after him. Surely he hadn't meant it? She'd done everything she could over the past few months to convince him that she was a lost cause. Whether she was reunited with Christopher or not, she couldn't see herself turning to Rhys. He deserved more than that, deserved to be first with a woman rather than know he would always be second choice.

And he *would* be second choice. Rosalind closed her eyes and tried to imagine Christopher's expression when he saw her. Would he be pleased or horrified? She couldn't decide how she felt about seeing him again. All she knew was that he'd stolen her heart, her mind and her body, and she would never be the same again.

Christopher pushed open the door of the Great Hall. The rush of night air was warm and scented with flowers. He breathed in deeply, allowed the fragrance to settle on him. Something was different. Everything looked the same, yet everything had changed. . . .

He looked around again. His mind was playing tricks on him. He could almost feel Rosalind in his arms, in his thoughts, even taste her. . . . He shook his head to clear the strange sensation. Rosalind was safe in deepest Wales, surrounded by her family, and attended by Rhys

Williams, who'd probably done his best to persuade her into his bed by now. Christopher slammed his hand against the oak door. And he, the fool, had let her go, convinced she would return to him.

Christopher muttered an oath and decided to seek his bed. He needed to be up early to make the journey to Hampton Court to attend the king. He followed the ragged path that led along the side of the Great Hall, his dagger at the ready, his mind unsettled.

A shadow leapt out at him as he rounded the corner of the massive structure. There were two men, and despite his best efforts, he couldn't withstand the attentions of them both. He was slammed face-first against the wall, his dagger hand wrenched up against his spine and a blade to his throat.

"Christopher Ellis."

He knew that voice, had trained alongside the man during his younger, more reckless years. "Sir Marcus Flavian."

"You remember me. Good." Marcus shifted his stance and jerked Christopher's wrist higher. "Then you will no doubt understand why I am here."

Christopher said nothing as he focused on controlling the pain.

Marcus laughed, the sound soft. "You are required to present yourself at our next meeting and explain your actions."

The summons wasn't unexpected. Ever since his betrothal to Rosalind had become public, Christopher had been expecting the Cult of Mithras to command his appearance. The only surprise was that it had taken so long. He fought back a groan as Marcus twisted his arm again.

"You will answer for your association with the Llewellyn bitch."

Fury rose in Christopher's gut, and he kicked out and caught Marcus on the shin and off guard. He spun around and pushed away from the wall with all his strength. The other man made short work of helping Marcus recapture him, but Christopher didn't care. As he was thrown back against the wall, he glared into Marcus's calm gray eyes.

"I will answer to my superiors, not to you."

"As you wish." The blade of Marcus's dagger flicked out and nicked Christopher's cheek. "Someone will let you know when the meeting is."

Christopher didn't acknowledge either the words or the blood now trickling down his face. There was nothing he could do to avoid the summons, and in truth, he didn't want to. It was high time for him to confess his doubts about the Cult.

What a pity that the only way to leave the Cult of Mithras was by death.

Rosalind slid the smallest of her daggers into her hanging pocket and retraced her steps down to the stables. As she walked, the stiff, embroidered green skirts of her favorite riding habit brushed against the lush summer foliage. The thought of getting on a horse again didn't please her, but she had no choice. She needed to see King Henry and to meet with Jasper, who had been watching over the king in her stead.

"Good morning, Rhys."

"Good morning, my lady." Rhys was already busy saddling her horse. "I assumed you'd want to follow the masses to Hampton Court this morning."

"Indeed." Rosalind made sure her headdress was securely fastened and pulled on her thick leather riding gloves. "You are going to accompany me, aren't you?"

"Of course, I wouldn't miss this for the world."

"I'm *hoping* to see the king and Jasper."

"Jasper, eh? Not Lord Christopher Ellis?" Rhys tightened the girth on her horse and stood ready to help her into the saddle. "I wonder why Jasper wrote to your grandfather."

"So do I. He's always been convinced he would be far better at guarding the king than I would, so asking for my help must have been hard for him."

"Well-nigh impossible, I should think. Things must indeed be bad." Rhys laced his hands together, waited until she placed her booted foot on his palms, and then threw her up into the saddle. She wanted to groan when her bottom hit the leather.

She waited until he mounted his horse with his usual easy grace, and then she set off after him. They passed through the great brick arch of the gatehouse. The clatter of the horses' hooves on the cobblestones made it impossible to speak or hear a thing.

As they emerged into the warm sunlight, Rhys glanced at her. "Are you still sore, my lady?"

"I'm quite well, thank you, Rhys," Rosalind answered and forced a smile.

He shrugged, making his muscled shoulders bunch in his leather jerkin. "As you wish, my lady. It isn't that far, less than twelve miles, I gather." He slowed his horse to come alongside her. "I hear that Cardinal Wolsey made Hampton Court a palace fit for a king."

"The king obviously decided the same thing."

Rhys chuckled and eased his horse into a smooth trot. "You might be right. They say Wolsey gave it to the king in a last desperate attempt to win back his favor, but obviously it didn't work."

Rosalind urged her horse into a trot. She could endure a short ride if it meant she was able to see Jasper and find out what was going on. Anticipation surged through her. After a year of almost no activity, she was anxious to return to fighting the Vampire foe. Excitement of another sort threaded through her as well. She might see Christopher again.

Eventually, they both gazed down at the moat and gatehouse leading up to the newly renovated Hampton Court. The gleaming red brick still looked pristine, the scars of the new building not yet concealed by the parks and gardens encircling the vast house.

"It seems the cardinal did very well for himself—very well, indeed, for the son of a butcher," Rhys said.

A cold shiver rippled through Rosalind. King Henry

never liked to be shown up by anyone, and this imposing structure was far grander than most royal palaces. It wasn't surprising that Wolsey had felt compelled to hand it over. "Too well, I suspect."

"Aye. The king's favor is a fickle thing." Rhys nodded in the direction of the gate. "Shall we go in?"

Rosalind followed him down the treelined avenue and waited as he inquired at the gate. One of the king's guards seemed to recognize Rhys, and they passed through without incident into the Basse court and then through an imposing archway into another courtyard. Rosalind's gaze was caught by the large astrological clock that dominated the enclosed square.

Rhys turned in the saddle to survey the lines of windows. "The guard said the state apartments are in this area. After we stable the horses, we should find the king there."

Rosalind followed him through to the vast and busy stables and waited as he ascertained that the horses would be taken care of. She'd forgotten how good Rhys was at getting people to do his bidding with just a smile and a polite turn of phrase—far better than she would ever be. It was a quality he shared with Christopher, who could charm the birds from the trees when he put his mind to it.

As her ears adjusted to the noisy bustle, she heard cheering from somewhere in the grounds. "Is the king outside?"

A passing stable boy answered her, his freckled face ablaze with excitement. "Indeed, he is, my lady. He and some of his courtiers are playing tennis in the pavilion."

Rosalind caught Rhys's attention and gestured toward the grounds. "Apparently, the king is playing tennis."

"Shall I find Jasper while you deal with the king?"

"Yes, please." Rosalind let out her breath. She'd much rather meet the king, and anyone else who happened to be included in the royal party, without Rhys at her shoulder. She picked up the skirts of her green riding habit and wished she was wearing something less heavy and concealing. It was hot in the sun, and she was sure she was red in the face. But it couldn't be helped. The king would have to take her as she was, as would everyone else.

She followed the roars and applause of the crowd, and came to a low, covered building with one side open to the air. Galleys filled with courtiers lined three sides of the enclosed space as the king and his opponent played a game of tennis on the court. Rosalind squeezed into a small space and wiggled her way forward through the packed courtiers. The king made another shot, and the crowd erupted.

By the time she reached the front, King Henry had finished his game and been replaced by another familiar figure, one that made Rosalind's heart beat faster. Christopher Ellis looked as lean and elegant as ever in his shirtsleeves and stockinged feet, his right hand gripping a racquet, his left holding the small ball in the air ready to serve.

He seemed quite friendly with his opponent, their laughing banter inaudible to Rosalind over the noisy crowd, but obviously not to each other. With a sigh, Rosalind sat back and watched Christopher. She'd missed him so badly, had cried for a month after leaving him.

She wrapped her arms around herself. She'd been too afraid to stand up to her grandfather and demand that he allow her to marry her family's worst enemy. Instead, like any silly woman, she'd skulked at home, waiting for her grandfather to resolve matters for her. But he hadn't resolved anything, and now she had to face Christopher again. In some part of her soul, it shamed her that she cared so much for Christopher that she was willing to abandon everything she had been brought up to believe in.

She turned to the man sitting next to her. "Excuse me, sir. Who is the man playing against Lord Christopher Ellis?"

"That is Lord George Boleyn, a gentleman of the king's Privy Chamber. Surely you must know of him?"

"I've recently returned from the countryside, sir. I don't believe I've met him before."

The man gave a snort. "If you stay at court, you'll meet him soon enough. Thanks to the influence of his sister, the man rides high in the king's favor."

That gave Rosalind plenty to think about. The match drew to a close, and George Boleyn claimed victory as Christopher laughingly complained. Rosalind stood with the rest of the crowd, her gaze fixed on Christopher as he headed for the exit. She stiffened as he and George Boleyn were surrounded by a bevy of beautiful court maidens. One of them even dared to mop Christopher's brow with her lace handkerchief. Not that he seemed to mind at all.

Rosalind set her jaw and stamped down from the viewing galley to the ground floor, her intentions unclear. Part of her wished to find Christopher and ask him whether he'd missed her at all; the saner part of her knew that would be a mistake and urged her to use her common sense and go find the king.

But it was too late; the group containing Christopher, George Boleyn, and their admirers was fast bearing down on her. Rosalind stiffened her spine and tried to look anywhere but at Christopher. A woman hung on each of his arms, and he was grinning like a fool who had not a care in the world.

Her smile died, and she raised her chin. She would not cower before him. She had nothing to be ashamed of. Christopher's laughing blue gaze swept past her and then returned.

"My lady, I didn't realize that you had returned to court."

"Obviously."

His smile was a challenge. "Did you imagine I would languish in despair without your presence?"

"That would have been nice, seeing as we are supposed to be betrothed."

"Are we?" He took two hasty steps toward her, blocking out the light, his chest still heaving, either from his recent exertions or from his current fury. She inhaled the scent of his warm skin and yearned to place her mouth over his and just breathe him in. "I wasn't sure, seeing as you haven't bothered to communicate with me for almost a year."

"How could I? It was a matter to be settled by our families."

"Was it?" He stared into her eyes, and she swallowed uncomfortably at the fire in his gaze. She had no sense of him in her mind at all. Perhaps the connection had been lost. "How foolish of me to believe that it was a matter between *us*."

His glare intensified as he looked over her shoulder. "Ah, here comes your watchdog. I'm sure I'll see you again, my lady. Tell Rhys I send him my greetings."

Christopher turned and stalked away, straight into the center of the laughing crowd of courtiers. The hint of the scent of fox drifted back to Rosalind, and she wondered which of the male courtiers was a Vampire, and whether Christopher had noticed it. He didn't look back, so Rosalind stayed where she was, her legs trembling and her heart racing so fast that she thought it might leap out of her chest. What right did he have to be so annoyed with her? What had he expected, a series of love letters?

She swung around and saw Rhys approaching her, his hand raised in salute. Beside him walked her cousin Jasper, who wasn't smiling. Not that he ever smiled much. Unlike most men, he tended to speak only when he had something important to say. He bowed and kissed her hand.

"Cousin Rosalind, I am pleased to see you again."

"And I you, Cousin."

"I'm glad that you were able to return." Jasper grimaced. "But this is not the best place for us to talk. Let us meet later tonight by the entrance to the maze. We will not be disturbed there."

Rosalind glanced uncertainly up at Rhys. "I'm not sure if we are staying here for the night."

Rhys looked resigned. "It seems as if we are now. I'll

go and seek some accommodation in the stables. I suggest you find a member of the queen's household and do the same."

"Is the queen here, Jasper?" Rosalind asked.

Jasper lowered his voice. "She is not welcome here. King Henry and his current companions have made that very clear."

Jasper took her arm and led her back toward the main buildings. "For all intents and purposes, the lady Anne Boleyn behaves as if she is the queen."

"Anne Boleyn?" Rosalind frowned. "I don't believe I've met her, although I just saw her brother playing tennis."

"She and her brother are much together, and their influence over the king grows daily. Anne returned to court a year or so ago. She was raised mainly in France."

"Is she here now?"

"Yes, though to keep the king's interest, she has been known to deliberately absent herself from court in a sulk." Jasper's smile wasn't pleasant. "I believe it is the first time in his life that the king has had to woo a woman for more than a day or two. He seems invigorated by the challenge."

Rosalind's unease grew. It seemed that the rumor was true. Queen Katherine had indeed fallen far from the king's favor if he was openly parading his new love in her place. And if that news wasn't bad enough, she dreaded what else Jasper had to reveal about their Vampire foes.

With a shake of her head, Rosalind went to find the controller of the queen's household and beg for a bed for the night. Whatever else happened, her mission to keep the king safe from the Vampire threat remained. It was far easier to focus on that than to delve into the unpleasant swirl of emotions Christopher aroused in her.

Hampton Court was crowded with the king's courtiers, and despite its size, the Great Hall seethed like an overcrowded ant hill. Rosalind arrived for the evening meal and made her way across to the trestle table, where some of the queen's ladies had gathered. She was greeted warmly, although there was also an undercurrent of unease among the women. Rosalind knew they were worried about their positions at court now that the queen was no longer in favor.

She glanced up at the High Table, where the king sat, surrounded by his favorites. To his right was his chancellor, Thomas Cromwell, dressed in his black-and-gray robes, a thick gold chain around his neck. To the king's left was a woman Rosalind hadn't seen before, no doubt the much talked-about Lady Anne Boleyn.

She wasn't beautiful by current court standards and was nothing like her sister Mary's gold-and-pink lusciousness. Her eyes were very dark, her chin pointed and her body slender. Not beautiful at all, but she had something that drew the eye.

Rosalind turned back to her dinner and tried not to look across the hall to the king's gentlemen. She'd already spotted Christopher's dark head bent toward George Boleyn. The two seemed companionable, sharing not only a trencher but an equal interest in the women who constantly paraded before them.

Rosalind set her teeth. Christopher might think he had a right to amuse himself when she wasn't there, but she intended to set him right on a few matters before they were done. Much depended on what Jasper had to say to her about the Vampires.

She looked up to see that his dark blue gaze had fallen on her and found that she couldn't look away. Part of her wanted to drop her guard and try to steal into his mind. Then at least she would know his true feelings. But she deserved the words, didn't she? If he was done with her, she deserved to hear it to her face rather than steal the thought from his mind.

She dropped her gaze and made stilted conversation with the ladies around her, aware of the movement of the crowds, the fact that Christopher had turned to speak to a woman and then disappeared. She could hardly expect him to remain celibate, could she? No woman should expect that from a man who wasn't bound by the ties of wedlock. Her fingers curled into fists. Except that if she ever caught Christopher in bed with another woman, she would have no hesitation in cutting off his—

"Lady Rosalind?"

With a start, Rosalind turned. "Cousin Jasper."

He smiled and indicated his companion. "I would like to present a friend of mine, Sir Reginald Fforde."

Rosalind held out her hand. "How do you do, sir?"

Sir Reginald bowed, his fair skin flushing. "Lady Rosalind, a pleasure. Indeed, a rare and glorious pleasure."

A corner of Jasper's mouth twitched upward as he met Rosalind's gaze. "Sir Reginald was most insistent on meeting you, cousin. He was— How did you put it, Reginald? 'Struck by your beauty.'"

"How flattering, sir." Behind Sir Reginald, Rosalind noticed the unmistakable looming presence of her betrothed. She smiled deeply into the stuttering young man's eyes. "If only all men were as poetic."

Sir Reginald turned quite red. "I'll write you a beautiful sonnet to your fine eyes. If you permit, of course."

Rosalind gave a small, tinkling laugh and clasped her hands to her bosom. "Oh, my, Sir Reginald. That would be delightful."

Incoherent now, his mouth opening and closing like a stranded fish, Sir Reginald allowed Jasper to lead him away, leaving Rosalind facing Christopher. She made as if to move past him, but he grasped her firmly by the elbow.

"If you desire poems written to you, ask me."

"With your surly and unpleasant attitude, sir, I would fear to read anything you might write." She tried to shake off his grip, but he refused to release her. "Sir Reginald was only being pleasant."

His eyebrows rose. "I can be pleasant."

"I haven't seen any evidence of it so far."

He leaned in closer until his mouth brushed her ear. "My, my, you have a very short memory, don't you?"

Tanya Huff

"The Gales are an amazing family, the aunts will strike fear into your heart, and the characters Allie meets are both charming and terrifying."
—#1 *New York Times* bestselling author
Charlaine Harris

The Enchantment Emporium

Alysha Gale is a member of a family capable of changing the world with the charms they cast. She is happy to escape to Calgary when when she inherits her grandmother's junk shop, but when Alysha learns just how much trouble is brewing, even calling in the family to help may not be enough to save the day.

978-0-7564-0605-9

The Wild Ways

Charlotte Gale is a Wild Power who allies herself with a family of Selkies in a fight against offshore oil drilling. The oil company has hired another of the Gale family's Wild Powers, the fearsome Auntie Catherine, to steal the Selkies' sealskins. To defeat her, Charlotte will have to learn what born to be Wild really means in the Gale family...

978-0-7564-0686-8

To Order Call: 1-800-788-6262
www.dawbooks.com

DAW 200